Praise for *Had a Good Time:*

"Butler inhabits these people with eerie emotional accuracy. He changes the narration to suit each character's voice, and brings wide swaths of early-twentieth-century America to life with a few deft strokes. . . . There is a great deal to admire in this collection—crisp writing, marvelous imaging, the discussion of large, existential questions that are as central to life now as they were a hundred years ago." —*The Boston Globe*

"A wonderfully varied third collection from Pulitzer-winning Butler that investigates diverse lives—and deaths—early in the twentieth century . . . Assured, accomplished, and another intriguing change of pace from an adventurous writer who refuses to be pigeonholed." —*Kirkus Reviews* (starred review)

"Only Butler could have crafted *Had a Good Time*. . . . [The] characters and situations absolutely *sing* in your mind as you read. And the most amazing thing—no two narrators sound alike. It's like reading short stories by a dozen different, immensely gifted authors." —*Fort Worth Morning Star*

"All of the stories are short and such good company that we read them in an afternoon. What's more, we had the feeling that Butler enjoyed them almost as much as we did." —*The Arizona Republic*

"Fifteen gloriously imaginative and utterly hypnotizing short stories . . . Scintillating, soulful, and surprising." —*Booklist*

"Butler has collected vintage postcards for ten years . . . and in his terrific new collection, he uses his findings to inspire mesmerizing excursions into loss and affirmation. From their smudged, often enigmatic messages . . . evolve tales that capture the rugged promise of the brand-new twentieth century."
—*The Tampa Tribune*

"Butler remains, unfortunately, a precious literary secret. . . . *Had a Good Time* is a legacy of supreme imagination, surely inimitable."
—*Fort Worth Star-Telegram*

"A collection of short stories that does nothing short of illuminating our humanity. A deeply moving book filled with emotionally gripping tales."
—*Curled Up With a Good Book*

"Butler's imaginative re-animation of anonymous lives from the past is both entertaining and informative, an alternate history of forgotten souls."
—*Pittsburgh Tribune-Review*

"Good Southern storyteller that he is, Butler sometimes writes with a comically absurd quality reminiscent of Flannery O'Connor."
—*Oregon Live*

"Picture postcards offer an unusually fertile vantage point from which to examine the traditions and complications of American life. In these terrific new stories, [Butler] uses his findings to inspire mesmerizing excursions into loss and affirmation."
—*The Denver Post/Rocky Mountain News*

"I would read a book like this by anyone, but Butler's an amazing storyteller, so it's even better."   —*Cargo*

"Butler is brilliant at shifting not only the fictional voices from story to story, but also each character's disposition, attitudes and shapes of thought, fooling you into believing each one. The author has quite a bit of fun here, and his playfulness is infectious."
                    —*Bellingham Weekly* (Washington)

"A thoughtful commentary on America at the dawn of a new century: while some Americans were buoyed by their confidence in technology and progress, others, at the mercy of a disease-ridden, hardscrabble existence, could trust only in their faith in God."   —*Publishers Weekly*

Had a Good Time

The Alleys of Eden

Sun Dogs

Countrymen of Bones

On Distant Ground

Wabash

The Deuce

A Good Scent from a Strange Mountain

They Whisper

Tabloid Dreams

The Deep Green Sea

Mr. Spaceman

Fair Warning

From Where You Dream: The Process of Writing Fiction
(Janet Burroway, editor)

HAD A GOOD TIME

Stories from American Postcards

ROBERT OLEN BUTLER

Grove Press
New York

The stories in this book first appeared in the following places: "Hotel Touraine," *Ninth Letter;* "Mother in the Trenches," *StoryQuarterly;* "The Ironworkers' Hayride," *Zoetrope;* "Carl and I," *Five Points;* "This Is Earl Sandt," *The Georgia Review;* "The One in White," *The Atlantic;* "No Chord of Music," *Hemispheres;* "Christmas 1910," *StoryQuarterly;* "Hiram the Desperado," *Glimmer Train;* "I Got Married to Milk Can," *Hemispheres;* "The Grotto," *Ploughshares;* "Up by Heart," *Image;* and "Twins," *Prairie Schooner.*

"This Is Earl Sandt" was created in its entirety on an Internet webcast, in real time, under the auspices of Florida State University. My sincere thanks to all those who made that event possible. The webcast is archived at www.fsu.edu/butler.

Published simultaneously in Canada
Printed in the United States of America

FIRST GROVE PRESS PAPERBACK EDITION

Library of Congress Cataloging-in-Publication Data

Butler, Robert Olen.
   Had a good time : stories from American postcards / by Robert Olen Butler.
     p. cm.
   ISBN 0-8021-4204-4 (pbk.)
   1. United States—Social life and customs—20th century—Fiction. I. Title.

PS3552.U8278H33 2004

813'.54—dc22   2003067771

Grove Press
an imprint of Grove/Atlantic, Inc.
841 Broadway
New York, NY 10003

05 06 07 08 09   10 9 8 7 6 5 4 3 2 1

For Elizabeth Dewberry

THE STORIES

LIST OF ILLUSTRATIONS

Had a Good Time

PICTURE POSTCARDS

The picture postcard manufacturer is your real modern explorer. You may flatter yourself that you have made a discovery when you happen, in the course of a foot tour, upon a neighborhood so remote that neither you nor any of your acquaintances has ever heard of its existence, many miles distant from railway and main travelled roads; but you will find the picture postcard awaiting you at the four corners general store. Its manufacturer has been there before you. He has explored the place and caught with his camera all its secrets of rustic charm and quiet, all its quaint delights of creeper-covered clapboard architecture. Nothing escapes the man with the commercial camera.

Is it the picture itself or the contracted space it leaves for writing that gives the picture postcard its vogue? Is its popularity due to the prevalent interest in illustrations of any and every kind, or to the fact that it furnishes an acceptable, and accepted, substitute for social and conjugal correspondence in the lazy days of summer? Does it primarily meet a sentimental or a utilitarian need? We know that in its wider international scope it has still another function—that of gratifying the vanity which first found expression in the label-bedecked suitcase. But whatever the motive, the use of the picture postcard has become a pretty custom.

from the editoral page of the *New-York Tribune*
Sunday, August 7, 1910

BOSTON, Mass. Hotel Touraine.

POST CARD

This is where the people who have more money than brains put up. They pay about 100 per month for 2 rooms furnished when they could afford to have a nice home of their own. I had a job in this hotel last year. Worked there for a week. Saw lots of style, but don't see as the people were any happier

Mason Bros. & Co., Boston, Mass.

Made in Germany.

HOTEL TOURAINE

This is where the people who have more money than brains put up. They pay about $100 per month for 2 rooms furnished when they could afford to have a nice home of their own. I had a job in this hotel last year. Worked there for a week. Saw lots of style, but don't see as the people were any happier.

My fifth day at the hotel I pretty near ran down John Stanford Barnhill in the corridor past the second-floor library. I was making time with a pitcher of water to a public room along the way, where some other swell was receiving guests like the whole place was his mansion and he was doing an at-home in his own parlor. The Oriental rugs are thick underfoot all over the Touraine and I was making no sound and Barnhill bolts out of the library door and I pull up sharp, tucking the pitcher into me so I'll take the splash instead of him. Which I do, down my bellboy jacket with the brass buttons, and he says, "Whoa, Dobbin," like I'm a spooked dray horse. I just keep my mouth shut. No *Sorry, sir* or *Excuse me, sir* like I know I'm supposed to do, but this guy's about my age, not much into his twenties, and he's in a serge suit with cigars sticking out of his pocket and he gets my goat in an instant. I'm still figuring out what to think about this job and I decide right off not to play the lackey to guys like this. This is even before I know who he is, exactly, heir to millions by being born the only grandnephew of somebody else who was born to millions and so on. I just take the splash and sashay around him and head on down to where I'm supposed to go. He could yell something after me, about my being a rude working-class bumpkin or some such, but he doesn't. I figure it's running through his head, though.

Then later that day I'm going out of the place in my own clothes, my uniform hanging in a wire locker in the changing room, and you'd think he'd never recognize me, but you'd think wrong. I'm going out of the hotel and he says, "You one of those bare-headed anarchists to boot?" *To boot* meaning bomb-throwing anarchist in addition to water-spilling bellboy, and the whole thing has been set off by my going without a hat, which has always been my way, unlike the vast herds of men in the world. But I don't like a thing to bind me in around my head. All of which sounds grand and free on my part, but I guess that'd be wrong too, because in response to his cheek I say, "No, sir," and I keep on going and I like to bite my tongue off.

I've picked up the habit of servant talk already, after just five days, and I shoot him a hard look over my shoulder and he's already turned away, wearing a Prince Albert coat and a high-crowned bowler, which he's just starting to tip to a woman in a veil going by. So I dash across Tremont, dodging a street-car and a couple of galloping horses and the express wagon they're pulling, and I cut into the Common.

This is *my* parlor, the Common, and I take a winding way through, slowing down, putting Barnhill out of my mind, though a bunch of guys like him are always floating through this place as well, usually squiring young women in big straw hats full of ostrich feathers. But I swing over to the open fields and the fellows there are playing baseball and one of them who thinks he's Tris Speaker makes a headlong dive for a hit into the outfield and he almost has it but not quite. Then he's in for it to get back to his feet and chase the ball down while the batter's making for third base. I don't blame him for trying, even if he'll never play for the Red Sox.

I turn away and move on and dig into my pocket for the pack of Meccas I bought in the lobby shop before I left the hotel. I open it and stick a smoke into my mouth and light it up and I'm starting to think about Barnhill again. Also there's some fat cigar of a guy in a bowler putting the mash on a sweet-faced girl on the path ahead of me. I go around them and I blow smoke at his right ear and I dig out my free card from the cigarette pack. They're still giving away Champion Athletes and I've got a guy with aviator goggles strapped on his head and a biplane up in the sky over his shoulder and the clouds are streaked with sunset and he's ready to go, this guy Arch Hoxsey. I stick him in my shirt pocket with the cigarettes and hustle up, moving smartly away from my fifth day of work at the Hotel Touraine.

Twenty minutes later, after skirting the edge of Beacon Hill where Barnhill's money was waiting in a marble-columned mansion for somebody to die, I climbed the steps of our tenement in the West End and there was a great caterwauling of kids and a stink from the third-floor toilet and Mr. Spinetti's voice was filling the stairwell from the top floor down, him being the Caruso of tenement-hollerers. I hesitated at our door and stubbed out a second cigarette I'd let myself have right away, just to get certain people out of my mind, and then I stepped in.

Mama was near the window, hunched over the side table, rolling cigars. Her back was to me. "Eli," she said, but she didn't turn around.

"Mama," I said. The smell of tobacco had thickened the air in the room. I stood for a moment getting up the strength to push through it. Maybe it was mostly not wanting to see her hands at work on these things that made me hesitate, but it felt more like I was struggling against the air being heavy with this smell. Then I did finally cross the room and I was behind Mama. Beside her on the floor on one side was a gunnysack of filler leaf and on the other a wooden box with the wrapper leaves, and her hands were moving, moving. I laid my own hand on her shoulder and I wanted to lift my eyes out the window, like the tenement across the way was some great landscape or something, but I couldn't help watching her hands rolling around and around this fancy man's cigar, the thing shaping up there, the loose leaves tightening as she rolled it and it would end up in John Stanford Barnhill's mouth, or somebody just like him, and Mama would get her eight mills pay. Now I looked out the window. Her sill pillow was there for later when she'd lean out into the night and talk to the women in the windows across the way.

"Just a moment," she said. "Let me finish this one."

I went and sat at the small round oak table where we ate and read and talked, the one piece we'd been able to keep from our plans for a house. Papa died under the hooves and wheels of a wagon hauling bricks, down at the wharf, right when we were going to be okay, when we were boarding in a nice house and Papa had plans to buy a bungalow from Sears and Roebuck and put it up out the streetcar line in some direction or other. I won't count the years it's been since. The night before, he gave me Rube Waddell of the St. Louis Browns from a pack of Sweet Caporals he'd smoked that day. Rube in portrait, no cap, his hair parted neatly down the middle. "This man made himself out of nothing," Papa said.

Mama sat down beside me now. I held her hand on the tabletop. She smelled of tobacco. Her eyes looked gray in the dim light. "How's it at your job?" she said.

"Okay," I said.

"You're doing right?"

"Sure."

"They'll take to you."

"I don't know," I said.

She took her hand from under mine and patted at me there, to reassure me. "I did a hundred twenty today," she said.

I looked away from her, landing on the wall where she had a chromo hung of the woman at the well and Jesus asking her for water.

"Nearly a dollar," she said.

That night I lay on my pallet propped up against the wall with a candle burning beside me. I was trying to read a Zane Grey but the cowboys with their horses and ten-gallon hats were steaming me up tonight for some reason. They think all you have to do is plug it or throw a rope around it or ride it to the ground and that solves everything. I could hear Mama breathing heavy in her sleep across the room. Somewhere on another floor some guy was yelling and somewhere else a baby was crying, but these sounds were dim, coming through all the walls in between. I reached into the pocket of my shirt hanging on a chair near me to get my cigarettes and I found Arch Hoxsey. He had a fur collar around his neck. It was cold high up in the air, I guess, no matter what the season. I turned the card over, and it said he started out working in a factory before he became a champion athlete automobile driver and then aeroplane flyer. He set a record and he rose to 11,000 feet. And then he died. He crashed trying to come back to earth on the last day of 1910. I turned his card over and looked him in the eyes. My papa would respect him. For myself, I couldn't figure if he was a fool to leave the ground.

The next morning I was sent to John Stanford Barnhill's rooms on the eighth floor. On the silver tray balanced on my palm was a bottle of whiskey. This was about ten in the morning, though I shouldn't sneer because even Papa started early some days. So I knock on his door, which is slightly open, and he calls for me to come in. I push the door and step into the place, a regular cut-velvet and leather sitting room. It smells strong of cigar smoke. He's left one lit on a saucer on the reading table. The gentleman himself is hanging out the open lower sash like the women in the tenements.

"Your whiskey," I say, and he draws his body in from the window.

"On the table," he says, and I put the tray down next to his cigar. I stare hard at the thing and I guess he sees me doing that.

"There hasn't been a good Cuban crop since 1908," he says, as if he knows I'd know something about cigars.

I look at him.

"They're charging seventy cents for the good ones down-stairs," he says.

Now I understand. Let the anarchist bellboy know how much money you've got, that you can spend better than a worker's daily wage on a couple of cigars.

"My mother does that," I say.

"What's that?"

"Hangs out the window. She talks to her friends and watches the street." I regret this at once. Trying to show him he's not so different from us, I've just made Mama look bad.

Barnhill flips his head to the side a little to acknowledge the window and he doesn't even crack a smile, much less a sneer. Instead, he says, "There's elms out there on the Common that John Hancock planted."

"You related to him, are you?"

Now I get a little sneery smile. "John Hancock is . . ."

"I know who he is."

Barnhill laughs. "Of course. No. I'm not related to him."

"So you like looking at trees."

"You want a drink?" he asks, and I think he's dead serious.

"There's easier ways to get me fired," I say.

Barnhill laughs again. He moves to the reading table and I back off a step. He touches the bottle but goes to thinking about something instead. His hand just stays there holding the neck of the bottle, and he's looking at it, thinking. I back up another step. It's time to get out of the room. I turn, and he says, "Not so fast."

I stop and face him again and he's digging in his vest pocket. He holds out his hand with a dime lifted by the thumb and forefinger. "Your tip," he says.

It's two steps away. It's twelve and a half cigars' worth of work. He's not moving. Neither am I. He gives the dime a little up-flip with his hand, like to say, Come and get it.

I lift my chin just a bit and I say, "Put it toward your next Cuban downstairs," and I'm out of that room in a flash.

Not that John Stanford Barnhill struck me as somebody real different from a dozen other guys I'd seen around the Touraine already, living in a hotel when they could so easily have what Papa had wanted all his life. A few of them even had wives with them, so they weren't all just helpless bachelors gagging on a silver spoon. They lived in a hotel so guys like me could hop for them and they could have a chambermaid come in and take away their soiled linens and they could just stroll downstairs and eat a fancy dinner with a little orchestra playing, but of course they could have that in homes of their own if they wanted, except for maybe the orchestra, so I just couldn't get myself to understand. Still can't.

Anyway, later in my sixth day at the Touraine, a bellhop from the next shift sent word he was sick and the manager asked me to stay on for a few extra hours and I said okay. And I run into Barnhill in the early evening while I'm at the front desk gathering up the bags of a man and his wife in automobile dusters. Barnhill is going out and he sees me just as I stand up straight with my arms and hands full and he tips his bowler at me going by, trying to get my goat. I just keep my face hard and steady and he puts his hat back down on his head and gives it a little tap as he goes out the door and into the night. A few minutes later I forget to talk like a servant to the guy in the duster, I guess—he asks me where the electric call bell is and I say, "Over there," and don't mention anything about sir or madam or let-me-lick-the-dust-off-your-boots—and I get a glare from him that I recognize for what it is right off, and still I don't say anything respectful to try to make it up. I don't get a tip and I don't blame him, I guess, seeing as what he's used to from a guy in my place, but I'm still working up an anger that I hope will stay put till this day is over. Then about ten or so the manager tells me things have slowed down enough, I should go on home, and I haven't popped anybody yet, so I'm glad to change from my bellhop suit fast and get out of there.

I don't cut through the Common but go up the mall along Tremont. There are lots of people around. That's good. I walk along among all these people, some in fancy dress and some in work clothes and some smoking a bummed cigarette and some a Cuban cigar, and we all just go on along together and there's a sharp breeze blowing, the first little whisper of the winter ahead, and then I'm coming up to the subway entrance at Park Street. The one-armed man with his two fox-colored dogs who walk around on their back legs is still selling the late edition. I pay a penny for it and then I see a crowd over by the little building where the steps go down to the train. I fold the paper and put it in my pocket and stroll over.

At the center of the crowd is an old man with a telescope on a tripod and he's got a sign up saying TEN CENTS TO SEE THE MOON. I stand watching for a minute. Some guy makes a big show of pulling out his ten cents for the girl he's with, and she sits on the little stool beneath the telescope, smoothing out her dress and pushing back her hat piled high with muslin roses, and then she looks into the telescope and she cries out like she's seen

somebody jump off a bridge. The crowd all goes to muttering
in wonder at her shock and somebody else steps forward to pay
a dime. For all I know, the guy and the girl in the big hat are
confederates of the telescope man and they've been put up to
this little show just to get the crowd going. But I find myself
wanting to look, all the same.

And then Barnhill is at my elbow. "You ever want to just
go to the moon?" he says.

I look at him. I get the feeling he's putting the needle in
me again, but if he'd like to have a go at me, I wish he'd just do
it straight, more like a man. All I know to do is keep my mouth
shut.

Then he says, "I figure I owe you a dime. Go look at the
moon, on me. Okay?"

He's got that dime up between us again. I take it.

"Good," he says.

We both square around and wait for some guy to finish
with his look, and I'm not even thinking to give the dime back.
I'm not sure why this telescope makes it different, about taking
money from John Stanford Barnhill, but it does. Then I get my
chance. I step forward and give Barnhill's money to the telescope man and I say, "I want to see something different."

The old man holds up a forefinger like he's got just the
thing. He crouches behind his telescope and looks in and swivels
it around and then moves aside. I step over and bend down and
I look. Against the dark is a small white globe, and it's ringed
all around. "The planet Saturn," the man says to me. Then he
tells the crowd, "This gentleman is now on the planet Saturn,
the sixth of our sun's eight planets," and he goes on with his

pitch. I just ignore him. I watch this other world moving along out there millions of miles away and I wonder who it is that lives on Saturn and what makes them tick. Then the telescope man's hand is on my shoulder and he says, "Time's up."

I straighten, and it takes a moment to get my bearings. I move off toward the Common, away from where I'd left Barnhill. The ring of gawkers opens for me and I'm into the dark, and then Barnhill is beside me again. "You went farther than the moon," he says.

"I went to your home planet," I say.

He laughs, though it sounds forced. "I've got my ticket back," he says.

He's walking with me now and it seems there's more to this than just trying to show up the bellhop. He smells of whiskey, but he's walking steady. "You don't like me," he says.

"Liking the guests ain't part of my job," I say.

"It doesn't make any difference," he says.

We're into an open part of the Common and the breeze has picked up pretty fierce. It's got a sting to it now.

"I'm finished at the Touraine anyway," Barnhill says.

I'm not paying any real attention to him. I'm just thinking about getting away from him. "I've got to get on home," I say, though the word catches in my throat: *home*. I've never had to call the tenement Mama and me live in by that name, and it makes me angry at Barnhill, his forcing me to say this.

We're both stopped now on the path, the empty field before us, the stars and the planets whirling around overhead. What he says about leaving the Touraine finally sinks in.

"Finished?" I say.

Barnhill kind of shivers. "You should wear a hat in this weather," he says, and I'll be damned if he doesn't take off his bowler and put it on my head.

It settles in perfect. I can feel the soft inner rim of it ringing across just below my hairline and on around my head and the hat's light there and it's even made it like the wind has stopped blowing, though I still can feel the bite of air on my face and hands if I try. But I'm fine inside the hat. I let it stay there. "You buying yourself a house?" I ask.

He runs a hand through his hair and lifts his chin a little. "Not quite," he says. "My aunt's cutting me off. She doesn't think much of me either, as it happens."

I'm not proud of it, but the first thing out of my mouth is, "I can get you on as a bellhop."

He looks at me and his face is white from the moon and I find myself wishing he had the guts to pop me. I deserve it and I won't raise a hand back at him. But he just looks at me and he doesn't say a word. So I reach up to his hat to take it off and he says, "No. Keep it."

That's the last thing I'm about to do. I lift the hat and I put it on his head and he doesn't resist. I feel the wind sharp on me again. We just look at each other and there's no more words. Finally I say, "Good night then."

"Good night," he says.

The next day, my last at the Hotel Touraine, I'm thinking about John Stanford Barnhill all morning. Then I'm hanging around the front desk and you can hear the call bell going over and over in the office and the manager comes out and says

Barnhill's room number. "I'll take it," I say, and the bell's still ringing as I walk away and I figure he's drunk and in a bad mood and something in me wants it to go like that, to make things simple again. All the way up in the elevator I'm getting ready for a blowup.

Then I step off on the eighth floor and the chambermaid is hopping around waiting for me and she's saying, "Come quick, come quick, he's gone, right in front of me," and I run down the hall and into Barnhill's rooms and the sash is thrown open where he was yesterday and the curtains are blowing in and I dash through the smell of his cigars and I go halfway out the window myself and I take in the chestnuts and Hancock's elms and the wide-open space with some guys out there playing baseball and people moving around, all this before facing what I know has happened. Then I look down, and Barnhill is there, far below, a crowd gathering around him, his arms open wide as if he leaped expecting an embrace.

I pull back in. I turn. The chambermaid is peeking in at the door. "Go get the manager," I say, and she vanishes.

I stand very still for a long moment, trying to read that moonlit face from last night. But my brain has shut down. There's nothing inside me except a clattering in my chest like horses' hooves. And then my eyes focus. The reading table. Cigar butts, long gone cold, in the saucer. And beside them is John Stanford Barnhill's bowler hat. I find myself panting like a dobbin. The room will be full of people very soon. I press myself to move. I take a step and another and another and I am at the side table and the hat sits there, the color of the night sky, and

I put my hand on it, I touch my palm to its high crown, and then I pick it up. I put it on my head and it settles on me right away, like it did last night, like when he put it on me with his own hand. And then I'm out the door, heading by the back stairs to the changing room. There's other things for me to do in this world. Other kinds of people. But he was right about me needing a hat.

THINKS HE'S SURELY INSANE

Woman Says Her Husband Reads Newspapers Upside Down

NEW YORK, AUGUST 6—Mrs. Belle Harper Hughes, who resides at the Plaza Hotel, is seeking through the courts to have her husband, Joseph B. Hughes, declared a mental incompetent, and to have a committee appointed to handle his estate, consisting of $300,000 in personal property. Mr. Hughes was one of the organizers of the tobacco trust and was Consul at Birmingham, England, under President Cleveland.

Mrs. Hughes, in order to show Hughes is insane, asserts:

That, with only $18,000 a year income, he imagines he is rich.

That he reads newspapers upside down for hours at a time.

That he always insists he has just returned from Cincinnati, whereas he has not been in Cincinnati in years.

That he frequently wanders around the hotel getting into beds where he doesn't belong.

Supreme Court Justice Bischoff today appointed a commission to inquire into the mental condition of Mr. Hughes.

Mr. Hughes is 61 years old and his wife is about 30. She was a member of Augustin Daly's theatrical company before she went to Paris to study music, where she met Mr. Hughes.

from the front page of *The Detroit Free Press*
Sunday, August 7, 1910

mother in the trenches

MOTHER IN THE TRENCHES

Mother in the trenches

W ith a world full of foolishly dangerous men, what's a mother to do? Like all the mothers of the world I am stuck with the barbarian Kaiser Wilhelm, a man full of himself but as hollow as a soufflé, and that well-meaning fool of a schoolmaster, Woodrow Wilson—I have known men like this all my life, being around preachers and teachers and also around my father, rest his soul, who was himself a bit of both, men who are certain they grasp things that no man can grasp for certain—and Black Jack Pershing, another kind of man, like the one I married, a man with quick, sure hands, I'd wager, and a single-minded bond with other men under whatever flag it may be—American, for General Jack and my own Jack—and there's nothing in the world to weaken that bond or soften those hands. My son is a man too, according to the Selective Service Act, but God help me if I'll let him be a man yet without a fight.

This is something I know like any mother knows. The boy is not fully a man if I can remember so clearly lifting his wee body up and placing it on a rectangle of cotton clean from the boiling pot and warm from the sun and I swaddle him up and hold him against me and he is gentle and he is quiet and I carry him away, carry him through the world, and all the while he is taking in the things I know as his mother, as a woman, but cannot say, cannot even put into words except to hold him close and whisper softly to him that he is a good boy and I love him.

They eat rats. I have heard people speak of this. They live in foul water so their feet swell and rot away. They cannot sleep for fear of the guns. They kill each other. My son was taken away to this kind of life. And so I packed a bag because my husband Jack was dead of influenza now and could not stop me and I boarded a ship and went to Paris and I hired a man who had already paid for all this madness of other men—one of his arms was merely a stump, from the early days of this war—and he drove me in a cart into the countryside and we slept in the fields along the way and it was June and there was no rain and he spoke a little English, and on one of the nights as we neared the front, he said, from the dark a ways off, behind some other tree, "Madame. You look at your son, yes?"

I knew what he meant. "Yes," I said. "*Oui.*"

There was a long silence, and then he said, "You are the mother of me also, yes?"

"I have my hands full," I said, which I'm not sure he understood. But he said no more.

I could hear a very faint thumping on the horizon down the road.

The next day there was a thin stream of civilians passing us. Most of them had already left this place up ahead, I assumed. These refugees had no sense of urgency, as one might expect, but moved with a terrible weariness about them. A mother on foot, carrying her infant, lifted her face as we passed, and her eyes seemed very old, though she was quite young. She was perhaps as young as my son. I could have been the infant's grandmother. I glanced over my shoulder as we passed and she, too, had turned her head.

I looked before me again. Edward was my only living child, Private Edward Marcus Gaines of the 108th Infantry, 27th Division, Company such-and-such. I had it written down in his letter. In a trench in a place in France. He had no infant child. He and I faced something together here in this foreign place. The end of our blood. I thought of the young woman we'd passed and of holding her child, just for a moment. Stopping the cart and she would have stopped too, and I would climb down and she would come to me and she would say, perhaps in her own language but I would know what she meant, *Here, she would say. Hold him.* And so I would and then I'd give him to his mother and I'd say, *Carry him off now. Quickly.*

There was a smell of burning in the air. The cart creaked in the ruts of the road. With each turn of the wheel there was a sound as if it would break. This one-armed man next to me muttered under his breath, I assumed to his horse. The explosions had ceased up ahead. I drifted into sleep and for a time I was in Yonkers, tending my roses, and the morning was bright and quiet and it was hot already. It was summer. The air hung heavily about my shoulders. In the dream it was only me and the roses and I was clipping the faded heads. I worked steadily but the garden was full of dead roses. The scissors *chinked* and *chinked* with a sound like a turning wheel.

And I awoke to tents passing and the rumble nearby of motorized vehicles with armor plating upon them and I got down from the cart and found my way through a trail of foolish men who were astonished to see me but compliantly helpful, and at last I was with an officer who had the authority to deal with my needs. We sat on reed chairs in a tent that smelled of grass and earth.

My son had written, *Mother the men suffer here greatly, those who have been here a long while. These are the French and the British and the Australians, mostly, where I am. I am filthy already, though it is all right because I feel like one of them.* This colonel before me was not filthy at all. He was quite properly clean and starched and his uniform rustled with gentility as he leaned forward and offered me tea.

"You've found the right place," he said, sitting back and holding his own cup with a steady hand before his face. "But I must ask you why. What is it that you wish to do here for your son?"

I had not put the question to myself with this sort of bluntness. The colonel reminded me of my husband. I had learned long ago, with Jack, to be prepared for the direct question. But he would ask for answers that were rarely as simple as he wanted them to be. I had not prepared myself for this similar moment with a stranger.

I sipped my tea.

The colonel waited, lifting his own cup to his lips. After both our cups settled back in their saucers and I kept silent for a moment more, he asked, "Are you opposed to our entry into the war?"

"I am an American," I said. "I am a patriot, as is my son."

"I'm sure you are," the colonel said. He nodded very faintly to me.

His face was long and heavily jowled, the face of a man with grandchildren.

I was still trying to find an answer to his question. For myself, as well. *I know there are things that need to be done,* my son wrote to me, *and I'm glad to be the one to do them instead of another fellow. But I have always spoken the truth to you, Mama. I am afraid.*

"My son did not ask me to come," I said. "He is a brave boy."

"He has a brave mother," the colonel said.

"I want to see him, is all." I could think of nothing to add to this.

The colonel seemed to consider taking another sip of his tea, but I knew men like him. He didn't actually like tea. He didn't like sitting in this delicate way with another person. He didn't like having to deal with emotions he could not understand. The colonel put the cup of tea on the table beside him. He squared around to me. It was time to get down to the business of a decision. "I cannot guarantee your safety," he said.

"I understand that," I said.

"How can I in good conscience put a civilian—a woman, no less—in harm's way?"

"It is a choice I have made for myself," I said. "I simply want to see him, to encourage him. And his friends as well." This last came to me all at once. I knew that military officers cared greatly for the morale of their men. "It will make them do better," I said, wandering even farther from some true answer to his question.

The colonel pursed his lips and lifted his chin. He looked away from me, out of the tent. Many men were moving around out there. I could hear their footsteps. And the hard whine of vehicle engines. But I kept my eyes on this man's face.

A long moment passed and finally the colonel said, "The trenches here are well established. There are three lines of them. One at the front. You can't go there, of course. Even if your son has been rotated forward already, which may be the case. You can't go to the support line, either. The German guns reach there quite easily, though it's not impossible for even this tent to receive a hit. I'll let you pass as far as the reserve line. You can return before dusk and the bombardments."

And so I was put in an automobile and a young officer drove me forward and we bounced hard in the rutted earth and there were large tents and the sign of the Red Cross and there were cries—muffled, but clearly men crying out—and I closed my eyes and put my hand on my chest to calm the fluttering inside me. And I thought of my son. Not Edward. It was the summer before he came into this world, when I lost my firstborn, George. I lost him in his second summer. So very many mothers lost a child in its second summer. It was the killing time for children. I should have given him a different name, or at least called him Georgie when I had the chance. He never had a child's name. He was named for my husband's father and Jack called him his *little man*.

And then at last I approached a vast wilderness of earth dead to the near horizon and a distant line of trees, and the earth was full of narrow pits stretching off as far as I could see and they were all broken and angled and ragged, never going for more than a dozen yards before breaking off briefly in some other direction. The young officer led me from the automobile and I insisted on carrying my own bag and he brought me to a set of rough wooden steps and I descended into the earth, as if we'd gotten it wrong all this time, the preachers and their followers: this thin man with bad teeth, dressed in a drab uniform, was all there was of angels, and you packed your bag and you followed him down some log steps into the earth and it was suddenly over, your life, you could not draw a breath, the air was thick with the stink of bodies and decay and the shadows were heavy on your eyes and the strip of blue sky above was just a faded memory of the life that was gone from you. I staggered a little bit and put the bag down.

"Are you okay?" the lieutenant asked, laying his hand on my arm.

"It comes to all of us," I said.

"Pardon me?"

I waved his concern away and picked up my bag again.

We moved along the trench, which was lined on its sides and underfoot with wooden planks. I watched where I put my feet, with puddled water all about, black shiny water, and there were little pockets of men huddled down together, a few sleeping in a lump, another group playing cards—a face lifted there and a man with a British accent said, "Mum," half in acknowledgment and half in wonder, and the other three faces lifted and they all watched me, startled but in an oddly muted way— and I moved on and another group of men were smoking and chatting softly and they too looked up and nodded at me. A solitary man lifted his hand, black with grime, and crossed himself—forehead, chest, left shoulder, right.

We turned a corner and immediately ahead were some men gathered around a great ugly black pot at full boil. They looked up and gaped at me and the lieutenant went ahead to guide me to the side of the pot but I stopped and said to these young men, "Do you know my son? I've come to encourage him. And you too. He's Private Edward Marcus Gaines, 108th Infantry, 27th Division."

"Eddie Gaines," one of them said. "I know him."

"Can you encourage our slumgum?" another boy said.

"Is that your stew you mean?"

"Our stew."

I peered into the pot and it was the color of the Hudson River on a stormy day. "Do I want to know what's in here?" I asked.

"No," came a chorus of voices.

"Mrs. Gaines," said the first one, who knew Eddie. I looked up through a column of steam from the pot, and the boy had a camera and the others retreated and he took my photo.

We all stood in silence over the stew, and for a brief, odd moment they were just a bunch of boys, my son's friends, and they'd dropped by for lunch, Eddie'd invited them and hadn't told me, and there we all stood, awkward like that in my kitchen.

Then I thought of my son and where, in fact, he was, and I moved around the pot and it smelled like the corner of a cellar and the boys were helmeted and dark from grime and this was another country and I moved up beside my lieutenant and we went along the trench until he touched my elbow and said, "Here."

We turned to the left and walked into a dark slash in the wall of the trench and he said, "Watch your step," and my eyes were rubbed hard by the dark, but I saw the dim downwardness of steps and I descended into a sharp cold smell of earth. I went down, as if this tattered angel had been from hell all along and hell was simply cold and dark, not fire at all.

But we came into a large dug-out room and there was a pallet and a hurricane lamp and another thin man who rose from a small table with papers before him. The two men exchanged a greeting, though there was no snapping-to, no saluting, and the lieutenant gave this new officer my letter from the colonel and the officer angled it to the lamp and read it.

"This is Captain Morgan," the lieutenant said, and he went away. The captain glanced up only briefly at this and gave a faint nod and he studied the letter and I could see his hands trembling slightly. His face was strange in the lamplight. I could not tell if he was very young or very old. Young, I decided, from his skin, jaundiced by the lamp but smooth still, though there was something else, perhaps in his eyes, like the eyes of the young mother I'd passed on the road. Who can say what that is? Another contradictory thing. A deadness, from what they'd already seen, but a faint, forced animation as well, knowing that there was more to come.

Finally he said, "I've read this twice."

He paused, as if trying to find more words. I waited. He opened his mouth, closed it, twitched a little at the shoulders. "Yes?" I finally said.

"I'll see if he's not forward," the captain said.

He left me without another word.

I stood waiting there for what felt like a long while. I did not think to sit down. This place was the captain's and he'd not said to have a seat or make myself comfortable, he'd just gone up the steps and left me inside the earth. His desk was covered with papers and a map spread out and a pistol lay there beside them as well. His bed was a pallet on a dug-out step of dirt. There was a table with a few books, some newspapers. A few photos were pinned to the earthen wall. I took a step toward them. The light was dim and the figures were small, standing on the porch of a wood frame house with dormers and a maple tree.

Then I felt something in this place. I turned. No one had entered. But still I felt it. Then my gaze fell to the floor and there in the spill of kerosene light was a rat as big as a squirrel. He was sitting on his haunches and calmly licking his paw and then wiping at his face, like a cat. He was grooming himself, this rat that would go out later tonight and dine on sewage and corpses. I am not a squeamish woman. I did not cry out at this sight. But I touched my chest, held myself hard there to stop the fluttering. Then the rat paused and he looked over his shoulder and lowered himself to all fours and scurried into the shadows.

A moment later, my son appeared. I took a step toward him as he descended.

"Mother," he said, his voice terribly flat.

This represented a change in him. I had always been *Mama*.

I was prepared to take him in my arms. But I stopped, as he had stopped at the foot of the stairs.

I found myself looking about for small talk. "Your captain," I said. "He seemed . . . burdened."

Edward furrowed his brow, not wanting to talk small and not knowing how to stop it. Finally he said, "He's been here nine months now. The officers are good for about six and then they start to fall apart."

I should have felt bad for Captain Morgan, but the sadness that dragged itself into my chest at that moment was for my son, for his having this knowledge of how it is that men fall apart. And for his calling me *Mother*.

"What have you done?" he asked.

"You're not happy to see me," I said.

"I'm a soldier," he said. "I'm in France. The front line is a thousand yards away. I may die there tonight."

"This is why I've come," I said, though I hadn't thought of it in these terms, that my child, my one remaining child, was thinking of dying. But of course he was.

"I'm rotating forward in a few hours," he said.

For a moment I thought of taking him up and carrying him away. There was a surge in me and I felt as if I was suddenly strong enough to sling this overgrown boy over my shoulder and carry him away. We should all do that, all the mothers of the world, I thought. Just pack a bag and come out here and carry these children home. The German mothers too. It would take all of us doing this at once. But instead, of course, we kissed them good-bye and told them we were proud and we packed a knit sweater in the bag they carried.

"Do you have your sweater?" I asked him.

"Mother," he said again, sharply, looking away.

I'd helped him pack his bag. I'd waved a flag at the train station. They'd given flags to all the mothers and fathers and sisters and brothers and wives and sweethearts and we waved them—with all forty-eight stars now—and a brass band played and we shouted hooray for the war. We'd cleaned their faces and sent them away.

"I shouldn't have come," I said.

Edward shrugged.

"Can I have a hug and a kiss good-bye then?"

"Sure," he said, and he crossed the space in two steps and his arms were around me, this grown child, this soldier, this man. We hugged and I kissed him on both cheeks and he kissed me on mine and he smelled bad, my son—he needed a bath—and then he was gone, up the steps, and I thought of lifting him dripping from his bath and wrapping him in a towel and I stopped this memory at once. That was a long time ago.

I sat down on the edge of the captain's bed. I could not stand. I looked at my bag where I'd left it in the middle of the room. I sat that way for a long while and I watched the circle of light on the floor, waiting for the rat to return, but he did not.

Then there was a sound at the top of the stairs. It was the captain.

"Is it all right?" he asked.

"Yes," I said.

He came down as quiet as the rat and he stood before me. I found that I wanted to cry and I worked on that, holding back the tears, before I looked up at him. Finally I did.

The captain's face was dark, with the lamp behind him, but I could see his eyes, darker than the shadows, and he said, "He hasn't been here long enough."

I didn't understand. He sensed it.

"To appreciate your gesture," he said.

I clenched back the tears for a final time. Captain Morgan jittered before me, trying to hold still, obviously, but he shifted ever so slightly from foot to foot, and his hands were shoved hard into his pockets, perhaps to keep them from trembling.

"Where is your mother today?" I asked.

"Omaha," he said.

I patted the pallet next to me, and for a moment he hesitated. "Please," I said. He sat down. I lifted my arm and put it around him. I could feel him trembling. Then he laid his head on my shoulder. Softly, very softly, I said, "You're a good boy. Your mother loves you."

UNIQUE GETAWAY

Dress With Buttons on Back Enables Woman Prisoner to Escape

EAST ST. LOUIS, ILL., AUG. 6—Frank Wible, sheriff of Sullivan County, Ind., came to arrest Mrs. Lizzie Clinger, 22 years old, wanted in Sullivan, Ind., and to-day is minus his prisoner and plus her baby. A gown that buttons in the back aided Mrs. Clinger in the clever ruse by which she escaped from him and Detective Purdy. "I can't go back to Indiana like this," Mrs. Clinger said when arrested. "I'll have to change my clothes."

Sheriff Wible courteously told her she could go into an adjoining room. "Will you please take care of baby while I dress?" Mrs. Clinger asked sweetly. Of course Sheriff Wible would. He and Detective Purdy amused themselves with the youngster while the rustle of feminine apparel came from the adjoining room. Then there came a plaintive voice:

"Oh, I must have some one to button my dress up the back. Can't one of you gentlemen do it."

Sheriff Wible blushed and Detective Purdy stammered. "Not for mine," the latter gasped.

"A couple of policemen got fired not long ago for being in the room while a woman prisoner dressed."

"Well, I'll have to get somebody," Mrs. Clinger cried through the portieres. "Let me run over to Mrs. Fleming, next door, and she'll button me up.

Sheriff Wible gave a sigh of relief and hurriedly agreed. Mrs. Clinger left the house and Sheriff Wible and Detective Purdy sat down to play longer with the baby, while they waited for Mrs. Clinger to return.

An hour later they went to Mrs. Fleming's to learn how many buttons were on the dress that required such a length of time to button. They found Mrs. Clinger had not been there.

from page 11 of the *New Orleans Daily Picayune*
Sunday, August 7, 1910

Performance now going on.

POST- CARD

Miss M. Bloss
219 Hartt Ave
San Francisco.
Calif

THE IRONWORKERS' HAYRIDE

Sunnyvale, Cal.
July 14, 1911

Miss M. Brose
219 Hearst Ave.
San Francisco, Calif.

Dear Mathilda,
Just a line to let you know I am still alive. I am not going
on that hayride. The young man that wants me to go with
his sister in law. But she has a cork leg. I am awfull tired
that is the main reason.

Regards to all. Milton

So this fellow at the new ironworks in Sunnyvale where I
am a cost-sheet man and he is a furnace man, he comes
over to me at the Ironman Saloon. I'm still in my blue serge
suit and collar, though the fellows in their overalls know me as
an okay guy, even if they mostly treat me like a hapless little
brother. But this one fellow, Zack, spots me as soon as he sets
foot in the place. I'm sitting on a stool at the bar counting the
smoked almonds I'm eating and sort of working the numbers
out—how many I need to eat to cover the cost of the beer in
front of me—and wishing I could dare pull out a scrap of paper
and do some downright figuring. But that would undercut my
standing among these fellows around me, who I'm here trying
to be part of, the sorts of fellows that used to daily snap my
suspenders and tweak my nose when we were all boys. So this

fellow Zack presses past his friends and makes straight for me and he claps me on the back, causing me to revise my almond count from twenty back to nineteen, most of the twentieth one attaching itself to the mirror behind the bar. "Milton, old man," he says, and he proceeds for the fourth time in four days to urge me to take his sister-in-law on the Ironworkers' hayride, which is now a mere two days off, even though he has confessed about her having a cork leg.

"I am awful tired nights," I say, an excuse I have not yet tried on him, and he perches on the stool next to me with a face crumpled in skepticism. I don't blame him. He shovels coal, I add numbers. He knows this. I know this. "My eyes," I say. "Tired eyes."

"It's dark," he says. "You got nothing much to look at except Minnie, and she's easy on the eyes, I'm telling you. And that other thing, you know, it wears a shoe and stocking like the good one."

I nod and begin gnawing the thin brown skin off a new almond. This is not my usual method. Minnie's brother-in-law is making me nervous.

He lowers his voice and leans near. "Look. Nobody but you knows about this leg thing. She walks real good. And she dresses up nice. The others will think you're a regular fellow."

I shoot him a sideways glance and turn the almond over, like a squirrel, to gnaw at the other side. I tote up all the sums of his remark. The others don't already think I'm a regular fellow. I'm not a regular fellow. If she can hide her cork leg, I can hide my irregular fellowness. Zack has let me in on a family secret with all the obligations and reciprocities attendant thereto.

Though I have to point out that I never solicited this secret. It was Zack who took the stocking off the rubber foot, so to speak. No. Erase that. *He let the cat out of the bag.* There's a reason for saying things the way everybody else says them.

"How 'bout it," Zack says.

I calculate it all, and the almond is bare and white in my hand. It gives me the willies. I slip it into my mouth, out of sight. I chew fast, knowing I'm about to get popped on the back again. I swallow and then turn to Zack, and I say, "All right."

This much I take pains to learn from Zack. Minnie's leg is missing from well above the knee. She is twenty-two. Her favorite flower is the poppy. And the leg isn't really made of cork. It couldn't be, if you think about it, cork being too soft a wood to bear the weight of a twenty-two-year-old girl, or even half her weight. The leg is of wood—willow, in fact—and years ago they made a swell wooden leg in the county of Cork in Ireland. Thus the name.

As for the reason, Zack says she lost her leg as a child to a runaway horse and an overturned carriage. She was riding in it. This gives me an idea. "Zack," I say. "Think. If she goes out in the night in a wagon being pulled by a horse, won't she be caused to dwell on that terrible event?"

He bends near, putting his great paw of a hand on my shoulder. It weighs quite a lot. I'm having trouble keeping from sliding off the bar stool under its pressure. "Look, Milton," he says. "I haven't been dogging you about this for your sake, much as I . . . like you. It's Minnie who wants bad to go on this hayride. I'm not about to disappoint her."

He squeezes my shoulder like he's trying to juice an orange and I know I better speak up quick. "Sure. Okay," I say, and he lets me go.

"That's my blue-serge pal," he says.

I want to say to him, Why me? I heard you hestitate before the word *like* in your recent declaration. *Pleasantly tolerate* is more what it is. So why choose a fellow like that for his sister-in-law? But I dare not ask. And I think I know the answer. He wants to keep from informing his pals in overalls about his sister-in-law's handicap. Not to mention he sees me as a safe choice, the last male in his acquaintance who'd ever play the masher with his wife's kin.

So this is how I come to be standing at the front gate of the ironworks in collar and straw hat holding a bunch of orange poppies. I am not alone. A few dozen couples—the guys from the various work gangs, mostly, and their girls in lacy shirtwaists and skirts—are all gabbling and promenading around me, trying to choose hay companions on the four large, sweet-smelling wagons that wait along the street. There is no sign of Zack and his sister-in-law. Then two piercing yellow eyes appear down the road—the headlamps of an automobile—and the horses start puffing and stirring, and up roars Zack in his father-in-law's Model T, to the great interest of all the couples. The Ford is as black as the night sky. Zack's father-in-law was one of the first to buy this wonder for a mere $845, and the prices have been coming down already in these past two years, the blue-serge boys in Detroit squeezing their production-cost numbers as tight as Zack squeezing my shoulder. I step forward from the crowd, which is already returning to the matter of choosing wagons. The driver's side of the auto is before me and Zack gives me a nod and I nod back. Then, stepping into the blazing beams of the headlamps is Minnie of the cork leg.

She pauses there, aflame from the lamps of the Ford, and I feel like the flowers are wilting in my hand. She is swell-looking. She's wearing a blue sailor dress with the big collar and the wide, knotted tie hanging down the center of her chest, and her head is bare, her hair all gathered up there with a wide, dark ribbon circling the crown, and there is a radiance all around her—thanks to the Ford, but radiance nonetheless—her whole head is surrounded with a bright glow, like a saint, a martyred saint who has lost her leg to an evil duke—a partially martyred saint—and her face is very pale and delicate of nose and brow and ear and so forth—my eyes are dancing around her, not taking her in very objectively, I realize—her mouth is a sweet painted butterfly. I'm squeezing the life out of the flowers in my hand, I realize, crushing their stems in my fist. I try to ease up, settle down. And now her face turns and she looks at me as if she knows who I am already. I flinch a bit inside, wondering how Zack described me, but it can't be too bad, because he's responsible for setting all this up. She steps from the light.

I observe this first step carefully. I am a detail man. That's my job. And I see with her first step which leg is descended from the land of Erin, so to speak. Her left. She has started from her right leg—she would surely start from her good side—and her left leg then follows a tiny bit slowly, perhaps dragging just a very little, almost imperceptibly, and it's true if I weren't look-ing for this and if I weren't a detail man, I'd never know, but I am and I am and I do. Now under way, she seems quite natural.

She has a blanket draped over one arm. Many of the girls have blankets. I noted that with envy when I first arrived. It is mid-July, and though it can get a bit chill in the valley even in July, I know these blankets are for spooning, and now Minnie is approaching me and she's been moved to bring a blanket. This is too much on my mind as she arrives before me.

"Milton?" she says.

"Are you subject to chills?" I say. Inexplicably. I do have a good, thick, gum-rubber eraser in my head always at the ready to wipe away my mistakes of judgment before they issue forth from my mouth. I am a man who arrives at the appropriate sum total before giving an answer. But on this occasion I have simply blurted forth the next, uncalculated thought in my head.

"I don't have an illness," she says.

My remark had nothing to do with her leg and I have to squeeze my lips shut hard to keep that assertion from coming out of my mouth now and just making things worse.

"Of course," I say. "Of course," I repeat instantly. And it only takes the briefest moment of silence following for me to add, "Of course."

"I'm Minnie," she says.

"Of course," I say, and the hand with the flowers shoots out as if my arm was artificial and the spring lever in the elbow had just let go.

But the flowers save the moment, I think.

"Poppies," Minnie says, her eyes widening at their sight, which is wide indeed because her eyes are already quite large as it is, large and dark as the skin of a Ford Model T, one of which is roaring off into the night, a Ford Model T, that is,

Zack's, leaving me alone with this girl. "They're my favorites. How did you know?" she says. "*Did* you know?"

"The flowers?" I say. "Oh . . ." I pause. I could suggest a deep intuitive bond here. I'm capable of that. I can't possibly expect strict, detailed honesty to be the best policy on a date with a girl with a wooden leg anyway, but in this circumstance I opt for it. "I asked Zack," I say.

Minnie laughs, lifting her face and not holding it back at all, not covering her mouth with her hand, like girls usually do. She says, "He had it drummed into his head by my sister around my last birthday."

A few moments pass and I'm not aware of it exactly but I'm just sort of gawking at her. She looks at me and tilts her head a little. "Are you trying to picture Zack's head being drummed on by his wife?"

I gawk some more.

Minnie lowers her voice. "She's a suffragette, you see."

I realize that if I don't take myself in hand I'll spend the rest of the evening two steps behind this girl without speaking a word. I manage to say, "I didn't know."

"Oh yes. I want to vote too. Does that surprise you?"

"No."

"Or put you off?"

"No," I say, and I manage to sound emphatic.

"I won't harangue you in the hay," she says. "Don't worry."

"Okay."

I'm finally catching up, I think, certainly enough to realize that I'm still holding the flowers straight out. I lift them up at her and she's been sort of in another place too, it seems. "Oh.

Sorry," she says, though it looks like she's talking to the flowers. She takes them and then fixes on me again. "You were swell to do this," she says.

So we get to the business of finding a place for the ride. Most of the other couples have already made their choices and are settling down in the hay. We drift down the row of wagons, Minnie moving along real natural next to me. We arrive at the last one, and I look inside and say to her low, so the others can't hear, "Do you know any of these people?"

"Not a one. And you?"

"Seen a couple of them around, don't know any of them."

"Any of Zack's pals?" she says.

"Not that I know of."

"Then this one's for us," she says and she's already trying to climb up into the wagon.

I step up behind her and my hands come out and sort of hang in the air on either side. She's not looking at me but she knows what I'm doing, even down to my hesitation. "You can just grab and shove if you like," she says.

So I put my hands, which I have to say are trembling more than a little, on each side of her waist and she is heavily corseted inside there and just thinking about her corset makes me go too weak to lift her. But I try. I help a little and somehow she's up on the wagon and I'm scrambling in after her.

She moves forward on her hands and knees pretty fast, heading for the far end of the wagon and I try to keep up, crawling past the other couples settling in. One guy that I've nodded to a few times at the Ironman I nod to again and he gives me a big wink, finally understanding I'm a regular fellow, I presume, and I have the problem of what to do with my face in return. A similar wink, as from a fellow fellow? Another nod, which, I instantly realize, might give an impression like some European king or somebody passing in a carriage? Nothing, just stay blank-faced or turn away? But would that be interpreted as a gesture of rejection or overreaching uppitiness? All this goes through me like turning the crank on the arcade mutoscope real slow, but my arms and legs are still moving in normal time and the decision is made by my indecision. I pass on with my mug fixed in what I'm sure is a mask of buffoonery. Then I look ahead and Minnie is just turning around in the spot she's found for us, and the whole batch of poppies are clenched in her teeth. She's got the stems in her mouth and the cluster of flower heads are bunched up at her cheek and she sees me seeing this and she flutters her eyebrows at me, and once again it's me and my face trying to figure out how to act in this world we're not quite suited for.

She has put the blanket on the straw to her right side and pats the straw to her left. I'm grateful for the instruction. I just set my face to the place where I've been told to go and I creep on. Meanwhile, Minnie takes the flowers from her mouth and lays them on the blanket. Happily, my mind catches up—she'd put the bouquet in her mouth to protect them as she crawled. This makes perfectly good sense. I have arrived safely, turning and falling into the hay beside Minnie, and we are side by side.

I lean on my elbows thrown back behind me and I cross my feet at the ankles. My mouth opens to say something and then snaps shut with no actual words coming to mind. Her wooden leg lies between us. The evening in hay lies before us. I figure I'm in trouble.

Not that I shouldn't be prepared simply to keep quiet. Especially considering I've been enlisted in this date by the girl's relative who happens to mostly know me from a bar and he knows how out of place I generally am and I've agreed to it only after I've said no a few times and even written to my sister in San Francisco that I was saying no in spite of she's the one who's always worried about me never looking up from the column of numbers in front of me to find a life with somebody, but here's a girl who's got a cork leg, not to say there isn't plenty of girl left in spite of that, but it's just the idea of this whole arrangement, which is: Let's choose Milton to take out this girl who other young men maybe would get uncomfortable around because Milton's hard up and he's also a safe choice because there's not really a red-blooded young man inside of him he's just got ink in his blood and ledgers in his brain and numbers on his lips. So under these circumstances why should I care if I don't say another word all night? I can just lie here in the hay and get through the whole thing and then everybody will leave me alone and let me go back to my numbers. See? That's the fate even *I* imagine for myself at the end of a hayride with a girl. Go back to my numbers. But in fact I do expect more from myself now. I want more. It was Minnie herself who brought this out in me. Minnie radiant in the Model T's headlights. Minnie who says just grab me and shove. Minnie who wants to vote. Why shouldn't she?

"Why shouldn't you vote?" I say, unexpectedly.

She looks at me. "Well, dog my cats," she says. "What a sweet thing to say, Milton."

And now, having been seized by one thing to say, the ink bottle in my head instantly spills all over the ledger—I'm not afraid to put it in these terms—I am who I am—and I figure I'm in an even worse predicament, since I've raised her expectations.

But Minnie seems happy to pick things up. Of course she deserves a vote, she tells me, and she goes on for a time about how women would have busted the trusts even quicker than Roosevelt and Taft—it was only this year—what a great year, though, it was, she says—that Standard Oil was finally dissolved and the tobacco trust was broken up, but even at that, look what's happening now, she says, the banks in New York are trying to monopolize the nation's credit. And Minnie is talking like sixty and I sort of settle back and let her words just carry me along about oil and railroads and steel and big corporations, and this should be working up my feelings for numbers and business and all, but that's not what's happening, the wagons have started up and I'm giving myself over to the stars above and the flow of Minnie's voice and her words are like music to me, like a fugue by Bach or something that you just take in and it shuts down all the unnecessary functions of your brain except the part that hears the music. I even feel like humming with her as she talks. Then Minnie finally has to nudge me a bit. I realize that her words have worked around to me, "You're going to cast your ballot in October, right Milton? For the woman's vote in California?"

"Of course," I say.

"Grand," she says. "Just grand." She stops talking and looks at me closely. I look at her closely. The moon is full and Minnie is bright white, like she's made of alabaster. "I'm sorry," she says.

"Why?" I say.

"I've harangued you in the hay," she says.

She seems sincerely regretful. Even in the moonlight I can read that in her face. I want to reach out and touch her, perhaps take her hand, though my own hands go rigid in panic at the thought of it. But I find I have words. "No," I say. "You've educated me."

Minnie sort of rolls her eyes. I think in pleasure.

"You've exhorted me," I say.

Her eyes focus hard on me now. She leans a little in my direction and her voice pitches low. "Thank you for saying so, Milton."

Then a choir begins to sing.

For a moment, strangely, it all seems to be happening just in my head. But the voices coarsen and the music is not Bach. In fact the sound is all around me in the wagons. The others on the hayride are singing. *Shine on, shine on harvest moon up in the sky. I ain't had no lovin' since January, February, June, or July.*

This is true, certainly. And you can tote up all my Januarys, Februarys, and so forth through the whole year. For all my years. Even just counting the ones since I hit adolescence, that's better than a hundred months. I can work up an exact sum tomorrow if I want. Now things go a little sour in my head. I realize that, given my ineptness at the lovin' and spoonin' and all, I'll be adding this present month of July to the tally in spite of this hayride.

The voices roll into a verse. *I can't see why a boy should sigh, when by his side is the girl he loves so true.*

I look at Minnie. She's not singing along, but she's smiling into the wagon, and then she lays her head back on the hay. So do I. And of course I sigh. Shine on, shine on harvest moon.

Minnie and I lie there and listen, side by side, the moon shining over us and the stars, as well, no more talk being necessary, and it's just grand, even as the singing ironmen and their girls move on to other songs, first to "Whoop Whoop Whoop, Make a Noise Like a Hoop and Roll Away," and then "Oh You Spearmint Kiddo with the Wrigley Eyes," not really catching the mood I'm in—but that's still okay, I'm beside Minnie lovely Minnie with the leg of willow—and they do go on to sing "I'd Love to Live in Loveland with a Girl Like You," and there's a lot about turtledoves and hearts beating in tune and babbling brooks and that's more like it and I'm definitely thinking about Minnie though I'm not touching her and I'm not looking at her and she might as well be a distant memory, for all that. And so she soon will be, I realize. This is my only chance with her and we are sliding along in the night and the time is ticking by and I'm acting like she's not even there and now they're singing, *Waltz me around again, Willie, around around around. The music is dreamy, it's peaches and creamy, O don't let my feet touch the ground.*

I sit up at once. It sounds like Minnie beseeching me. Waltz me, Milton, don't let my feet touch the ground. That's what I would need to do. I see myself sweeping her up and it makes no difference what her legs are made of, with me she need never touch the ground.

"Are you all right?" Minnie's voice slips in under the last chorus of the song. I look at her. She's sitting up, too. *I feel like a ship on an ocean of joy—I just want to holler out loud, "Ship ahoy!"* And she turns her head to the wagon and she opens her mouth and sings with the others, *Waltz me around again, Willie, around, around around.* I can't take my eyes off her. There's straw caught in her hair and I want very much to lift my hand and take it out but I'm as paralyzed as ever. Then everyone is laughing and applauding themselves and the music is over and Minnie turns her face back to me.

And she winks.

I have, of course, no earthly idea what she means by this, exactly. But I dare now to think that I'm pretty much okay for the moment. With this very progressive girl. With this girl who would bust the trusts and still has it in her to wink. The madness of speech comes upon me again. "I'm going to vote in October," I say, apropos of nothing but the chaos in my head. So I add, "Like I said before." Which needs further explanation. "For women to vote," I say, and I try to lock my jaw shut.

Miraculously, she seems to understand, even though I don't. She leans close. "You're right," she says. "That's just the way to waltz me around and around, Willie."

I'm glad my jaw is still locked because I'm about to impulsively correct her about my name. But I stay quiet long enough to get what she means. How clever she has made me out to be. Then, inspired, I wink.

She smiles and turns away. "Aren't you feeling a little bit chilled?" she says.

"No," I say. I am, in fact, feeling quite flushed.

Probably from the rapid disintegration of my brain cells. I turn to see what Minnie is seeing and several other couples are opening their blankets and disappearing under them.

"Yes," I say.

Minnie looks at me and of course I'm driven to explanations. "The valley gets chilly," I say. "It's all the orchards," I say.

"I think they somehow, the fruit trees, absorb the heat perhaps, to make it chilly. There's no real statistics on that, however. It's probably just Northern California. The climate, you know." I stop myself at last. I'm breathless from this madness.

"So you're chilly?" she says.

"Yes," I say.

She reaches beside her and gently sets the flowers on the hay. She flashes open the blanket and lifts it and it settles over the two of us up to our shoulders and she says, "How's that?" and I say, "Fine."

We lie back to watch the night sky. We do that for a while, not saying anything, and we're still not touching at all, except maybe just barely along the upper arms, though that might only be my imagination.

It is true that the Santa Clara Valley is like one big orchard. After the earthquake, Sunnyvale started wooing San Francisco companies to reestablish themselves down here, offering free orchard land to build on. That's how the ironworks got started. But mostly it's fruit trees up and down and all around. Which is where the wagons end up, now that the singing is done and the giggling and low talk and spooning have begun. We head out into one of the big apricot orchards.

There is still a smell of sulfur smoke lingering in the air from the curing houses. "You remember last year?" Minnie says.

I know at once what she's thinking and I know it's because of the night sky and the acrid smell.

She says, "When we were all waiting to pass through the tail of Halley's Comet? Did you think that life on earth would come to an end?"

This happens to be a topic I know something about. When the astronomers decided that the tail was made up of deadly cyanogen gas I knew the numbers had to be in our favor, which was soon confirmed in news reports that plenty of people decided to overlook.

"Not for a moment," I say.

"Not for a moment?" Minnie asks, real soft.

I blunder ahead. "The tail looked pretty substantial across the sky," I say. "We passed through forty-eight trillion cubic miles of it and of course it was highly reflective of the sunlight. But you have to understand there was only about one molecule of poison per cubic yard, and since it takes ten thousand sextillion cyanogen molecules to weigh one pound—these were all known numbers well in advance of the encounter—then a little figuring would have told us that the sum total of poison gas the planet earth was about to pass through weighed barely half an ounce."

Minnie's arms emerge from beneath the blanket and she cradles the back of her head in the palms of her hands. She studies the sky and then says, "I was frightened for a while."

And I understand at once how it is that even correctly gathered and accurately calculated numbers can sometimes be irrelevant. I also understand how much I adore this Minnie of the willow leg. I turn a bit onto my side, gently, without disturbing her gaze at the sky, so that I can look at her. And there is a comet of desire streaking through me, its tail thick with something much denser than Halley's poison. I am suddenly desperate to touch this girl, just lay a hand on her arm or brush at her hair with my fingertips—*something*—but I have neither the courage nor the confidence. And I am seized by a plan.

Even as Minnie goes on about her fear of the comet. "No matter what the scientists announced," she says. "Scientists are constantly saying things and taking them back."

I think of her artificial leg lying between us, hidden beneath the blanket.

"It's not a rational thing," she says.

The leg is part of Minnie, but it really isn't.

"We're not always rational creatures," she says.

So it stands to reason that a touch there would not constitute an actual offense, that is to say the flagrant act of a masher. Though it's a leg, after all, which is a powerful part of a girl indeed, it's not really a leg, it's a piece of wood, it's really as if you were with a girl who walked with a cane and you touched the cane, which is no offense at all, and yet, from my own private comet's point of view, it is her own personal sweet willow leg and it is attached to her and so it would still be a thrillingly tender connection to her while at the same time being a connection that no one in the world would know about, not even her, especially under a blanket, and even if they did know about it, it's not like touching the actual girl.

"Sometimes you have to face a difficult thing," she says.

I turn my attention to my left hand, but the hand is only too willing to dash ahead and I glance down the length of the blanket, gauging the contours, and my hand slithers along humpbacked under the cloth, like a mole making for the roses, which in this case is a place just below her artificial knee.

"You think you might die," Minnie says, "and even if that never was so, just the thinking of it is more or less the same."

I am drawing near and I fix on her profile, edged in moonlight, though as beautiful as she is, my attention is elsewhere.

Moles are blind but they have other highly refined senses and so it is with my hand, which expertly arrives on the scene and lifts and curls and descends, slowly, delicately, and Minnie sighs and says, "I didn't have it too bad, though."

Then I touch her. Or it. Or more precisely her skirt, the cloth is rippled beneath my palm, and her wooden leg is further within, a distant thing still, which is all right, I am very happy.

"Did you know that people actually took one look at the comet and died?" Minnie says. "Heart attacks, mostly."

My hand settles in. I surround Minnie's leg. I even squeeze it, ever so faintly.

"There was a woman named Ruth Jordan in Talladega, Alabama," Minnie says. "I read all this in the newspapers. She stepped onto the porch of her home and she looked and fell over dead. And there was another woman, in St. Louis, who was fine looking at the comet thinking it a cloud, but when they told her what she was seeing, she died."

I squeeze Minnie's leg again. And I realize I was actually *thinking* too much both those times, thinking about squeezing and thinking about having squeezed, and all the while I didn't actually *experience* the act, so I squeeze her leg again, trying to concentrate just on feeling it. Then I move my way up to the knee and even across it—Zack said the wooden part goes far up—and I feel my way back down again, squeezing all along.

"Some were simply driven insane," Minnie says. "Especially in Chicago, for some reason."

Squeeze, squeeze, move along, squeeze some more. I'm a bit breathless now. I'm growing dizzy. I love her willow leg.

"Perhaps that's just where the reporter was who wrote the story. But there were people on Chicago streetcars praying and weeping about the end of the world."

Now I slow down for moment. I make the squeezes long and lingering. Here, sweet knee, take this long caress.

"That's not necessarily insane, I suppose," Minnie says. "Something more like religious ecstasy, I guess. But there were suicides. One woman, afraid of the gas of the comet, inhaled the gas from her lamp."

Here, sweet thigh, just above the knee a long caress for you. And then another quick one further up, and then further down.

"Sometimes," Minnie says, "we are compelled to embrace the thing we fear the most, don't you think?"

But her face doesn't turn to me with this question. It's just as well. I wouldn't be able to say much at the moment. It's all I can do to keep my eyes from rolling back in my head in something like religious ecstasy.

"I can understand that, I suppose," Minnie says.

I am vaguely aware of a stir, and I look down the length of the blanket and I nearly gasp. Mr. Mole is racing furiously up and down there, absolutely crazed. I watch for a moment in awe. Up and down the leg. Up and down. It's my hand, I know.

Frenzied with love. It's my own hand. I can stop it, if I choose. And so I do. I concentrate on my hand and I have this bad news for it and I send out the message, and it stops, my hand. Though it's still lying on her leg. Okay. I let myself have this one last touch.

Minnie turns her face to me. "Weren't you a little afraid, even for a moment?" she says.

"Yes," I manage to say.

"That's natural," she says.

I gently move my hand off her leg and back to my side. I focus on catching my breath.

"Shall we find all the constellations?" Minnie says suddenly, lifting her face to the night.

"Yes," I say. "I know something about that."

And so we trace them out together, these patterns in the sky, and I count the stars that make them up while she talks about bears and archers and hunters with swords. And we go on to talk about this and that and we all sing some more songs after the others emerge from their blankets, and when the wagons have returned to the gates of the ironworks, I help Minnie down, grabbing her firmly at her waist, and for a moment it feels as if I am ready to waltz her around and around with her feet never touching the ground.

Though I don't. The Model T is idling nearby and Minnie and I stand before each other, about to part. She says, "Thank you, Milton. This has been grand."

"Yes," I say. And at this moment it does not occur to me whatsoever that Minnie would want to see me again. But what do I know? My judgment is trustworthy only to the bottom of a column of figures. For Minnie takes a step nearer to me, and she dips her face just a little without letting her eyes leave mine, and she says, "You come call on me, all right, Milton?"

I am once again without words, but I manage to nod my head so as to say yes yes I will I will. And then she smiles a sweet slow smile and says, "Just for future reference, Milton. It's the other leg."

SEER'S DOPE MADE GOOD BY FRIGHT

Scared Hoosiers Die of Heart Disease Because Astrologer Said They Would

LOGANSPORT, IND., AUGUST 6— P. A. Graves, a local "astrologer," two months ago made the prediction that during the next two years heart disease would become prevalent and that residents of Logansport would die on the street, sitting in chairs and while at work, and that no one with a weak heart could exercise violently without dying. He said that this condition would result because of the fact that Saturn has become a fixed planet and as such exerts a baneful influence on the heart.

The deaths of four persons in the past five days from the disease, coupled with the fact that there were seven deaths in July, has greatly excited many of the residents and the doctors are being besieged by hundreds of the ignorant for treatment. Physicians say that the excitement and the fear incident to the situation is doing much to justify the prediction.

from the front page of *The Detroit Free Press*
Sunday, August 7, 1910

I CAN QUITE SEE THROUGH IT NOW

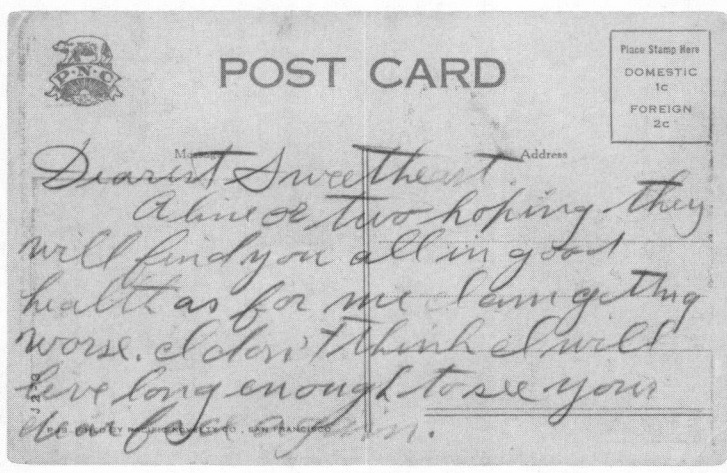

POST CARD

Place Stamp Here

DOMESTIC
1c

FOREIGN
2c

Dearest Sweetheart
A line or two hoping they
will find you all in good
health as for me I am getting
worse. I don't think I will
live long enough to see you

CARL AND I

Dearest Sweetheart
A line or two hoping they will find you all in good health
as for me I am getting worse. I don't think I will live long
enough to see your dear face again.

Three nights after I married Carl Peterson, we watched Sarah Bernhardt die of consumption on a bed strewn with camellias. She was very beautiful, her face a sad white mask, her eyes enormous and dark, her voice rising from the stage and filling the Lyric Theatre, though as the courtesan Marguerite Gautier she was capable of barely a whisper, dying as she was from the tubercular bacilli breeding in her lungs. Her sins had been cleansed, Marguerite Gautier's, by her suffering and by the goodness of her heart and by the sacrifice she had made, giving up for his own sake the one man she had ever loved. I grasped my Carl's arm on the seat next to me as Maguerite died, for he was the one man I had ever loved and now we were married, on the previous Saturday, December 16, 1905, and the church was filled with red camellias. The newspapers said that Sarah Bernhardt slept in her own coffin, transporting it with her wherever she went, and she had died nearly twenty thousand times in her life, just as she was dying before us, and she took a cloth from her bosom as she lay on her deathbed, and she coughed terribly into it.

Now Carl has written to me from Attleboro that he is dying. He left for the sanitarium barely a month ago and he has lost hope. So quickly. The death is coming upon him very quickly. This sometimes happens. Like John Keats, who wasted and died at the age of twenty-six. The British writer Robert Louis Stevenson, on the other hand, resisted for decades before being overwhelmed. As Dr. Gilbert would say, the bacilli have found "fertile ground" in Carl's body. Oh, had you only been as barren as I, my Carl.

He did not send me a view of the sanitarium. None of his postcards have been of this place I have never seen, where he will die. He says it is vast and made of gray stone the color of our birdbath. He could not resist a romantic postcard, even considering. Two lovers sitting at the edge of the sea and she has raised her parasol to shield what they are doing, but their silhouettes are visible. They are about to kiss. He put the postcard in an envelope so the postal carrier would not share his words. *Dearest Sweetheart,* he said to me. I grew weak at this. And he tried hard to put his bravery down on the card, going quite formal for a moment. *A line or two hoping they will find you all in good health,* he said. All in good health. Wholly in good health. Completely in good health. As I seem, in fact, to be, which gives me no comfort. *As for me,* he said, *I am getting worse. I don't think I will live long enough to see your dear face again.*

He turned his face to me when we tucked the quilts around him in the backseat of the automobile that came to take him. He was as white as Sarah Bernhardt dying in the Lyric Theatre. As white as Marguerite Gautier. As white, I'm sure, as John Keats.

I gave out John Keats's book of poems this very morning to a
sallow-faced boy at the library. I am a Carnegie Maid, dispens-
ing the words of all the writers of the world, some still living,
but destined to die at last, and most who have died already, some
of this disease, some not. One in seven who dies in the world,
dies of this White Death. Some leave words behind, some do
not. I have kept all the postcards Carl has sent to me. They are
in a teakwood box. He wooed me with postcards. And he continued to write them even after we were married. He would be
at work and I would come home from the library before him,
and waiting in the mailbox would be a card from him. *Oh, you
sweetheart,* he wrote, in his love of a good catchphrase. This was
not so very long ago. *Oh, you daisy field and up along the creek on
that log or under the big tree. Oh, you. I wish I could go there now
and pick daisies with you.* His face was white and his eyes were
terrible dark when he left for Attleboro.

    I must write him now in return. He will not let me come
to visit. He says I've been exposed long enough to the contagion, he could not bear for me to get sick. And he doesn't say
it, but he's ashamed of how he's grown weak, how he's lost so
much weight. He has always been a man to take off his coat
and roll up his sleeves and have at some physical thing. My only
recourse is a penny postcard that lies before me now in the
center of the little flattop desk in our bedroom. I've chosen a
card from among the romance cards with all the come-hithering
and the oh-no-not-now-sirs, but this is of a woman sitting with
her hands clasped around a knee and her eyes are cast down
and beneath her is the printed word *heartbroken.* I'm regretting

the choice. The card was intended for a woman whose beau has not written to her, has not asked her to the dance. But I am, in fact, heartbroken. Carl will understand.

I look out the open window and across the yard to the sugar maple and to the laundry I'd hung this afternoon, the sheets and my nightgowns and underskirts and two of his dress shirts and I cannot look at his shirts. They lift slightly in a wisp of breeze and I cannot look. I'm finding more things I cannot look at in this house. The overstuffed armchair in our front room where he would read his newspaper of the evening. The porch swing. The cotton handkerchief near my feet. I wish I'd found it before I'd done the laundry. It was caught in the narrow dark space between the wall and his bed, near the headboard. It is folded tightly over the things he brought up from his lungs in his last days in our home. I can see the stains, the color of dried camellias. I found it an hour ago and dropped it at once and I washed my hands, as Carl would wish me to do.

I have filled my fountain pen.

I turn the card over.

I look at it for a long time, its blank, divided back. Finally I take a stamp from the folder in the drawer, a green, one-cent Benjamin Franklin, the image of a man who died when he was eighty-four and who wrote a poem, which I was compelled in school to memorize, that said, "Death is a fisherman, the world we see / his fish-pond is, and we the fishes be." I lick the stamp and put it on the card, and then I sit for another long time, feeling irritated with this old man, for him to live to such an old age and to say this vapid thing about death. This man our country reveres, an old fool is.

But I no better am. I've written nothing yet to my husband. My mind is seizing idly on this and that. The chased hard rubber of my Waterman pen. The ticking of the clock from the front room. The faint snap of the sheets in the breeze. The stirring of the maple tree. We first kissed under a vast maple tree, Carl and I. Decoration Day, 1904. We'd met in a late March snow that year. I came out of the general store and I had my shopping bag clutched to my chest. The air was unexpectedly full of snow and I was dazzled by this. I lifted my face as I stepped out and turned and I even closed my eyes to let the flakes fall on my eyelids and I ran into Carl Peterson, a great tall oak of a man whose arms went around me even before I had looked into his face, though he was a perfect gentleman, Carl was always a gentleman and his arms were there simply to keep me from falling. As soon as I was steady on my feet he withdrew and we looked into each other's face and he did not seem particularly handsome to me in those first moments. I am an overly critical sort, I think. It is my nature. His eyes were rather too close together and his face too round and too ruddy and though he was clearly a young man, he had deep-shadowed furrows across his brow above his nose and defining his cheeks from nose to lips. I would come to love these places on his face. I would run my fingertip in these soft grooves of his face. Even when I had long prayed for that ruddiness to return, and when his face had begun to go gaunt, I would lie beside him and run my fingertip in these places and he would close his eyes and perhaps dream of how we met.

He suddenly bent forward and I took a step back, startled. Then he rose up with the tinned milk that had fallen from my bag. "I make these," he said.

"Yes?" I said, not comprehending at first, though the new Pet Milk factory was a source of civic pride in our town. Flakes of snow were clinging to his kersey cap.

"Well, so to speak," he said, lifting the can and considering it, his lower lip pushing up thoughtfully. Too thoughtfully to be serious.

"I'd say cows made those," I said, surprised at myself that I'd suddenly banter with a strange man.

The deep furrow across his brow dipped down sharply, but not for a moment did I think I'd made a mistake. We knew at once, both of us, what we were doing. He said, "Well now, miss, do you think the cows run all the kettles and vacuum pans and heating chambers and cooling tanks to make this stuff pure and safe?"

"So the cows work for you?"

"And then there's the canning." He lifted the tinned milk high. "No cow can do a double seam on a tin can."

"All right," I said. "I'm prepared to give you credit. . . . You own the company, do you?"

He drew up to full height and he laid the can in the center of his chest. "Please," he said. "I'm a proud member of the working class, which does the real work. Neither cow nor tycoon can usurp our importance." He paused to let that sink in for a moment and I duly stood there looking up at him, agape. Then he winked at me and said, "I *am* a foreman, however."

And that was how we met, Carl Peterson and I. And we kissed under a maple tree up along a creek where we lingered, sitting on a log, and we talked, and there were daisies all around and then we kissed under the big tree, and this was on Decora-

tion Day, 1904, the Pet Milk factory picnic, and all the work-
ingmen tipped their hats to Carl and he was dressed in coat and
collar and tie and I wore my lingerie dress and I carried a
parasol, and without a fuss we walked away from all the others,
and on the log, before we got to the maple tree, we sat silent
for a long while, a few daisies drooping in his large hand that
rested on his knee, and he was unaware of them, he had picked
them thinking, I'm sure, to give them to me, but something
else had come to his mind and he'd forgotten. I was feeling
very tender about this absentmindedness in him and I was
watching that hand, its stillness, the yellow flower faces leaning there. He was thinking hard. And then he said, with no
preamble, no clearing of his throat or shuffling around, without that hand and the daisies stirring even a little bit, he said
just straight out, having quietly worked up the courage, "I love
you."

"Well," I said after only a single quick breath, "I love you
too."

I slept in the yard last night in a reclining chair, my body
swaddled like Carl's. I want to share this sanitarium life of his.
Yesterday I ate raw eggs and milk and did exercises, moderately,
morning and evening, and I lay in that chair under the sky all
day long, trying to think of nothing, resting my body and mind,
resting completely and activating my body's own defenses out
in the fresh pure air. On the day we found out for sure that our
worst fears about his persistent cough, his afternoon flush, his
weakness were true—this was still before the blood—on that
day, Dr. Gilbert, who has always looked pale and gaunt himself, truth be told, sat behind his massive desk and his glasses

hung round his neck on a cord and he told us straight out. "Mr. Peterson, you have tuberculosis of the lungs."

I was calm, at this. And, of course, Carl was calm. We had known for a while, though the words had never been spoken between us. But Carl, even from the first, would smother his coughs in some bit of cloth or other, and he would rise up abruptly and walk out of the house to a corner of the yard to spit. Carl and I held hands before Dr. Gilbert, who was going on in a voice tainted with sarcasm about "that German germ hunter who has made us imagine the very air full of contagion." Then Dr. Gilbert shrugged and said, "These bacilli, though they may well exist, must necessarily fall on favorable soil, fertile soil, to grow and live. So we must build up the soil."

He had used the same metaphor—apparently the only one he knew—when he'd told me the year before that my ovaries were not properly formed and my womb was tilted. So I cannot have children? I said, not really a question. You have no fertile soil, he said. I imagine him bending over a man suffering a heart attack to say, Your heart lacks fertile soil for beating. He is a fool with his words. I held Carl the night we discovered my barrenness and for several nights thereafter. I held him till morning, my arms around him as if to cradle him. We both shed tears, though with no sounds, no words about this turn of events. There would be no children for us. Though so many die young, anyway. When yellow fever and cholera and smallpox aren't going around, there's always influenza and pneumonia and typhus and scarlet fever and measles and whooping cough and diphtheria, to name a few, and there is always a bit of poisoned meat or milk or something else that a child can eat and die from, and, of course, there is tuberculosis. Let *us* die then, Carl and I, but not a child. It's better for us not to have a child than to bear a child that will die young, is it not?

It is not. But I have no other consolation.

I rise up from my desk. The postcard is still blank, except for my husband's name and his final address in this world, the Attleboro Sanitarium, Attleboro, Massachusetts. I turn away from the desk. I cross the room and stand in the doorway from the bedroom to the living room. I look at his armchair by the window. I turn and face into the bedroom. I look at our bed. He wrote me a postcard from Attleboro soon after he arrived to say that the nurses all admired him, how he followed procedures. He wrote, *I will surely win next month's Careful Consumptive Award for sputum management.* I wrote and asked if there was money for that. I knew he would laugh. He knew I had laughed. I will soon lose this house to the savings and loan. I can go to Worcester and live with my mother. Carnegie has put a library there, I'm sure.

I wait for another thought. I wait for words to say to my husband.

We were so careful. He was always a careful consumptive, even at home, and I let him. I regret that. Standing now looking at our bed I understand that I should have kissed him more. I should have turned his face to me when he was coughing so terribly in the night and I should have taken his face in my hands and kissed him in that moment when he needed something no one could give. I should have kissed him on the lips.

I move to the desk now. I sit. I pick up my pen. I think to call him sweetheart. I think to say, *My darling I love you and always will. I kiss your dear face, your darling lips.* But I write none of this. These are foolish words. True, perhaps, in their way. But foolish in their bland abstractedness. They have nothing to do with the life Carl and I now share.

And then I know what to say.

I remove the cap of my pen, and I angle the card just so, and I write: *We'll meet in death.*

And I know what to do. I put the pen down and I push my chair back and I bend to the handkerchief on the floor. I hold it with my two hands, Carl's handkerchief, and I unfold it. I expose the remnants of his tortured breath and I lift it to my face. And I breathe in, deeply. I breathe into myself my husband's life, and I pray that I am fertile soil.

Heartbroken.

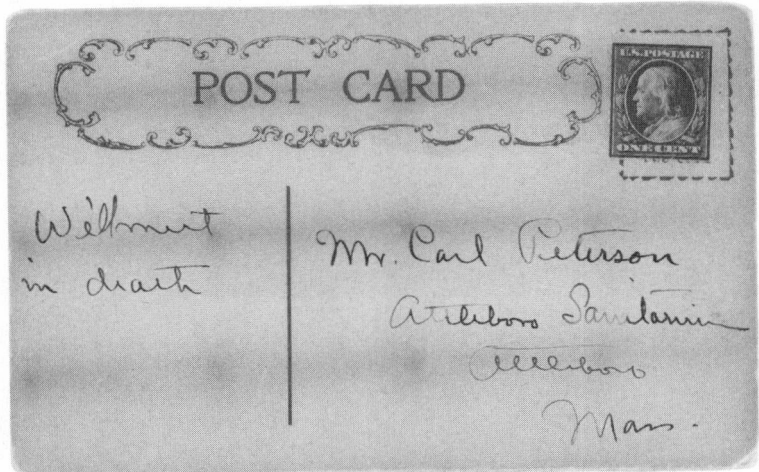

POST CARD

U.S. POSTAGE
ONE CENT

Wëlhnut
in death

Mr. Carl Peterson
Attleboro Sanitarin
Attleboro
Mass.

FLIES OVER ALL PITTSBURG
30,000 PERSONS
SEE GLENN CURTISS SOAR

Comes Down Without Having Been Asphyxiated —600 Persons Wanted to Go Up With Him, of Whom 75 Were Women—Baldwin Hasn't Any Luck

PITTSBURG, AUG. 6—The wind favored the aviation meet this evening for the first time in three days and 30,000 people on the hills surrounding Brunot's Island witnessed three successful flights by Glenn Curtiss.

The boss aviator of the Pittsburg exhibition had a narrow escape in his early attempts this afternoon while trying out the machine he used at Reims, France. The machine had been rebuilt and the wires attached to the rudder had become crossed.

Curtiss started for a straightaway flight across the Brunot's Island grounds and when he was about fifteen feet above the ground the plane ducked downward. Curtiss shut off his motor and landed with a jolt which threw him off his seat. He discovered on examining the Reims machine that the rudder was not working right, so he put it away.

Curtiss made three good flights. The last was at dusk. He sailed over Brunot's Island twice, then headed out over the north shore of the Ohio River, passing over the smokestacks of the mills in Allegheny, over the Western Penitentiary and across the hills to McKee's Rocks on the south shore, then over the mills and back to the island. The 5,000 spectators on the grounds cheered him wildly as he grounded in front of the grand stand.

Capt. Baldwin had trouble with his "red devil" and had to quit for the day after making unsuccessful straightaway flights. Mars also made several straightaway flights, but his machine was too light to work against the wind, which was blowing about ten miles an hour at the time.

Curtiss in one flight took a newspaper writer up with him. He had 600 applicants, among them seventy-five from women, who wanted to accompany him.

from page 4 of *The Sun,* New York
Sunday, August 7, 1910

POST CARD

PLACE
STAMP
HERE

CORRESPONDENCE HERE NAME AND ADDRESS HERE

This is Earl Sandt of
Erie Pa in his Aeroplane
just before it fell

THIS IS EARL SANDT

*This is Earl Sandt of Erie Pa in his Aeroplane just before
it fell*

I've seen a man die, but not like this. There was silence
suddenly around us when he disappeared beyond the
trees, silence after terrible sounds, that hammering of his
engine, the engine of his aeroplane, and the other sound,
after.

He had climbed miraculously up and he had circled the
field and we all took off our hats as one, the men among us.
Mine as well. Hooray, we cried. My son cried out, too. Hooray.
This was why we'd come to this meadow. We would peek into
the future and cheer it on.

And Earl Sandt hammered overhead and down to the far
edge of the pasture, defying the trees, defying the earth. The
propeller of his engine spun behind him and he sat in a rattan
chair, as if he was on his front porch smoking a cigar. Then he
came back from the tree line, heading our way.

I reached down and touched my son on the shoulder. I
had never seen an aeroplane and something was changing in
me as it approached. I suppose it scared me some. I had no
premonition, but I needed to touch my son at that moment.
The plane came toward us and there was a stiff wind blowing—
the plane bucked a little, like a nervous horse, but Earl Sandt

kept him steady, kept him coming forward, and I felt us all ready to cheer again.

Then there was a movement on the wing. With no particular sound. Still the engine. But there was a tearing away. If I had been Earl Sandt, if I had been sitting in that rattan chair and flying above these bared heads, I might have heard the sound and been afraid.

I lifted my camera. This had nothing to do with the thing happening on the wing. I was only vaguely aware of it in that moment. I lifted my camera and I tripped the shutter, and here was another amazing thing, it seemed to me. One man was flying above the earth, and with a tiny movement of a hand, another man had captured him.

Earl Sandt was about to die, but he was forever caught there in that box in my hand. I lowered my Kodak and for a moment the plane was before me against the sky and all I felt was a thing that I sometimes had felt as a younger man, riding up into the Alleghenys alone and there would be a turning in the path and suddenly the trees broke apart and there was a great falling away of the land.

A falling. He fell, Earl Sandt. The aeroplane suddenly reared up on its left side, as if it wanted to turn to the right, but the nose went down and there was so little sky below, so little, and then the aeroplane tried to lift itself, briefly, but the wing was tearing away and the engine hammered loud and Earl Sandt turned sharply right again pointing to the earth and his aeroplane looped, the engine crying out, and he fell, disappearing behind a stand of pine.

There was a heavy thump beyond the trees, and I have nothing in my head to compare it to. Not a barn collapsing, not a horse going down, not the dead sugar maple, forty foot high, I had felled only yesterday in our yard. This sound was new.

And our silence followed. We all of us could not take this in. He had flown, this Earl Sandt, he had raised his goggles to his eyes and stepped into his machine and he had run along the meadow and had lifted into the air, and now I looked into the empty place where he had been, only a moment before. In my head I could see once again the two great wings and the spinning of the propeller and then he was gone.

"Papa?" It was my son's voice drifting up to me from the silence.

I looked into his face.

"It's all right," I said, though I knew it was not. I could feel Matthew's bones beneath my hand, which still lay on his shoulder.

"He's gone," my son said.

I looked to the others. There was a stirring. Some of the women began to cry.

"Mother of God," one man said and he moved in the direction of the pines. He was right. We had to do something now.

I let go of my son and put the camera in his hand. I turned to the place where Earl Sandt had vanished. "Stay here," I said.

We ran, perhaps a dozen of us, across the meadow grass and into the pines and I could smell burning and there was smoke up ahead and I could smell a newly familiar thing, a smell of the automobiles that had come to our town, their fuel. Then we broke into a clearing and the aeroplane was crumpled up ahead and beginning to burn.

I was behind several of the men and we were in our Sunday clothes, we had left our churches this morning and had come to see the exhibition of this wonderful thing, and now we were stripping off our coats and winding them around our hands and arms to allow us to reach into the flames, to bring Earl Sandt out. Two men were ahead of me, already bending to the tangle of canvas and wood and metal and smoke. I felt myself slow and stop.

I did not know this man. I had seen him only from afar, only briefly. He had raised his goggles and hidden his eyes and he'd had some intent in his head—to fly, of course; and he did. But he was a man, flesh and blood, and he was lying broken now, ahead of me. There were others to help him. The ones ahead, and still others now, rushing past me. I continued to hesitate, and then I turned away.

Matthew had followed me. He was standing a few yards behind, in the trees. I lifted my hand to acknowledge him, and I found it swathed in my suit coat, expecting the fire.

I moved to my son, unwrapping my arm.

"The others are helping," I said to him, so he would understand why I had turned away.

"I want to see," he said.

"No."

"Pa."

"No," I said, firm. I turned him around and we stepped out of the trees. I looked once more into the sky where Earl Sandt had been.

Matthew and I walked from the meadow and through the center of town, passing the Merchants Bank, where I had an office, where I was vice president, and we moved beneath the maples of our street, old trees, dense above us, and we were quiet, my son and I. The meadow, the open sky, all of that, was left behind. Then we reached the place along the road where I could see my house ahead.

The maple was gone from the front edge of my property, dead from blight and felled by my own hand. I looked away, not wanting to, but I felt suddenly bereft of this tree. I was sorry for its passing, this tree. Matthew broke away from me now, began to run. I looked.

His mother was coming down the porch steps. My son ran hard to her, not calling out. She turned her face toward us, saw him approaching, sensing, I think, that something had happened.

I stopped, still separate from them. My daughter, a tall gangly girl, my sweet Naomi, emerged from the house, and for a moment they all three were before me, and the house itself, a fine house, a house we'd lived in for four years now, a solid house with its hipped roof and double-windowed dormer and its clapboard siding the color of sunlight in the brightness of noon.

My wife went down on one knee, and Matthew reached her and he threw his arms around her neck. I knew I should move forward, to explain. But what would I say? Naomi came to the two of them, put her hand on her crouching mother's shoulder. There was a seizing in my chest. I wanted to take them all three up into my arms, but instead, I stood dumbly there, watching.

Finally, Rachel's face lifted to look at me over Matthew's shoulder. I felt heavy now, rooted to this earth, as if I'd decided to take the place of the dead maple. But I made myself move. I took a step and another and there was a loosening inside me as I moved toward my family. My wife tilted her head slightly, a questioning gesture, I think. Naomi looked at me too, came around her mother, and I was glad she was drawing near, and she put her arms about me, I felt the bones in her arms pressing at my back. I held her tight.

"What was it, Daddy?"

"An accident," I said. "It was just an accident."

"Matty said he was dead, the man."

"We don't know that for sure."

"He fell?"

"Yes."

She said no more, but she needed me to hold her closer and I did. "It's all right," I said. "We're all right."

Matthew could not sleep. The house was dark and my wife and I had just extinguished the lamp, alone and undistracted at last. Then we heard his cry, wordless, and Rachel rose. I knew what it was about. As she disappeared, I looked toward the dark gape of the bedroom doorway and I gripped the sheet as if to put it aside and to rise. But I hesitated. I should not have hesitated to go to my son, but I did. For one moment and then another.

I forced myself to throw back the sheet and put my feet on the floor. I stood. I made my way across the room and down the hall, and my son's tears were fading as I approached. I stood in his doorway and his mother said to him, "It's okay, Matty. God decided he wanted an aeroplane pilot in heaven."

"Like he wanted Henry for an angel," my son said.

I turned away. I moved back down the hall and then stopped, neither here nor there. Matthew's first cousin Henry, my brother's son, had died of smallpox. My son had already encountered death. Of course he had, we had all encountered death, it was a part of our daily lives. Always, we waited for the first sneeze, the first cough, the first spot on our skin, we waited to be carried away, if not from smallpox then from influenza or from scarlet fever or from diphtheria or from pneumonia or from tuberculosis. It was the way of the world. I believed in God, that he managed our lives, that he would call us when he chose to. And I was glad my son could picture his blood kin, a child of his own age, as an angel and not as a corpse in the ground.

But I stood in the middle of the hallway and I dragged my forearm across my brow and I was having trouble drawing a breath.

I waited in bed, sitting propped up in the dark, sweating still.

Finally Rachel appeared in the door, quietly, pausing there in the dim light, her white nightgown glowing faintly, as if she were a ghost. I spoke to her at once, to drive that image from my mind. "Is he all right?"

"I don't know," she said, and she floated this way.

"Rachel," I said.

"Yes?"

She was beside the bed now. I had spoken her name without anything more to say. I just needed to say her name.

"Nothing," I said.

"What happened out there?"

"The plane crashed," I said. "These machines aren't safe."

Rachel drew back the sheet and sat beside me. "Paul."

I looked toward her.

Her face was there, turned to me, featureless in the dark. She touched my hand and repeated, almost in a whisper, "What happened?"

"I don't know."

I was Earl Sandt. Sitting in my rattan chair. I looked down and the faces all turned upward and the mouths all opened to cry out but the only sound I could hear was the rush of air about me as I flew, I flew and the lift was not in my wings it was in my chest my very chest I was buoyed up and moving quickly and there was nothing around me now, not the aeroplane, not the rattan chair, only the wide bright air. I looked down again and there was only one face below and it was my own.

Mine. I woke. I sat up quickly, expecting to rise from the bed and up through the ceiling and out into the night sky. But I was awake. I was sitting on my bed. Nevertheless, I lifted my eyes, and I saw the aeroplane, its broad wings, the fragile bones holding them in place, the bones stretching behind to the smaller back wings, the tail. And then suddenly the beast veered and showed me its dark underside and it dashed down.

And then the sound.

I jumped up from the bed, knocking into the bedstand.

"What is it?" Rachel cried.

"I'm all right," I said.

"Was it Matty?"

"It was a dream," I said.

I do not require silence at the breakfast table. We eat together each day, my wife and my son and my daughter and I. Even when my children have one leg skewed out from under the table, ready to run into the summer morning. They have their duties in this house, but the mornings are theirs. It is best to let a child feel his freedom in the morning. And they are free to speak, as well. I like to listen to the movement of my children's minds.

But this morning there was silence. A long period of silence. And their legs were under the table, in spite of it being early summer. And without urging, Matthew was eating his eggs, studiously sopping up the last bits of yolk with a piece of bread.

I had not picked up the newspaper that lay folded beside my plate. I could see, in large bold type, in the upturned quarter, the words AVIATOR KILLED. It was not uncommon for me to read the newspaper at the breakfast table, but only after we'd all had a chance to speak of the day to come.

I looked at Rachel. She was lifting her coffee cup to her lips and I could see that her eyes were on Matthew. He was intent on the bread, running it around and around the plate. Naomi was looking out the kitchen door. I followed her gaze. The sun was bright. The trees quaked. A scrap of paper blew across the yard—lifting briefly into the air—and then it fell and tumbled along.

I placed my hand on the newspaper but I did not open it. I looked at my hand. It covered the words in the headline.

Finally I said, "It looks like a fine day."

Matthew lifted his face at this. "May I be excused?" he said.

"Yes."

He pushed back his chair and he rose and only now was I hearing the flatness of his voice. He was a boy. This was the moment of the day that should have been relished above all others.

"Matty," my wife said. "Are you all right?"

My son had moved toward the door. He stopped now and turned to us. His two shoulders lifted slightly and fell. It was a very small gesture, really, this shrug, but it made my eyes close so as not to see it, this gesture in my son that was not the gesture of a child at all. Too late.

I opened my eyes. He was pushing through the screen door, not having spoken a word.

A Monday morning in the year of our Lord 1913. A desk in a bank. A newspaper tucked under my arm and then put away in a drawer. I sat and my hands were flat and unmoving on the top of my desk, my mahogany desk, and above me was a high window, and I have always liked the column of sky looking over me and I have liked the hush of the bank. It is not blasphemy to say that the hush was like that of a church. We protected the money of the people of this town, and their money was a measure of their hard work, and their hard work rightly gave them the things of this world, the things of a world changing rapidly now. The hush of the bank, and there were low voices murmuring, and I knew their words, I could hear *terrible* and I could hear *aeroplane* and I could hear *fire* and I could hear *dead*. I wanted to stand up and cry out to my tellers and my customers, Go about your business, all of you. Just go about your business.

But I did not stand. I swiveled in my chair and raised my eyes to the window, to the empty morning sky. I had myself gone up into that sky. Higher even than Earl Sandt. I had stood in the air.

I had stood and looked out on a great city, on a world of business and banking, a world of making goods and buying and selling and building houses and factories and I looked out on steamships and trains and bridges and, far off, a vast sea, and I was standing within a thing as great as all of that. The Singer Building. The highest building in the world at that moment in the summer of 1909 when my host, a fellow banker, lifted his office window on the thirty-eighth floor, and I trembled like a horse before a fire. I crept forward and I felt my chest swell, I grew large with fear and happiness to look at this city, vast and multiform in its stone and marble and terra-cotta, the work of human hands.

I stepped closer still. I grew bold. The air moved on my face. An air only the clouds knew. But I was part of a race of creatures of the earth who were remaking themselves into something new. I took the last step a man could take and not fall. I pressed against the sill and I bent forward at the waist and looked across the rooftops below—rooftops that themselves were higher than any tree on earth, but far below me now—and I looked beyond the docks and masts and smokestacks, I followed the bright thread of the Hudson River to Ellis Island and the statue of Madam Liberty, her arm lifted high.

Earl Sandt, I lift my arm to you. I stand in the meadow beside my son, a blazing torch in my hand. Come here to me, guide your plane this way, fly down to this flame and land safely beside me. I look from where I sit in the rattan chair, my hands on the steering handle, I see the flame below, and my wing has not yet torn. I nudge my aeroplane gently downward, down toward the man and the boy. I will be safe.

But I am not Earl Sandt. He is dead.

I have seen men die before. My father, long ago, his lungs bricked up solid with pneumonia. A man in the Alleghenys, broken beneath a felled tree, when I was young and working in timber. And another in New York City on that day in 1909 when I went out of the Singer Building and into the streets that were dim even near noon, streets narrow and full of rushing men and the hammering of metal and the whine of wheels and the mutter of automobile engines and the clatter of a distant elevated train, and I turned to look up at the place where I'd stood, in the middle of the air, and my eyes went up and up, impossibly high, up the great bluestone and redbrick column, up to its great mansard roof and cupola and the bright sky beyond. "Step lively," a voice said, and I looked and I could not pick the speaker out of a hundred bowlered men moving all about me.

I stepped away, up the street, which was cloaked in the shadows of skyscrapers as far as I could see. I moved, and suddenly before me there was a gathering of men and some bowlers were coming off and I came up.

He was in a greatcoat in spite of the heat. He was sprawled facedown, his arms outstretched, his legs spread wide. The men about him were quiet. I thought to look up. A gray stone building loomed over us, perhaps two hundred feet high. I looked back down to the dead man. A policeman pushed past me and bent to the body.

I found myself standing beside my desk in the bank on the morning after Earl Sandt died. I could not recall the act of rising from this chair. I extended my arm, touched my hand to the corner of my desk, stiffened my fingertips, held myself up. I had to go out, I realized.

I moved to the coatrack and took my hat and I put it on my head and I stepped from my office and my secretary looked up and I said to her, "I'll be back shortly." She lifted her eyebrows ever so slightly. This was unlike me, of course. But I did not pause to explain. There was no explanation.

I stepped into the sunlight before the bank and turned toward the woods where he had gone down.

A wagon was moving toward me from the tree line as I approached. I stopped. The horse had its head lowered as if the load were heavy, but the wagon moved easily, quickly. I stepped away from it. The driver turned his face to me. A man I knew, a collector of scrap goods. He nodded, but I could not return the nod. I was leaden now in my limbs. The wagon slipped past and I glanced into the bed of it: twisted metal, charred wood, a panel of canvas. I looked sharply to the side. This whole thing was a mistake, to come here again. I thought to back away, to face toward the town, the square, the bank, the maple trees, face toward my house where I would surely live the rest of my life.

I could not. I had to press on, into the stand of pine. But I had to catch my breath first. I felt as if I'd been running a long way. I bent forward and put my hands on my knees.

Above me was the sky where Earl Sandt had spent his last moments of life. I did not look. I leaned hard onto my knees. I closed my eyes. I held tight to the steering handle and there was something terribly wrong. These wings that felt like my own limbs—I sensed them stretching out from me and lifting me up— these wings went weak and so did my limbs of flesh, I was instantly aware of the very surface of my skin, the beating of my heart. And I felt a question rise like a gasp into my throat: What was it I believed? Did I sense a God all about me in the sky? Was it he who lifted me and would take me now into his arms?

Forgive me, no.

This thing I had expected to be familiar—my own death— was all new. I fell. I fell from him. His hands receded and the trees reached up and I fell.

I could not breathe at all. I rose up from where I'd been bending and I stood straight and dragged the air into my lungs and I opened my eyes, and before me was the tree line, the pines, and beyond them was the clearing where he fell and burned, Earl Sandt. And he knew something now. Right this moment. Something that I desperately wished to know. He had been alive above me, in the sunlit air, just yesterday, and now he knew the great truth of it all.

I stepped forward, moved toward the trees. My breath had returned. Fragile. Easily taken away. But I breathed deep once, and again, and I walked into the darkness of the trees and I was filled with the smell of pine all about me and the smell of the duff beneath my feet and with other smells, not of the forest, faintly still of smoke in the air and the fuel of the aeroplane.

I pressed on, my face lowered, feeling the trees on the back of my neck, in my shoulders, in a faint wrenching upward in my chest. I've been around trees often in my life, I made a life from the forests before I became who I am, a man with a desk in a bank and a Georgian revival home and a wife and a son and a daughter and a special pew in a church where the deacons sit, and I know nothing about anything, I know only that I must press past these last few trees and into this clearing, which I do.

It is empty. It is empty. Earl Sandt's aeroplane was here and now it is gone. I move out to the center, I am surrounded by high pine, and there is something. A shapeless patch of burnt earth. I slow and stop before it. He burned here. He vanished from this life here.

I take another step. I stand precisely where he fell. For a moment I stretch out my arms, as if to fly, and they are contained within this black bareness. I hold fast to the steering column and my wings are still whole and I am racing toward those distant pines, and a thought occurs to me. I sit on the back of a horse. I am high up, above the tree line, on a slender thread of a path. Not even the smell of the pines has risen this high. I pause and I look below me. Faces turn up, their hats raised high in the air. Treetops point up to me and I have nothing inside but an enormous quiet. I find myself separated from all that I've known, from every touch every word every face, I have lifted up into the air, high on this mountain with nothing around me but the empty sky, high in the air above this meadow. And I think: This is how it feels. To be free. To be utterly alone. And my hands clench on the reins. There is only one more thing to feel, to know. My hands clench harder, wanting to slip hard to the right, to leap into that empty sky beneath me. Earl and I.

"Papa."

For a moment I do not recognize the voice.

"Papa."

It has drawn near. I look.

It is Matthew.

He stands before me. His face is smudged. His hair is tousled. His eyes are fixed hard on mine.

I want him to go away from this place, quickly. I lift my hand to him, a vague gesture, and I cannot find words. "Matty," I say, just that. I am within the circle of Earl's fire and my son is outside. I try to step to him, but I am rooted here. I look at the trees all around. And then back to my son. His face is turned up to me, waiting.

I know too much. I want him to run away now, not just from this place but from me.

"Go on home," I say.

His brow furrows very slightly.

I step from the circle, I reach out, my hand goes to him, my thumb lands gently on his brow, tries to smooth the furrow away.

He backs off.

I didn't mean to frighten him. I carry too much in these fingertips now.

But suddenly he smiles.

"Papa," he says. "Look."

His hand comes from behind his back. I don't recognize the object at first, hanging limply over his fingers.

"It's his," Matthew says.

And now I can see. Earl Sandt's goggles.

"I found it," he says.

I struggle once again to draw a breath. The moments I have yearned to share with Earl Sandt: he entered them looking through this thing in my son's hand.

But before I can think of what to do, Matthew grasps the goggles at each end and he lifts them high and the strap goes quickly over his head and the goggles slide down and are on his face and I can see his eyes for a moment, his child's eyes, the eyes of my boy, faint there and distant, and his face angles and his eyes vanish, the panes of glass go blank from the light.

And my son lifts his arms. He lifts them like wings, and he turns to his left and he begins to run, he runs swooping and lifting and falling. "Look, Papa," he cries. "Look. I'm Earl Sandt!"

REAL PERIL

Familiarity with his father's adventures in the search for the South Pole has apparently bred contempt in the mind of Lieutenant Shackleton's small son.

He was heard not long ago asking his mother for "a story with danger in it."

"I don't want to hear anything more about papa," he said. "Tell me about the baby that was drowned in his barf."

from page 3, section 5,
of *The Daily Tribune,* New York
Sunday, August 7, 1910

POST CARD

A A ☆ ☆ A
A PLACE A
☆ STAMP ☆
○ HERE ○
A A ☆ ☆ A

CORRESPONDENCE HERE | NAME AND ADDRESS HERE

After the battle notice the pretty Senoritas in this photo. The one in white does my laundry.

THE ONE IN WHITE

After the battle notice the pretty Senorita's in this photo.
The one in white does my laundry.

B unky Millerman caught me from behind on the third day of Woody Wilson's little escapade in Vera Cruz. Bunky and his cameras and I had gone down south of the border a couple of weeks earlier for the *Tribune*. I'd been promised an interview with the tin-pot General Huerta who was running the country. He had his hands full with Zapata and Villa and Carranza, and by the time I got there, *el Presidente* was no longer in a mood to see the American press. I was ready to beat it back north, but then the muse of reporters shucked off her diaphanous gown for me and made the local commandant in Tampico, on the Gulf Coast, go a little mad. He grabbed a squad of our navy bluejackets ashore for gasoline and showers and marched them through the street as Mexican prisoners. That first madness passed quick and our boys were let go right away, but old Woodrow had worked himself up. He demanded certain kinds of apologies and protocols, which the stiff-necked Huerta wouldn't give. Everybody started talking about war. Then I got wind of a German munitions ship heading for Vera Cruz, and while the other papers were still picking at bones in Tampico, I hopped a train over the mountains and into the *tierra caliente*. I arrived in Vera Cruz, which was the hot country all right, a godforsaken port town in a desolate sandy plain with a fierce, hot northern wind. But I figured I'd be Johnny-on-the-spot.

Anyways. That Bunky Millerman photo of me. It was almost three years later and I was in Clyde Fetter's office at the *Tribune*. His steam heat was running behind a gale off Lake Michigan and we were hunching down into our collars and blowing on our fingertips and hashing out the details of me heading to Europe to get ahead of things again. I'd be on the docks of Le Havre when our first boys arrived. Wilson would have to pull the trigger soon.

Then I see the postcard up on the cork wall behind his desk. It's surrounded by clippings and Brownie shots and news copy but it sort of jumps off the wall at me. Clyde's paused anyway, trying to relight his cigar with frozen fingers, and I circle around him and look close.

It's me, all right. Bunky snapped me from behind and I'm walking along one of the streets just off the Plaza de Armas and there's been a gun battle. Bunky had it printed up on a postcard back for me, and I sent it off to Clyde. I've inked an arrow pointing at a tiny, unrecognizable figure way up the street standing with a bunch of other locals. In the foreground I'm striding past a leather goods shop. The pavement's wide and glaring from the sun. Even from behind I've got the look of a war correspondent. There but not there. Unafraid of the battle and floating along just a little above it all. Not in the manner of Richard Harding Davis, who came down for a syndicate after the action got started and who wore evening clothes every night at his table in the *portales*. Not like Jack London either, who was in Vera

Cruz looking as if he'd hopped a freight from the Klondike. I've got a razor press in my dark trousers and my white shirt is fresh. We boys of the fourth estate love our image and our woodchopper's feel for words. It's an image you like your editors to have of you, and so I sent this card, even though by the time I did I'd learned a thing or two I couldn't put in a story for the *Tribune* or anybody else.

I pull the card off the wall now and turn it over. I've scrawled in pencil, *After the battle notice the pretty Senorita's in this photo. The one in white does my laundry.* I draw my thumb over the words, compulsively noticing the dangle of the first phrase, which was meant like a headline. I should have put a full stop. After the battle. And I've made *Senorita's* singular possessive, capitalizing it like a proper name. Maybe this was more than sloppiness in a hasty, self-serving scrawl on a postcard. It was, in fact, true that I had no interest in the other girls. Just in whatever it was that this particular señorita had inside her. Luisa Morales.

Clyde takes a guess at where my mind has gone. "Good thing we've got a copy desk," he says, a puff of his relit cigar floating past me.

"If I were you I wouldn't trust a reporter who bothered to figure out apostrophes anyway," I say. But I'm not looking at him.

I've turned the card over once more and I'm looking at Luisa, dressed in white, far away. And I'm falling into it again, the lesson I was about to learn seemingly lost on me. Because what I'm *not* looking at in the picture or even while standing there in Clyde's office, really, are the two dead bodies I've just walked past, still pretty much merely arm's length away. A couple of snipers, also in white, dead on the sidewalk. That's what they pay us for, Davis and London and me and all the rest of the boys. To take that in and keep focused. I get the head count and work out the politics of it, and I can write the smear of their blood, their sprawled limbs, their peasant sandals without a second glance. I can fill cable blanks one after the other with that kind of stuff while parked in a wisp of sea breeze in the *portales* over a glass of blue agave. If I get stuck finding the right phrase for the folks on Lake Shore Drive or Division Street or Michigan Avenue, I just tap a spoon on my saucer and along comes a refill and inspiration, delivered by an hombre who might end up on the sidewalk tomorrow showing the bottoms of his sandals.

"So what became of your señorita, do you suppose?" Clyde says.

I look over my shoulder at him. He's drawn his craggy moon of a face out of his collar and has it angled a little like he's sprung a horsewhip of a question on a dirty politician.

I ruffle around in my head trying to think what I may have said to him about her. I'm not coming up with anything. "Did I get drunk around you sometime I'm not remembering?" I say.

"Nah," Clyde says. "Call it a newsman's intuition."

I shrug and look away from him again. But I'm not talking.

She sort of came with the rooms I rented in a little house just off the zocalo. I'd barely thrown my kit on the bed and wiped the sweat off my brow with my wrist when she peeked her head in at the door, which I had failed to close all the way. These two big dark eyes and a high forehead from her Spanish grandfather or whoever. "Señor?" she says.

"Come in. As long as you're not one of Huerta's assassins,"
I say in Spanish, which I'm pretty good at. I figure that accounts
for the smile she gives me.

"No problem, señor," she says. "I'll take your dirty things."
She's swung the door open wide now and I see a straw basket
behind her, waiting.

"Well, there was this time with Roosevelt in San Juan . . ."
I say, though it's under my breath, really, and I let it trail off,
just an easy private joke when I'm roughed up from travel and
needing a drink.

But right off she says, "You keep that, señor. Some things
I can't wash away." She does this matter-of-fact, shrugging her
thin shoulders a little.

"Of course," I say. "It's probably a priest I need."

"The ones in Mexico won't do you much good," she says.

She keeps surprising me and this time I don't have a response. I'm just looking at her and thinking what a swell girl,
and I'm probably showing it in my face.

Her face stays blank as a tortilla and after a moment she
says, "Your clothes."

My hand goes of its own accord to the top button on my
shirt.

"Please, señor," she says, her voice full of weary patience,
and she points to my kit.

I give her some things to wash.

"What's your name?" I say.

"I'm just the local girl who does your laundry," she says,
and I still can't read anything in her face, to see if she's flirting
or really trying to put me off.

I say, "You've advised me to keep away from your priests even though I'm plenty dirty. You're already more than a laundry girl."

She laughs. "That was not for your sake. I just hate the priests."

"That's swell," I say. Swell enough that I've said it in English, and I speak some equivalent in Spanish for her.

She hesitates a moment more and finally says, "Luisa Morales," and then she goes out without another word, not even an adios.

I put her aside in my mind and beat it down to the docks where I find out the location at sea of the German ship, the *Ypiranca*, said to be carrying fifteen million rounds of ammunition. Then I stop at the telegraph office where Clyde has wired me. It seems that half the Great White Fleet is also headed in my general direction, including the troopship *Prairie*, the battleship *Utah,* and Admiral Fletcher's flagship *Florida*. Things are getting interesting, but for now all there is to do is wait. So I end up at a cantina I reconnoitered near my rooms.

Not that thoughts of Luisa Morales come back to me while I'm drinking, not directly. I soak up a few fingers of a bottle of mezcal and sweat a lot at a table in the rear of the cantina with my back to the wall and I watch the shadows of the *zopilotes* heaving past, the mangy black vultures that seem to be in the city's official employ to remove carrion from the streets, and I think mostly about what crybabies Wilson and his paunchy windbag of a secretary of state Bryan have turned out to be. I lift my glass to Roosevelt and toast his big stick.

I did that same thing in Corpus Christi a couple of weeks earlier with a guy who knew how it would all happen. I was waiting in Corpus for my expense money to show up at a local bank. I found a saloon with a swinging door down by the docks, but the spot I always like at the back wall had a gaunt hombre with a stuffed bandolera and beat-up Stetson sitting in it. He saw me look at him. Coming in, I'd passed a couple of Johnnies rolling in the dirt outside gouging each other's eyes and I didn't want to add to the mood, so I was ready to just veer off to the rail. But the guy in the Stetson flipped up his chin, and the other chair at the table scooted itself open for me, a thing he did right slick, timed with the chin flip, like the toe of his boot had been poised to invite the first likely looking drinking buddy.

So I found myself with Bob Smith and a bottle of whiskey. He didn't like being called a "soldier of fortune," if you please, he was an *insurrecto* from the old school, 'cause his granddaddy had stirred things up long before him, down in Nicaragua, and his daddy had added to some trouble, too, somewhere amongst the downtrodden of Colombia before all the stink about the canal, so this was an old family profession to him, and as far as personal names were concerned, I was to address him by how he was known to others of his kind, that was to say, Tallahassee Slim.

I said, "There's a bunch of you Slims in all this mess, it seems."

He agreed happily, listing a few. Chicago and Silent and San Antonio and Death Valley. He and Dynamite Slim had even spent time side by side with Villa last fall. Now Tallahassee Slim had come north to regroup himself and dally with some white women before heading south again. We traded war stories and I got around to complaining about Wilson, who I took to be a lily liver.

"Not exactly," Tallahassee Slim said, leaning a little across the table and rustling the ammunition strapped to his chest. "At least a lily liver has a straightforward position. This guy isn't one thing or another. You hear how the man talks? Teddy would put his pistol on the table and call it a pistol. Old Woody sneaks his out and calls it the Bible. He preaches about upholding civilized values, stabilizing governments, giving the Mexicans or the Filipinos or whoever a fine, peaceful life. Not to mention protecting American interests, which means the oilmen and the railroad men and so forth. And as for the locals, you simply try to persuade the bad old boys who happen to be running a country we're interested in to retire to the countryside. Problem is, the *cojones* that got those fellas into power in the first place will never let them walk away. So when it comes down to it, Woody's going to go to war. Over a chaw of tobacco, too, when it's time. Mark my words."

So we drank to Teddy Roosevelt, and I did mark those words. One thing I'd learned filling cable blanks from various *tierras caliente* for a few years already was to listen to anybody with live ammunition who called himself Slim. You can keep your three-named windbags with bow ties.

And I also lift my glass that first afternoon in Vera Cruz for Tallahassee Slim. A couple of times. I drink mezcal till it's too hot to stay upright and I decide to follow the example of those who actually live with the infernal bluster of *el Norte* and take a nap.

When I get back to my rooms I find my shirts and my dark trousers folded neatly at the foot of my bed, which leads me to notice a quiet babble of female voices somewhere nearby.

I step out into the courtyard and Luisa and two other señoritas are over under a banana tree, hugging the shade and talking low. So she sees me looking at her and she rises and steps into the sunlight, crossing to me but taking her time.

"Señor?" she says as she approaches. "Your shirts are clean, yes? Your pants are pressed just right?"

Even in the United States of America, land of equality, when a girl who works in a shop or a beanery or who does laundry, for a good example, gets a little forward, you take it in a different way from a girl of money and fancy family who you meet somewhere official. I've had a few blue-blood girls say some pretty cheeky things in my presence in this day and age. But the shirt-washing señorita Luisa Morales standing before me, as beautiful as her face is, with maybe even some granddaddy straight from Castile, she's sure no *sangre azul,* and she's already been plenty forward with me, and she doesn't have to get up and come over and ask about my laundry based on me just looking in her direction. So given all this, it's natural to think she's ready to spend some private time together.

I speak pretty good Spanish, but my vocabulary has some gaps. The few things I know to say in this situation I picked up in cantinas and a *burdel* or two, and though I figure she's ready for the substance of those words, I'm not feeling comfortable with the tone of them. She has a thing about her that I'm not understanding. So trying to go around another way, I say, "Why don't you come on in and we check out the crease in my pants."

She puts on a face I can't decode. Then I say, "I speak softly and carry a big stick."

Maybe Teddy loses something in translation. Or maybe not. She's gone before I can draw another breath. I remember those big eyes going narrow just before she vanished, an after-image like the pop of Bunky's flash.

Right off, I have a surprisingly strong regret at this. Not just the missed opportunity. The whole breakdown. But I've still got too much mezcal in me and the afternoon is too hot, and so I go take my siesta.

Before I see my señorita again, it's two days later, the German ship arrives, and so does the U.S. Navy. Bunky and I go down to the docks first thing and the German ship is anchored, just inside the breakwater, with the American fleet gathered half a mile farther out. There doesn't seem to be any serious action out there and it's only a few blocks inland to the Plaza de Armas. So I figure I have time to write a dispatch to Clyde.

I take what I've decided will be my usual table in the *portales* and even have a couple of beers. Bunky, as usual, is off on his own snapping what strikes him as interesting, and he swings back to me and gives me a nod now and then. For a teetotaler from Kansas, Bunky is a straight guy. Then, well into the morning, the local Mexican general, a guy named Maass, marches a battalion's worth of government troops into the Plaza. I figure it's getting time for the off-loading of the *Ypiranca*. I'm also the object of some nasty looks from a major on horseback as I finish my beer while the locals are discreetly heading for cover.

So Bunky and I beat it back down to the docks and it's begun. I count ten whaleboats coming in, full of American marines, which I later learn are from the *Prairie.* No sign behind me, up the boulevard, of Maass sending his troops down to meet them. I've got my notebook and pencil stub in hand and Bunky takes off to find his camera angles.

It all goes fast and easy for our boys and for me during the next hour or so. The marines, who number about two hundred, are followed by almost the same number of bluejackets from the *Florida,* and they bring the admiral's Stars and Stripes with them. We take the Custom House without a shot being fired.

I'm still waiting for the Mexicans to come down and put up a fight, but there's no sign of them. Meanwhile, a bunch of locals are gathering on the street to watch. A peon in a serape and sombrero calls out "Viva Mexico" and throws a rock, and even before the rock clatters to the cobblestoned street twenty yards from a couple of riflemen, he's hightailing it away. The riflemen just give him a look and the crowd guffaws and it's all turning into a vaudeville skit.

Then a detachment of marines clad in khaki and wrapped with ammunition starts to march through the street along the railway yards. They turn like they're heading for the Plaza. I signal Bunky and take off after them. They're going down the center of the cobbled street, the *zopilotes* hop-skipping out of their way and giving them a look over their shoulders like these guys could be lunch. I'm hustling hard and gaining on the marines and they're passing storefronts and balconied houses. Mexicans are strung along the street watching like it's the Fourth of July.

Just as I'm about to overtake the captain in charge of the detachment, I see Luisa. She's up ahead with some other señoritas nearby but she's standing by herself and she's dressed in white and she's standing stiff with her chin lifted just a little. I've got a man's business to do first. I'm up with the captain and I slow to his pace and he gives me a quick, suspicious look when I first come up, but then he sees I'm American.

"Captain," I say, and I lift my arm to point up ahead. "You've got about two hundred Mexican soldiers waiting for you in the Plaza."

He gives me a nod of thanks and turns his face to halt his detachment, and at that moment I look toward Luisa, who is just about even with me but I pass her with my next step and my next, and I slow down, even as the detachment is coming to a halt, and it registers on me that Luisa has been watching me closely and I feel a good little thing about having her attention but at that moment the gunfire starts. The crack of a rifle and another and a double crack and the marines are all shifting away and I spin around, knowing at once that the rifles are up above, that the Mexicans are on the roofs, and Luisa has her face lifted to see and I leap forward one stride and another and my arms open and I catch her up, Luisa Morales, I sweep her up in my arms and carry her forward and she's impossibly light and I press us both into the alcove of a bakery shop, the smell of corn tortilla all around us.

"Stay down," I say, and I put my body between the street and her and I realize I've spoken in English. "They're firing from the roofs," I say in Spanish. "Don't move."

She doesn't. But she says, "They're not shooting at me."

"Anyone can get hit."

"They're shooting at you," she says.

"I'm all right," I say. "This is old news to me."

A rifle round flits past my ear—I can feel the zip of air on me—and it takes a bite out of the wall of the alcove. I twist a little to look into the street—I'm missing the action—this is news happening all around me—and as soon as I do, I feel Luisa slip out past me and she's moving quick along the storeline heading away. Another round chunks close in the wall and there's nothing I can do about my spunky señorita and I press back into the alcove to stay alive for the afternoon.

It isn't a bad spot, actually, to watch the skirmish. The marines do a quick job of sharpshooting the Mexicans, some of them falling to the pavement below and others going down on the roofs or beating a fast retreat.

Then it's over. I step out of the alcove. Bunky is coming up from the direction of the docks and he's doing his camera work. I stay with the marines while they regroup and tend to a couple of wounded. The Mexicans on the roofs turned out to be poor shots and the marine captain thinks they weren't regular troops. Meanwhile a scout comes up and says Maass's men have moved out of the Plaza and off to the west. Later in the day the Mexicans will go over the hills on the western outskirts of town to flank the battalion of marines in the railway yards and along Montesinos Street by the American consulate. The boys on the *Florida* will see what they're doing and break them up with the ship's guns and Maass and his men will all run away.

But for now the marines muster up and march off toward the Plaza and I cross onto the wide sidewalk in the sunlight and saunter in the same direction. I'm starting to shape a lead paragraph in my head. I pass a couple of dead Mexicans. I've seen plenty of dead bodies. My business is getting stories. You're dead, and your story's over.

Then up ahead I notice a figure in white. I'm very glad to see her. She got through the bullets okay. I head for Luisa and she sees me coming. I'm still not in talking distance and she says something to the girl next to her and moves off. I stop. The girl Luisa spoke to looks at me with a blank face and then looks away. I'm not a masher. A little dense sometimes, maybe. I'm ready to leave Luisa Morales entirely alone, if that's what she wants.

Early the next morning, long before the sunrise, I wake abruptly to the scratch of a match. I turn my face and see a candlewick flare up and glide to the night table, and before I can quite comprehend it all, the business end of a pistol barrel is resting coldly on my left temple. Floating in the candlelight is Luisa's face.

"You were working for them," she says.

"Who?"

"The American invaders."

I'm reluctant to get into a political argument with my laundry girl who has a pistol pointed at my head. I choose my words carefully. "I'm a newsman," I say.

"I saw you with the American officer, directing him."

The pistol is getting heavier. If her weapon is cocked and her bearing in on me is unconscious, her tired hand could do something it doesn't necessarily intend. I try not to think about that. There are some other pressing issues. For one thing, her attitudes aren't adding up. I need to talk to her about this, but I have to make the point carefully. I don't remind her of her hatred of Mexican priests—they're all I can think of in her culture that might speak against her pulling the trigger. But I bring up the logical next thing. "I don't think you're a supporter of General Huerta," I say.

"I hate Huerta. Do you take me for a fool?" She nudges my head with the pistol in emphasis.

"No. Of course not. But these Americans. They're here to help free Mexico of Huerta. That's all."

"Did you see who was dead in the streets?" she says.

Lying sweating in my bed, a pistol muzzle to my temple, I'm still unable to set aside the impulse to deal in either the literal facts or the political rhetoric that are the goods of my trade. Rhetoric would be dangerous, and I'm short of facts. I didn't look closely enough to identify the bodies. I'm not saying anything, and I feel an agitation growing in Luisa. I feel it in the faint, nibbly restlessness of the steel against my head.

"Did you see who was dead in the streets?" she says again, very low, nearly a whisper.

"No," I say.

"Mexicans," she says, and she cocks the hammer.

My breath catches hard in my chest and I wait. She waits too. Weighing my Americanness, I suppose. Weighing my life. Charting a path for herself.

Then the hammer uncocks and clicks softly back into place. The muzzle draws off my skin. The candle flame vanishes in a puff of her breath and I lie very still as she slips through the dark and out of the room and out of the life she's left for me.

Not that my lead paragraph the next day and the next are any different from what they would have been. The weeks go on and General Huerta resigns and is exiled to Long Island. Venustiano Carranza becomes president. I stay and write more stories and the bandstand in the Plaza goes back into business after a week off. German bands play American tunes. The Mexican couples return to the ballrooms at the bigger hotels and they promenade to the Cuban *danzón*. Down at the docks the marines willingly restage the taking of the Custom House for the Pathé moving picture cameras. That newsreel plays all over America as an image of the actual event and nobody is any the wiser. Seven months later the U.S. troops leave Vera Cruz with several hundred Mexicans dead. Wilson tries to control Carranza over the next few years. And then he takes us into the European war saying that the world must be made safe for democracy. Not that any lesson you learn is simple. The first Mexican president of the revolution, the one before Huerta, a former big landowner, foresaw his revolutionary future in a Ouija board. And the peasants who rose up on his behalf did so because they were convinced Halley's Comet had been a sign from God to change their government.

But standing in Clyde Fetter's office that cold February in 1917, I took a moment to look at the two men dead on the street.

Whatever the madness on both sides, they'd died for their country, trying to help some Americans die for theirs. I gave them a little nod. As for Luisa, I suspect she went off to join up with Villa or Zapata or one of the others. She was a swell girl, and to this day, I haven't stopped wishing I could have done something to make things good for her.

CROSSED CONTINENT ON DARE

Vassar Girl Makes Biplane Ascent After Auto Trip

SAN DIEGO, CAL., AUG. 6—Miss Blanche Scott, of Rochester, a Vassar College student, arrived yesterday in an automobile which she had driven across the continent on a dare. Later in the day she made an ascent with E. M. Roehrig in a biplane. Roehrig and Miss Scott were in the air several minutes and flew a mile and a quarter.

from page 12 of the *New-York Tribune*
Sunday, August 7, 1910

Quanah, Texas
Nov. 29 - 1906.

No chord of music has yet been found—
To even equal, that sweet sound—,
Which to my mind, all else surpasses!—
An auto engine, and its puffing gasses.
— By - C. M. H.

Lillie: May first. Don't this picture recall many a pleasant ride over the beautiful drive-ways?

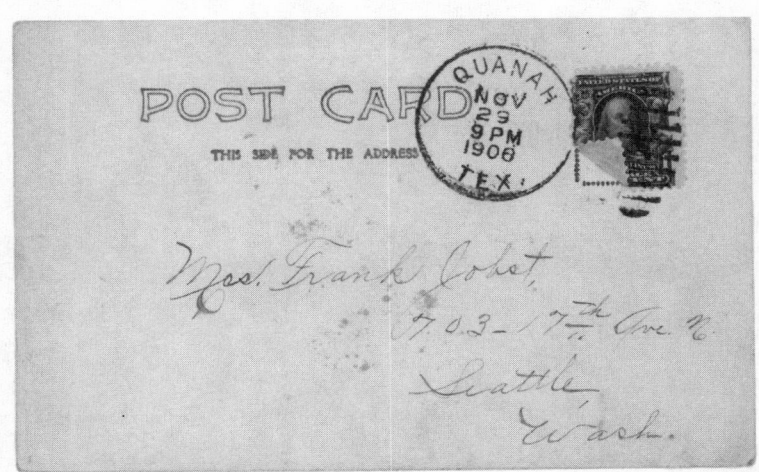

POST CARD

THIS SIDE FOR THE ADDRESS

QUANAH
NOV
29
9 PM
1906
TEX.

Mrs. Frank Colet,
4703 - 17th Ave. N.
Seattle,
Wash.

NO CHORD OF MUSIC

Quanah, Texas
Nov. 29—1906

Mrs. Frank Jobst
703 17th Ave. N.
Seattle, Wash.

Hello: Mrs. Jobst—
Don't this picture recall many pleasant rides over the
Beautiful Drive Way?

No chord of music has yet been found—
To even equal, that sweet sound,
Which to my mind, all else surpasses:
An Auto engine, and its puffing gases.

—By C. M. H.

There was George, off a ways from the automobile, behind the Kodak, and the driver's seat in front of Esther and me was empty, and it was then that I got the idea. Esther was so pretty in white and so much in love with Frank, who so preferred his horses that he had stayed on our porch in spite of the perfect day. My idea came from that too, I think. From the empty seat, but also from Frank with his arms folded on his chest, sitting on the porch, and Esther in a perfect whirl of guilt about going off with us while her husband sat there like that.

I whispered to Esther as George squinted into the camera's peephole, "Well, Mrs. Jobst, I have an idea."

She crossed her arms like it was an answer to me, the poor little dear. She didn't want to hear it.

"Hush now and hold still," George said.

Hush now and hold still. Really.

There I sat on an almost spanking-new 1906 Mitchell, model D-4, not two months off the train from Racine, Wisconsin, and its body was still ticking like a clock, calming down after its run from the house, and I was to hush and hold still. I did so, of course. I was hushing and holding still on a perfect September day—we were not, around our house, mentioning it was Labor Day, which belonged to the immigrants and the big city folk, the *North* for heaven's sake—but I was keeping my own counsel on that whole subject, with a day off from my own labor, and I was out on a good, hard road— a veritable Drive Way—out among the scrub cedar and shinnery oak, and the North Texas plains rolled away as far you could see, and I was corseted and dressed in black and I was on a backseat holding still. I cocked my head at George and wondered what was coming over me. The shutter clicked on the camera and George lifted his face and smiled and said, "Now *there* are three fine ladies." The Mitchell being the third.

And we veritably flew home. I was breathless. George was hulking on the seat before me, holding the wheel straight and true and working the throttle and the spark and the change-speed lever as needed—I'd been watching all this very carefully the dozen times we'd taken a run on the auto—and I patted Esther on the arm and nodded at her and winked. She smiled back and turned her face at once into the rush of the air and the smell of the earth and she closed her eyes and I knew she was as thrilled as I. I would have to touch that special feeling that was happening in her. My plan was intended for two women. I could not do it alone, though I wished I had it in me to be truly bold.

That evening Esther and I helped Mrs. Grant lay out the dinner and I'd still not had a chance to present the idea to her. The men were leaning toward each other over the table, going on about the horse auction tomorrow. George Junior was there with them, his fifteen-year-old brain working full steam, studying up what it was like to be a man across a dinner table, and his hands were fiddling ceaselessly with the silverware from the excitement of going along. After Esther and I had insinuated the bowls of new potatoes and fried chicken and snap beans in front of our husbands, barely able to press these jammering men back out of the way—I was inclined to float the gravy boat along in just such a way that George would dip his lapels in it, but I'd had that inclination before in these circumstances and I'd never done it, nor did I do it now—so after we'd put all the food on the table and sat down ourselves, Esther and I, they finally sat back in their chairs, these two men. George Junior had said thanks for putting the food out, but that impulse would soon pass.

George the Elder didn't even bother to look at me. He launched right into the prayer, and he blessed not only the food but the quest for horses tomorrow. I caught Esther peeking over her tented, prayerful hands as George went on and on to God about the horses and I gave her a wink—a regular I've-got-a-secret-plan wink—and this time she lifted one eyebrow ever so slightly. She'd only been married to Frank for a year and she was young and she hadn't started in with children yet, but she had spirit, my young friend Esther, and I was sure I hadn't misjudged her. I smiled at her over our praying hands and George said "Amen" and then we all ate in absolute silence. George likes silence at his dinner table during the eating part, though he did give at least two separate winks to Frank which spoke loudly of their plans for the morrow. Just fine by me.

Finally, with the men smoking on the porch and the man-to-be outside with the horses and with the table all cleared, I sat Esther down in the parlor and said to her, "Now listen, Mrs. Jobst, you and me need to have a little adventure of our own."

"It's an adventure merely to return to Texas, Mrs. Hunt," she said.

"Yes?" I said, not divining her tone, exactly. "And has your new state of Washington chilled all the spunk out of you, dear?"

She rainbowed her face to the window, that is to say, describing a perfect arc and showing a little color. "Perhaps so," she said. "Life takes its natural shape, doesn't it?"

To be honest, I had no straight answer for that. It was a new century, but a lot of past centuries tended to be alike in certain ways. I sat back in my chair and plopped my hands on my knees. I sighed a heavy sigh and took the opposite tack.

I said, "Well, as the poet so eloquently put it, 'To give thy life to him you wed / Means glory, dear, when you are dead.'"

"Who said a confounded thing like that?"

"I believe that was the esteemed Clara Lauer Baldwin."

"What's your plan?"

"That's my Esther," I said. "Tomorrow we will go for a ride in the auto. Just you and I."

Esther drew in a sharp, quick breath. I understood that to mean yes.

Our ranch is very near the town of Quanah in Hardeman County in the great state of Texas. The town is named after Quanah Parker, who was the last chief of the Comanche on the Staked Plains, bringing his tribe into the white man's reservation only after a protracted struggle. Then—what do you ever know?— he turned around and became a big advocate among his people for assimilation with the white folks he'd fought so hard. He himself raised some cattle the white man's way and he invested in the Quanah, Acme & Pacific Railroad and became a wealthy man. He built himself a twenty-two-room Queen Anne up in Lawton, Oklahoma, where he lives to this day, and he's even a good hunting buddy of Theodore Roosevelt, though they say he still eats peyote and it's definitely known that he kept his seven wives. But just look at his mama, if you want to understand. She was a white girl named Cynthia Ann Parker who'd been kidnapped as a nine-year-old by the Comanche in a raid on Parker's Fort. This was in 1836. Five years later all the other captives of that raid had been returned to their families, but she decided she wanted to stay with the Comanche, and she did. She later took an Indian husband and she had three children by him, including Quanah.

This is relevant because I had my eye on the Medicine Mounds, which were south of town. I could have been thinking about going north to the Red River, which was the direction we most usually went, the Drive Way being very nice the whole distance, but I wanted to take the auto to the Mounds, which were four cone-shaped hills all in a row that the Comanche thought could work good and powerful medicine. It was also the place where Cynthia Ann Parker—to her everlasting regret— was recaptured by white folks when she was thirty-three years old.

So when George and Frank and my son went off in the buggy to the auction and I'd dispatched Mrs. Grant and her husband to do some errands in town, Esther and I went out to the barn and stood before the auto. Our Mitchell was heavy and swarthy and had a broad flat nose of a radiator and its front fenders were angled up like two great eyebrows registering surprise to see me. George was unquestionably wrong. Mitchell was not a lady. Mitchell was a man.

"Oh, Catherine," Esther said, "are you sure you know how?"

Until she asked the question, the answer would have been yes. But upon hearing these words, my chest knotted up like it was my wedding night and I'd just put up my hair and pinned it and I was ready to turn to my new husband. Certainly I knew how to do *this* better than I'd known how to do *that*. But did I, in fact, know enough? I didn't have an answer.

So I replied to Esther, "Of course I'm sure."

I motioned her to take a seat, which she promptly did. She sat on the first of the two rows of touring seats behind the single driver's chair. I stepped up and slid in behind the wheel, which I grasped in my two hands.

"Don't you have to crank it?" Esther asked.

"Yes, dear, but first I'm just getting acquainted." I squeezed the wheel hard and took a deep breath and then I began to do all that I'd carefully observed George do. I grasped the standing change-speed lever and moved it to the second notch, which was the neutral position. I pulled the other stand-up lever back, thus engaging the emergency brake. The levers felt solid in my hand and yet they yielded at once to my touch. I was gaining confidence. I pressed in the clutch pedal and locked it in place and I found the spark lever, marked s on the inside of the steering wheel. I moved it to a spot about an inch from the forward end of the metal ring through which it slid. Then I moved the T lever, the throttle, about halfway along its metal ring.

"Ready," I said.

I climbed down and circled our Mitchell to face him head on. I drew near and I wanted to say some sweet, encouraging thing to him, but I couldn't find the right words. Below me was his crank and his spark was already going and his fuel was flowing and I had to act. I leaned down and took the crank in my hand and it was loose there and cool to the touch. I lifted it slightly and slipped it back a bit and I could feel it fit the grooves or whatever it was inside that would send his flywheel spinning. I'd heard George speak of the danger at this moment. He knew men whose wrists were broken or their shoulders separated by back kicks when they cranked. It was too much spark, he'd said. I thought of that particular lever setting again. It was the best I could do. So I said, low, to my sweet young Mitchell, "Be good now."

I have a strong right arm. Not just for a woman. I have a strong right arm for anyone. And I gave the crank a swift, firm lift and it rolled over and the engine started right up, grumbling back to me, throaty and beautiful, and the crank disengaged right away. All was well.

I straightened up. And Esther raised her right hand and saluted me, just as if it were the Fourth of July and I were a passing parade. I saluted her back, and for a moment, oddly, it felt as if I'd done all that I'd intended to do. But suddenly I heard the engine begin to labor and I stirred and sprang into action. Levers needed adjusting. I moved around the auto and mounted into the driver's chair and I advanced the throttle and the spark until the engine was veritably humming.

I looked at Esther and we nodded to each other and she drew down her veil. I was about to do the same, but then I remembered something beneath the seat. I felt about and found George's goggles. I put them over my eyes, drawing the strap tight. I almost lowered my veil at that point but I stopped myself. I was the driver. The begoggled driver. And as such, I needed no veil, and I unlocked the clutch and released the brake—I was thinking very clearly, very methodically now, I realized—and I advanced the change-gears lever into the first position and slowly lifted up on the clutch.

The Mitchell began to move. And with a wild scattering of astonished chickens and a barking hound, we were out of the barn and passing the front of our house and I advanced the throttle some more and also the spark and we gathered speed and the house was growing small behind us and the air was pressing at us and I felt the auto bucking a little under my hands trying to veer this way or that with the ruts of the path and what he wanted was for me to tell him with the wheel in my two hands which was the right way to go and he listened to my promptings and did what he was told and I held a true course and I throttled up and we were going faster.

Then the engine began to whine like somebody'd burnt his dinner and with a jolt I realized I was forgetting to change gears. Which I did right then, into second position and later into third position, and we dashed off into the gathering heat of the Texas morning, Esther and I.

It was a lovely run we had, Mitchell puffing and muttering away, Esther and me keeping a perfect silence, the bluestem and cord grasses and the mesquite rolling by, the engine pounding a little on some uphills and me retarding the spark just enough to make everything smooth again and then advancing the spark to run on along on the downslope, and it was like breathing in and breathing out, Mitchell and me together.

There was a horse or two that fretted and flinched as we went by and I slowed down for them—spark and throttle, throttle and spark—and the men who were driving them gaped at us going along and I paid them no mind. We just kept on going and mostly it was just the three of us and the prairie and all the sunlight around.

Then the Medicine Mounds were in sight up ahead and I turned to Esther and I cried out over the rush of air, "Don't this just beat all, Mrs. Jobst?"

"It certainly does, Mrs. Hunt," she called back to me.

There'd been no rain for over a week anywhere in Hardeman County, so I didn't hesitate a moment to turn Mitchell onto the remains of an old buffalo trail that led straight toward the tallest of these hills, the one with a top as flat as a mesa. I throttled back on Mitchell, softened down his spark and changed him to a lower gear. In short, we approached at a buffalo's pace, or an Indian pony's.

Esther leaned near me and said, "Catherine. How can we ever go back?"

This was a good question. I was thinking about it when I caught sight of a dark shape up ahead. It was tiny still, from this distance, but I knew instantly what it was. Another automobile. It sat at the foot of the hill and Mitchell and I straight-arrowed for it. It grew and grew and the hill loomed now before us and this other auto had the same general shape as mine, but with some striking differences that now came clear. The night lamps were brass and sat low at the front, great snoopy owlish eyes, while my Mitchell's eyes were set far back, at either end of the front seat, and this other auto's radiator was narrow and refined, a patrician nose to my Mitchell's hired-hand pug.

And what's more, the back seat was stuffed full of round little Comanche wives wrapped in blankets. There were four of them, three in the seat and one wedged in at their feet. They turned their heads as one as I drove up, and I slowed down and put on the brake and stopped and throttled back to an idle.

"Who are they?" Esther whispered.

This other auto was shiny black and the seats were fine leather and the brass gleamed, not just on the lamps but around the edge of the radiator. It was a fine auto, not taking anything away from Mitchell who sat beneath me humming to himself. "I'm beginning to think," I said.

And sure enough, around from the back of the auto came an old Indian gentleman in a high turn-down collar and a black three-button frock suit. He was wearing what my Sears, Roebuck Catalogue calls a black stiff hat but I've also heard it called a derby and his long Indian pigtails hung down over each shoulder.

In short, I knew him to be what I whispered out of the side of my mouth to Esther: "It's Quanah Parker himself and four of his wives."

"No," she whispered back.

He bucked a little when he saw me and I lifted my goggles to look at him properly.

"I've seen an engraving in *Harper's Weekly*," I told Esther.

She gasped a little, not from the thought of the engraving but from Quanah Parker's approach.

He came as far as my front fender and he removed his hat and said, "Where is your driver, madam?"

"It should be clear that I myself am the driver," I said.

He took this in and assimilated it in the blink of an eye, for he said almost at once, and with no further to-do about my place behind the wheel, "You own a Mitchell."

I was conscious of his four wives moving their faces ever so slightly to follow our conversation: to their husband when he spoke, to me when I spoke.

"You're right," I said.

"I own a Pope-Toledo," he said.

"It's a very beautiful auto," I said.

"This Pope-Toledo means I can visit more often this place of my young days. And I can bring some of my wives."

"I have brought my friend."

"Have you come on a Vision Quest?" he said.

I wasn't sure what that was—an Indian ritual of some sort, I knew—but it sounded about right. "Yes," I said.

"My wives' quest came in childbirth. But you have a Mitchell."

"I do," I said.

"Then may your eyes be opened," he said, and he bowed and put his hat back on and he turned and moved to his auto. He slipped up behind the wheel, adjusted his levers, returned to his crank and bent gracefully to it, giving it the easiest of pulls, and his Pope-Toledo started right up, making a fine, sweet puffing. In a flash he was behind the wheel again and he was rolling away. He turned his face one last time to me and nodded very slightly, his four wives turning too and smiling a faint smile in unison. And then they were gone in a cloud of dust down the buffalo trail.

That evening Esther and I sat on the porch waiting for the men to return.

We didn't say much, she and I, but at some point my friend Esther leaned toward me and asked, "Can you still feel it?"

"What?"

"The auto. Even sitting here, I keep thinking I'm moving."

"Yes," I said. "You're right."

And she was.

CLUB FUGITIVE SWIMMER

Boatmen Use Oar on Man Who Breaks from Randall's Island

Louis Scafaro escaped from the school for the feeble minded of the Department of Charities, on Randall's Island, about 5:30 o'clock yesterday afternoon and jumped into the East River. He struck out toward 123rd street.

In the channel at the time was a rowboat, containing Joseph Suckey, of No. 1443 Second avenue, and William Kennedy, of No. 433 East 120th street.

They saw Scafaro and pulled quickly toward him. He resisted their attempts to get him into the boat and bit Kennedy's right hand as the latter sought to grab him.

Kennedy and Suckey beat him senseless with an oar, hauled him into the boat and later turned him over to Lieutenant Dwyer, of Harbor Squad B, who put out in a launch from the Harbor Squad sub-station, at 120th street.

Dwyer took Scafaro, who was still ugly when he came to his senses, back to the island.

from the front page of the *New-York Tribune*
Sunday, August 7, 1910

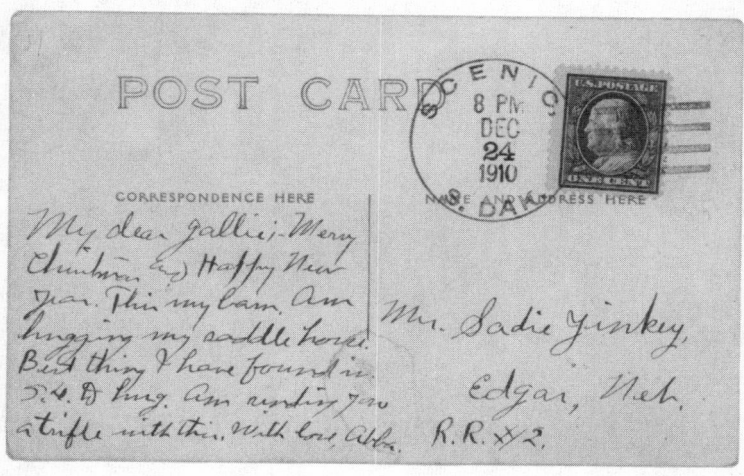

POST CARD

CORRESPONDENCE HERE

My dear Gallie: Merry
Christmas and Happy New
Year. This my barn. Am
bringing my saddle horse.
But they & have found in
S. & D ling. Am renting you
a trifle with this. With love, Abba.

Mr. Sadie Yinkey,
Edgar, Neb.
R. R. x 2.

CHRISTMAS 1910

Scenic, S. Dak.
Dec. 24, 1910

Mrs. Sadie Yinkey
R.R. #2
Edgar, Neb.

My dear gallie: Merry Christmas and Happy New Year.
This [is] my barn. Am hugging my saddle horse. Best thing
I have found in S.D. to hug. Am sending you a trifle with
this. With love, Abba.

My third Christmas in the west river country came hard upon the summer drought of 1910, and Papa and my brothers had gone pretty grim, especially my brother Luther, who was a decade older than me and had his own adjacent homestead, to the east, that much closer to the Badlands. Luther had lost his youngest, my sweet little nephew Caleb, to a snakebite in August. We all knew the rattlers would come into your house. We women would hardly take a step without a hoe at hand for protection. But one of the snakes had got into the bedclothes and no one knew and Caleb took the bite and hardly cried at all before it was done. And then there was the problem with everybody's crops. Some worse than others. A few had done hardly ten bushels of corn for forty acres put out. We weren't quite that bad off, but it was bad nonetheless. Bad enough that I felt like a selfish girl to slip out of the presence of my kin whenever I had the chance and take up with Sam my saddle horse, go up on his back and ride off a ways from the things my mama and papa and brothers were working so hard to build, and I just let my Sam take me, let him follow his eyes and ears to whatever little thing interested him.

And out on my own I couldn't keep on being grim about the things that I should have. There was a whole other thing or two. Selfish things. Like how you can be a good daughter in a Sodbuster family with flesh and blood of your own living right there all around you, making a life together—think of the poor orphans of the world and the widows and all the lost people in the cities—how you can be a good daughter in such a cozy pile of kin and still feel so lonely. Mary Joseph and Jesus happy in a horse stall, forgive me. Of course, in that sweet little picture of the Holy Family, Mary had Joseph to be with her, not her brothers and parents with their faces set hard and snakes crawling in your door and hiding in your shoe.

So when the winter had first come in, there hadn't been any snow since the beginning of November and it was starting to feel like a drought all over again, though we were happy not to have to hunker down yet and wait out the dark season under all the snow. There was still plenty of wind, of course. Everybody in our part of South Dakota shouted at each other all the time because of the wind that galloped in across the flatland to the west and to the north with nothing to stop it but the buffalo grass and little bluestem and prairie sand reed, which is to say nothing at all. But the winter of 1910 commenced with the world dead dry and that's when he came, two days before Christmas, the young man on horseback.

We were all to Luther's place and after dinner we returned home and found the young man sitting at our oak table in what we called our parlor, the big main room of our soddy. He'd lit a candle. The table was one of the few pieces of house furniture we'd brought with us from Nebraska when Papa got our homestead. Right away my vanity was kicking up. I was glad this young man, who had a long, lank, handsome face, a little like Sam actually, had settled himself at our nicest household possession, which was this table. And I hoped he understood the meaning of the blue tarpaper on our walls. Most of the homesteaders used the thinner red tarpaper at three dollars a roll. Papa took the thick blue at six dollars, to make us something better. People in the west river country knew the meaning of that, but this young man had the air of coming from far off. We all left our houses unlocked for each other and for just such a wayfarer, so no one felt it odd in those days if you came home and found a stranger making himself comfortable.

He rose and held his hat down around his belt buckle and slowly rotated it in both hands and he apologized for lighting the candle but he didn't want to startle us coming in, and then he told us his name, which was John Marsh, and where he was from, which was Bardstown, Kentucky, county of Nelson—not far down the way from Nazareth, Kentucky, he said, smiling all around—and he wished us a Merry Christmas and hoped we wouldn't mind if he slept in the barn for the night and he'd be moving on in the morning. "I'm bound for Montana," he said, "to work a cattle ranch of a man I know there and to make my own fortune someday." With this last announcement he stopped turning his hat, so as to indicate how serious he was about his intentions. Sam's a dapple gray with a soft puff of dark hair between his ears, and the young man sort of had that too, a lock of which fell down on his forehead as he nodded once, sharply, to signify his determination.

My mama would hear nothing of this, the moving on in the morning part. "You're welcome to stay but it should be for more than a night," she said. "No man should be alone on Christmas if there's someone to spend it with." And with this, Mama shot Papa a look, and he knew to take it up.

"We can use a hand with some winter chores while we've got the chance," Papa said. "I can pay you in provisions for your trip."

John Marsh studied each of our faces, Mama and Papa and my other older brother Frank, just a year over me, standing by Papa's side as he always did, and my younger brother Ben, still a boy, really, though he was as tall as me already. And John Marsh looked me in the eye and I looked back at him and we neither of us turned away, and I thought to breathe into his nostrils, like you do to meet a new horse and show him you understand his ways, and it was this thought that made me lower my eyes from his at last.

"I might could stay a bit longer than the night," he said.

"Queer time to be making this trip anyway," my papa said, and I heard a little bit of suspicion, I think, creeping in, as he thought all this over a bit more.

"He can take me in now," John Marsh said. "And there was nothing for me anymore in Kentucky."

Which was more explanation than my father was owed, it seemed to me. Papa eased up, saying, "Sometimes it just comes the moment to leave."

"Yessir." And John Marsh started turning his hat again.

Mama touched my arm and said, low, "Abigail, you curry the horses tonight before we retire."

This was instead of the early morning, when I was usually up before anyone, and she called me by my whole name and not Abba, so it was to be the barn for John Marsh.

Papa took off at a conversational trot, complaining about the drought and the soil and the wind and the hot and the cold and the varmints and all, pretty much life in South Dakota in general, though that's the life he'd brought us all to without anyone forcing us to leave Nebraska, a thing he didn't point out. He was, however, making sure to say that he held three hundred twenty acres now and his eldest son a hundred sixty more and that's pretty good for a man what never went to school, his daughter being plenty educated for all of them and she even going around teaching homesteader kids who couldn't or wouldn't go to the one-room school down at Scenic. John Marsh wasn't looking at me anymore, though I fancied it was something he was struggling to control, which he proved by not even glancing at me when Papa talked of my schooling, in spite of it being natural for him to turn his face to me for that. Instead, when the subject of me came up, his Adam's apple started bobbing, like he was swallowing hard, over and over.

I slipped out of the house at that point, while Papa continued on. I walked across the hard ground toward the little barn we kept for the saddle horses, Sam and Papa's Scout and Dixie. When Papa's voice finally faded away behind me, I stopped and just stood for a moment and looked up at the stars. It's true that along with the wind and the snakes and the lightning storms and all, South Dakota had the most stars in the sky of anywhere, and the brightest, and I had a tune take up in my head. *I wonder as I wander out under the sky. . . .* Christmas was nearly upon us and I shivered standing there, not from the cold, though the wind was whipping at me pretty good, but because I realized that nothing special was going on inside me over Christmas, a time which had always all my life thrilled me. Luther had even put up a wild plum tree off his land in a bucket of dirt and we'd lit candles on it, just this very night. And all I could do was sit aside a ways and nod and smile when anyone's attention turned to me, but all the while I was feeling nothing much but how I was as distant from this scene as one of those stars outside. And even now the only quick thing in me was the thought of some young man who'd just up and walked in our door, some stranger who maybe was a varmint himself or a scuffler or a drunkard or a fool. I didn't know anything about him, but I was out under this terrible big sky and wishing he was beside me, his hat still in his hands, and saying how he'd been inside thinking about only me for all this time. *How Jesus the Savior did come for to die, For poor ornery people like you and like I.* Ornery was right.

I went on into the barn and lit a kerosene lamp and Sam was lying there, stirred from his sleep by my coming to him at an odd time. His head rose up and he looked over his shoulder at me and he nickered soft and I came and knelt by him and put my arm around his neck. He turned his head a little and offered me his ear and waited for my sweet talk. "Hello, my Sammy," I said to him, low. "I'm sorry to disturb your sleep. Were you dreaming? I bet you were dreaming of you and me riding out along the coulee like today. Did we find some wonderful thing, like buffalo grass flowering in December?"

He puffed a bit and I leaned into him. "I dream of you, too," I said. "You're my affinity, Sammy." Like John Marsh not looking my way when Papa spoke of me, I was making a gesture that was the opposite of what I was feeling. My mind was still on this young man in the house. I suddenly felt ashamed, playing my Sam off of this stranger. In fact, I was hoping that this John Marsh might be my affinity, the boy I'd fit alongside of. I put my other arm around Sam, held him tight. After a moment he gently pulled away and laid his head down. So I got the currycomb and began to brush out the day's sweat and the wind spew and stall-floor muck and I sang a little to him while I did. "When Mary birthed Jesus 'twas in a cow's stall, With wise men and farmers and horses and all," me putting the horses in for Sammy's sake, though I'm sure there were horses around the baby Jesus, even if the stories didn't say so. The stories always made it mules, but the horses were there. The Wise Men came on horses. There was quite a crowd around the baby, if you think about it. But when he grew up, even though he gathered the twelve around him, and some others too, like his mama and the Mary who'd been a wicked girl, he was still lonely. You can tell. He was as distant from them as the stars in the sky.

So I finished with Sam and then with Scout, and Dixie had stood up for me to comb her and I was just working on her hindquarters when I heard voices outside in the wind and then Papa and John Marsh came into the barn, stamping around. I didn't say anything but moved behind Dixie, to listen.

And then Papa said, "I'm sorry there's no place in the house for a young man to stay."

"This is fine," John Marsh said. "I like to keep to myself."

There was a silence for a moment, like Papa was thinking about this, and I thought about it as well. Not thought about it, exactly, but sort of felt a little wind gust of something for this John Marsh and I wasn't quite sure what. I wanted to keep to myself too, but only so I could moon around about not keeping to myself. John Marsh seemed overly content. I leaned into Dixie.

"I was your age once," my papa said.

"I'll manage out here fine."

"Night then," Papa said, and I expected him to call for me to go on in the house with him, but he didn't say anything and I realized he'd gone out of the barn not even thinking about me being there. Which is why I'd sort of hid behind Dixie, but he'd even ignored my lamp and so I was surprised to find myself alone in the barn with John Marsh. I held my breath and didn't move.

"Hey there, Gray," John Marsh said, and I knew he was talking to Sam. "You don't mind some company, do you? That's a fella."

I heard Sam blow a bit, giving John Marsh his breath to read. It was not going to be simple about this boy. Him talking to my sweet, gray man all familiar, even touching him now, I realized—I could sense him stroking Sam—all this made me go a little weak-kneed, like it was me he was talking to and putting his hand on. It was like I was up on Sam right now and he was being part of me and I was being part of him. But then I stiffened all of a sudden, got a little heated up about this stranger talking to my Sam like the two of them already had a bond that I never knew about. I was jealous. And I was on the mash. Both at once. In short, I was a country fool, and Dixie knew it because she rustled her rump and made me pull back from her. She also drew John Marsh's attention and he said, "Hello?"

"Hello," I said, seeing as there was no other way out. I took to brushing Dixie pretty heavy with the currycomb and John Marsh appeared, his hat still on his head this time and looking like a right cowboy.

"I didn't know you was there," he said.

"Papa was continuing to bend your ear, is why," I said.

John Marsh smiled at this but tried to make his face go straight again real quick.

I said, "You can find that true and amusing if you want. He's not here to take offense."

John Marsh angled his head at me, trying to figure what to say or do next. He wasn't used to sass in a girl, I guess. Wasn't used to girls at all, maybe. I should have just blowed in his nose and nickered at him.

"He does go on some," John Marsh said, speaking low.

I concentrated on my currying, though it was merely for show since I was combing out the same bit of flank I'd been working on for a while. Dixie looked over her shoulder at me, pretty much in contempt. I shot her a just-stand-there-and-mind-your-own-business glance and she huffed at me and turned away. I went back to combing and didn't look John Marsh in the eye for a little while, not wanting to frighten him off by being too forward but getting impatient pretty quick with the silence. The eligible males I'd known since I was old enough for them to be pertinent to me had all been either silly prattlers or totally tongue-tied. This John Marsh was seeming to be among the latter and I brushed and brushed at Dixie's chestnut hair trying to send some brain waves over to this outsized boy, trying to whisper him something to say to me. *Which horse is yours?* Or, *You go around teaching, do you?* Or, *Is there a Christmas Eve social at the schoolhouse tomorrow that I could escort you to?* But he just stood there.

Finally I looked over to him. He was staring hard at me and he ripped off his hat the second we made eye contact.

"I'll be out of your way shortly," I said.

"That's okay," he said. "Take your time. She deserves it." And with this he patted Dixie on the rump.

"You hear that, Dixie?" I said. "You've got a gentleman admirer." Dixie didn't bother to respond.

"Where's your horse put up?" I said.

"Oh, he likes the outdoors. Horses do. It ain't too fierce tonight for him."

"My Sam—he's the gray down there—it took a long time for him to adjust to a barn. But I like him cozy even if it's not his natural way."

"I'd set him out on a night like this," John Marsh said.

"He's better off," I said.

"I'm sure you love him," John Marsh said.

We both stopped talking and I wasn't sure what had just happened, though I felt that something had come up between us and been done with.

John Marsh nodded to me and moved away.

I stopped brushing Dixie and I just stood there for a moment and then I put down the currycomb and moved off from Dixie and found John Marsh unrolling his sleeping bag outside Sam's stall.

I moved past him to the door. "Night then," I said.

John Marsh nodded and I stepped out under the stars.

Then it was the morning before Christmas and I'd done my currying the night before and I'd had a dream of empty prairie and stars and I couldn't see any way to go no matter how I turned and so I slept on and on and woke late. As I dressed, there were sounds outside that didn't really register, their being common sounds, a horse, voices trying to speak over the wind, and then Papa came in and said, "Well, he's gone on."

Mama said, "The boy?"

"Yep," Papa said. "He wants to make time to Montana. He's got grit, the boy. The sky west looks bad."

I crossed the parlor, past the oak table and Papa, something furious going on in my chest.

"I was his age once," Papa said.

Then I took up my coat and I was out the door. It was first light. Papa was correct. To the west, the sky was thickening up pretty bad. A sky like this in Kentucky might not say the same thing to a man. Even thinking this way, I knew there was more than bad weather to my stepping away from our house and

looking to where John Marsh had gone, maybe only ten minutes before, and me churning around inside so fierce I could
hardly hold still. Then I couldn't hold still. I told myself I needed
to warn him.

I dashed into the barn and Sam was standing waiting and
I gave him the bridle and bit and that was all. There was no
time. I threw my skirt up and mounted Sam bareback and we
pulled out of the stall and the barn and we were away.

There was a good horse trail through the rest of our land
and on out toward the Black Hills that rippled at the horizon
when you could see it. But there was only dark and cloud out
there now, which John Marsh could recognize very well, and
Sam felt my urgency, straight from my thighs. I hadn't ridden
him bareback in several years and we both were het up now
together like this, with John Marsh not far ahead, surely, and
we galloped hard, taking the little dips easy and Sam's ears were
pitched forward listening for this man up ahead, and mostly it
was flat and winter bare all around and we concentrated on
making time, me not thinking at all what it was I was doing. I
was just with Sam and we were trying to catch up with some
other possibility.

But John Marsh must have been riding fast too. He wasn't
showing up. It was just the naked prairie fanning out ahead as
far as the eye would carry, to the blur of a restless horizon. What
was he running so fast for? Had I frightened him off somehow?
Was it so bad to think he might put his arms around me?

I lay forward, pressing my chest against Sam, keeping low
before the rush of the air, and I heard Sam's breathing, heavy

and steady, galloping strong with me, him not feeling jealous at all that I was using him to chase this man. I closed my eyes. Sam was rocking me. I clung to him, and this was my Sam, who wasn't a gray man at all, not a man at all, he was something else altogther, he was of this wind and of this land, my Sam, he was of the stars that were up there above me even now, just hiding in the light of day, and we rode like this for a while, rocking together like the waves on the sea, and when I looked up again, there was still no rider in sight but instead an unraveling of the horizon. Sam knew at once what my body was saying. He read the faint tensing and pulling back of my thighs and he slowed and his ears came up and I didn't even have to say for him to stop.

We scuffled into stillness and stood quiet, and together Sam and I saw the storm. All across the horizon ahead were the vast billowing frays of a blizzard. I had a thought for John Marsh. He'd ridden smack into that. Or maybe not. Maybe he'd cut off for somewhere else. Then Sam waggled his head and snorted his unease about what we were looking at, and he was right, of course. He and I had our own life to live and so we turned around and galloped back.

The storm came in right behind us that day before Christmas in 1910, and there was no social at the schoolhouse that year. We all burrowed in and kept the fires going and sang some carols. *Stars were gleaming, shepherds dreaming, And the night was dark and chill.*

After midnight I arose and I took a lantern and a shovel and I made a way to the barn, the new snow biting at me all the while, but at last I came in to Sam and hung the lantern, and he muttered in that way he sometimes did, like he knew a thing before it would happen—he knew I'd be there—and I lay down by my horse and I put my arms around him. "Aren't you glad you're in your stable," I whispered to him. "I brought you here away from the storm." And I held him tight.

HIS HICCOUGHS ARE STOPPED

But Heroic Remedies Necessary May Result in Death of Elmer Smith, Mio Farmer

BAY CITY, MICH., AUGUST 6— After 11 days of hiccoughing Elmer Smith, the wealthy Mio farmer who was brought to Mercy hospital because his physicians could not stop the spasms, local physicians today succeeded in bringing about a complete cessation of the affection, but Smith is in such state from exhaustion and the effects of heroic remedies that his life is hanging by a thread.

Enormous doses of chlorotone and whisky almost completely paralyzed the man, the physicians announcing beforehand that they might kill the sufferer with the drug. Relief was also afforded by mechanically paralyzing the phrenic nerve, nurses sitting for hours at a time pinching it between their fingers.

from page 10 of *The Detroit Free Press*
Sunday, August 7, 1910

PUBLIC SCHOOL, CHARLESTON, WASH. #339 DAWES, SEATTLE.

POST CARD

CORRESPONDENCE HERE

NAME AND ADDRESS HERE

Dear Omer— This is
the school where
Cousin Hiram reigns
supreme & curries
the town ruffians.
All's well— Chas

Mr. O. E. Malsberry
Instrument man P.R.R.
Gorgona C. Z.
N. Y. Foreign
Panama

Miraflores

MAY 10
530PM
C

HIRAM THE DESPERADO

Charleston, Wash.
Apr. 24, 1908

Mr. O. E. Malsberry
Instrument man P.R.R.
Gorgona, C.Z. Panama

Dear Owen—This is the school where Cousin Hiram reigns supreme & curries the town ruffians. All's well. Chas.

S ay, don't you think they need somebody to tell them what to do? These kids all around me? Another kid to tell them, I mean. Me. Not like the things they hear plenty of already. Elbows off the table and quiet down and be in this room on that tick of the clock and add up these meaningless numbers and eat your greens. But things that have something to do with something. So for instance I tell the six- and seven-year-olds to steal cigarettes for me from their dads, just one every other day and only from a near-full pack, nothing the old man'll even realize is gone, and for this I'll keep the big kids off their backs, and then I tell the thirteen- and fourteen-year-olds not to rough up the six- and seven-year-olds and I keep them in cigarettes for going along with it. I perform a service for everybody, and it has to do with what they really need, in this case protection and smokes. And sure, along the way in this one particular part of the doings, I keep a few extra cigarettes to smoke for myself and I get a few extra favors from the biggest of the older kids. That's only fair.

Say, we're just trying to get out of childhood in one piece, all of us. It's a new century, so they keep reminding us. There's some swell stuff going on. But I'm sitting around in a kid's body and I'm waiting for influenza and diphtheria and dengue fever and the black cholera and if you go out to play, one of those swell automobiles will run you down or an aeroplane will crash on your barn with you in the hayloft or a sixteen-foot cedar cut will roll off a logging sled and right over you or maybe your dad will drink the whole pailful of beer in about one hour flat not to mention half a bottle of whiskey and he'll beat you near to death for breathing too heavy or you can get knuckled to death by anybody who happens to have been born a few years before you—they say kids have died having their brains scrambled up by a good knuckling to the temple while in a headlock—and there's always being bored to death sitting in a schoolroom all day with George Washington staring down from over the blackboard looking like he's as bored as you, not to mention a Sunday afternoon when it rains all get-out and you are doing so bad you still have your church-going collar on and no strength to even take it off, this Puget Sound rain is coming down so hard. Kids have been known to seize up and keel over dead sitting in a window seat or on a porch swing with the rain coming down on a Sunday afternoon.

The boy who moved in next door—he was twelve, same as me, though I never got a chance to play with him—had himself a growth on his neck. He was a Catholic and went to parochial and so he wasn't on display at our school, where we hadn't had a good goiter for several years, and I made better than a dollar selling nickel views of him from our attic window, which could see down into his fenced backyard and him sitting there in the sun. Then last week he was gone and they put up the black wreath and I guess it was something worse than a goiter and that kid didn't need anybody telling him to divide thirteen into a hundred and four or to sit up straight. I don't know what his dad was like.

So ain't I already saying how I can be fidgeting to death in a front desk of a classroom on a spring day that's working up to rain as soon as the bell rings? I'm not in that front desk out of choice or even the alphabet. I'm put there to be in knuckle-striking range and where I can't whisper worth a hoot or pass a note, and it's like that from the first day of class anymore, me being a known desperado. It's the price I pay. I saved others but myself I couldn't save, which is one true thing, at least, that I learned while being brought to the brink of death-by-boredom at my weepy mother's side in church.

Anyways, I'm sitting there in school one day this spring and I can't find a place in that chair where my tailbone is happy about anything and there's a terrible itch in my left heel and digging at it with the toe of my right shoe isn't helping and Mrs. Pickernose is droning on about something, which isn't her real name but I saw her with her finger up her nose once after school when she thought nobody was looking and I'm still waiting to give out that information in some useful way sometime. But I'm sitting there when I see out the classroom door and Miss Spencer walks past.

Say, I can be in love, can't I? I don't have to explain any of that. If most of the hundred-something other boys in this school would ride me down the hill to Port Orchard Bay on a saw blade and dump me in if they figured I was mashed on a girl, not to mention a full-grown woman, not to mention a teacher, then that's just why I'm the guy who runs things and not them, because they're all a little backward is how I see it and I don't have to 'fess up to nothing, much less explain myself. Not that I ever got any advice about this sort of thing. Pa don't talk about nothing. The few boys who some girls think of as their beaus, they haven't got the first idea about it. It's something I just know to do. She's past that door in one second flat but she's as clear as can be in my head. She's got her hair all twisted up in the back like that princess who Cupid was stuck on that's in our reader. Miss Spencer has never been my teacher, and I guess it's better that way, her not having a direct chance to think of me as rotten, though if she had to crack my knuckles with a ruler I'd be pretty happy just to have her thinking that strong about me at all.

This has been going on for a few months already. On this particular day, after the bell, I go out and she's walking away fast, her purse and her books tucked hard against her chest, and I follow her for about a quarter of a mile past the logger cutoff and she's still walking fast like she's got serious business downtown, but I've got things to do and I let her go.

I've only ever spoken a little bit to Miss Spencer. Once, she came upon me out back of school collecting dues from a mollycoddle who didn't understand the workings of the Grand Fraternal Lodge and Benevolent Association of Cedar Weevils.

"But when do we meet?" he says to me.

"We don't meet," I say.

"So why do I pay dues?" he says.

"Say," I say. "Don't you have even a little sense? There's privileges."

"What sort?" he says.

I'm not quite ready to knuckle his brains. He's two years younger and kind of on the small side and that's always a final argument, but I've found there are fewer problems if you use reasoning. "The secret handshake," I say, wiggling my fingers at him. "The code of honor. And ain't I letting you skip the terrors of initiation? Do you think a privilege like that ain't worth ten cents? What would your fellow weevils think, them having paid up *and* also bearing the scars of the rites of initiation? You need to take into account how subject you could be to this and that."

Which is when Miss Spencer walks up, right as I'm doing a serious forefinger tap into the center of the kid's chest and he's finally getting that look in his eye like logic is going to prevail.

"Hiram," she says, and I didn't even realize that she knew my name.

I stuff my hands into my pockets and turn to her. Her face is swell, is all I can say.

"Are you playing rough with this little boy?" she says.

I smile slow. She knows my name but not his. "Not at all," I say. "We was just discussing."

"We *were* just discussing," she says, stressing the word I already knew I got wrong. I'm not stupid. I pick up more than they realize. "And what might that be?" she says.

I say, "Oh, *this and that,*" which the weevil-to-be under-
stands right off.

"This and that," he repeats and I look at him and give him
a very friendly nod. He gives me a nod back, like we understand each other. Miss Spencer made the mistake of calling him
a "little boy" and that reminded him of who he really depends
on. I even turn to him and grab his hand like I'm shaking it but
I sort of jiggle it around a few times right and left and he's beam-
ing now with his first weevil secret, he thinks, the handshake.

"That's all right then," Miss Spencer says.

I turn back to her, wanting the conversation to go on. I
say, "Nice weather we're having, Miss Spencer, isn't it?"

She looks at me with just a little pinch in her forehead,
like she's not sure she wants to talk about the weather to a kid.
Then she says, "If you like rain."

"You're not used to rain?" I say, and I'm thinking what I've
heard about her, which she now tells me.

"Last year I taught in California," she says. "It's very wet
up here by contrast."

"That's what puts the *wash* in Washington," I say. I'm pitch-
ing like Christy Mathewson here, but she has to go.

"All right, boys," she says. "Be good."

"Sure," I say. And that's the longest conversation I've ever
had with the woman I love.

So it's a couple hours later on the day when I follow her
from school. It's working up to time for Pa to come home and
I go into the kitchen and get the beer pail. It's sitting next to
the door so I can just step in and take it without any talk. Ma is
rolling out some dough and usually she's all over me about

something I've done, but she acts like I'm not even there, which is how it goes at pail time.

I head on down the hill toward the bay and I can see the smokestacks of the USS *Iowa* in dry dock at the navy yard, which is pretty swell, and I dream a little about somehow having control of this view and I'm selling admission and I'm toting up dollar after dollar. And I dream a little, too, about the Great White Fleet that our president has sent off to circle the world and show them all who's boss, sixteen battleships and six torpedo boats, and I feel bad for the *Iowa* that got left behind, it being a big hero in Cuba and all. Even battleships can get a raw deal. This all is what's going through my head with Pa's beer pail swinging in my hand, when I get down to Front Street and I see Miss Spencer.

I've made the turn up toward the docks, heading for the saloon, and the trade's a little rough along here, and there she is, the last person I'd expect to be walking along. She's on the other side of the street heading the opposite direction from me, and at first all I see is her—there's nothing else on the street, or in the whole state of Washington, for that matter—her in her white shirtwaist and black skirt. Her face is lowered a little like she's concentrating on where she's walking, which is a pretty good idea around these parts, actually. Then I realize there's a guy at her side, a navy guy in his blues. I don't know he's with her till I see them go a few steps and keep alongside each other. But she's not looking at him and he's not looking at her and they're not saying nothing. She'd have me put that different, I know. I'd always talk perfect around Miss Spencer, because I can if I want to, and it'd make her happy.

I think they're heading for the nickel motion picture show up the street. But I don't like how her face is down and how they're acting. Something's wrong here. I cross the street and follow them. He's a little guy, not even quite as tall as Miss Spencer, which makes me real edgy inside, like this could be me beside her as likely as him. They pass the motion picture show right by and the brickyard and they cut in at a footpath through the waterfront park. They circle the bandstand and nothing's changed about how they're walking. There's a little space between them like they're trying not even to accidentally bump into each other and there's no talking as far as I can tell and she's still got her head down. Yet it's not like they've just met or something. There's a real familiar feel going on between them too. Like you pick up from somebody's parents, my own Ma and Pa even, when she gets him to go off to church once in a while and I'm walking behind them. Finally Miss Spencer and her bluejacket slow and stop and they start to turn around to sit on a bench and I duck off the path and into some shrubs and I crouch down and wait for them to get settled. A Port Orchard steamer out on the bay toots its whistle. Another couple walks by and the guy shoots me a look, and I'd give him a *bugs* or a *dry up* except I don't want to draw attention to myself. But even this dope has his girl's arm through his and then I peek out at Miss Spencer and this guy she's spending time with who's maybe a problem for her.

They're sitting side by side all right, pretty close now, and he's talking and then she's talking but they're not looking each other in the eye and then they just sit for a while. I settle down where I am. I've got a Piedmont in my pocket and a dry match and I light up and puff away. I don't look at the pail. I know it's there and time's passing and I'm going to catch something bad for doing this, but I'm not ready to leave Miss Spencer out here with this guy. Though I'm not looking at them, either. I'm just sitting in the middle and smoking a cigarette.

When I look at them again, they're just starting to stand up. One thing I notice. She puts her hand just below her stomach, but very light, like it hurts. I know right off what's been going on, like I knew the first time I saw them on the street. Pa's smart. He don't like me showing his handiwork, usually. Ma cares about that. She's got to tote me off to church and she don't want folks knowing how bad a boy I really am. When it's not a strap or a lath or a switch across the back of me from my collar to my shoes, it's a fist right where she's touching.

They're coming this way and I duck down and hunker into the bush. They could see me if they turn, but they don't. They drift past like a dark cloud and I wait a bit and I'm pretty angry and trying to think what to do to this guy. For now I follow them. And there's two more things I notice. On the footpath, with nobody around and Front Street coming up, he tries to take hold of Miss Spencer's hand and she jerks it away. That just shows me I'm right. And if he wants to get tough with her right here for taking her hand away, I'm ready to run up on him and do what damage I can with this pail across the side of his head and my fingers in his eyes and my teeth taking chunks out of his ears. But he doesn't do a thing. He keeps walking. Which figures. It's a public place. Guys like this know how to keep it all private.

Then the other thing I notice comes a few minutes later, along Front Street. He tries to take her hand once more and she

lets him. She holds his hand for a moment like it's still okay
between them, and then they let go, but they move a little closer
to each other as they walk.

Say, don't I know how that happens? Don't I realize I have
to stop and let these two go on to wherever they're going and
don't I double back to my Pa's favorite saloon and go around to
the back door? Some woman with a tired face is there ahead of
me and she's just starting to move off with a pail of beer, and I
guess she loves her man, and I'd rather do this myself than have
Ma come down to Front Street every day. Fat Ed in his apron
takes my pail, and he's okay, Fat Ed. He gives me a couple of
cigarettes and a handful of radishes from the free eats and I pop
the radishes on the way home and they're real good, they taste
sharp, a little bitter, just what I need.

The next day the father of our country is watching me
squirm to find a way to sit in my desk that don't hurt too bad
and he's not changing that little smirk on his face. Being father
of the country, he had his hands full with all the backs to whip,
I guess, about a million. So I keep my mind on what to do with
this bluejacket who normally I'd think is pretty swell, him fighting for his country and having a swell uniform to show for it,
but say, there's only so much you can allow somebody for
being whatever else they are. The main thing is he's hurting Miss
Spencer.

So I go to my two best hard-boiled eggs, a couple of fourteen-year-olds who I find smoking out over the knoll behind
the school and who I've done some things for way beyond the
Piedmonts they're sucking on right now. Joe's dad is a logger
and Joe's taller by a hand than the guy I'm after. Billy's only a

little over my size but he would bite an ear clear off if he needed to. I see their plumes of smoke and I come up over the knoll and they jump up fast from where they were crouching.

"Yay, Hiram," Joe says. "I thought you was a teacher."

"Yay, Joe," I say. "Yay, Billy."

"Yay, Hiram," Billy says.

"I may need another note from my mom soon," Joe says.

"You know where to come," I say. My handwriting is a lot better than any of the teachers realize. I say, "I need a favor from you too. Both of you."

Joe lifts a clenched fist before his face. "You just point me," he says.

"Bet your knickerbockers," Billy says, lifting his own fist.

"Good men," I say. "Good men. And you're right about needing this." I lift my fist with theirs. "The three of us."

"We need to recruit some more weevils?" Joe says.

"There's a sailor in town we've got to teach a lesson," I say.

The fists fall and the eyes widen. It's true this is nothing like what I've asked of them before. Or of myself, either.

"A *sailor*?" Joe says.

"A *grown-up*?" Billy says.

I don't need to listen to any more. I suddenly understand I'm standing here with children. I turn and head up over the knoll. "The note for my mom . . ." Joe calls after me.

Sailors drink. This is something I know. They get drunk and then they stagger around Front Street late at night. I'm a kid. I still look like one. Nobody notices a kid or thinks a kid can do certain things. I don't need some damn army of children crusaders with me to do what I have to for Miss Spencer.

So my pa has some old logging tools in the stable out back and I fetch his beer and tonight he passes out before he can get angry, which happens four nights out of five, to be honest, and Ma is passed out too, mostly from tiredness, and I go to the stable and find me a billhook, which is just right, pretty short and easy to swing but with a nasty curved blade and it still has a good gouging point to it and it's even rusty so I can give him lockjaw on top of whatever else. I wrap it in burlap and put it under my arm and I go into the night and down the hill and there are electric lights shining all around at the navy yard, you can even see the *Iowa* sitting there half lit up against the dark, and I guess maybe Miss Spencer's bluejacket is from the battleship, though he's too young to have been at Cuba, that was ten years ago, when I was still pretty much a baby and this guy was probably knuckling little kids at his public school. Not for me, he wouldn't have. Not this guy. He's bad seed, as Pa likes to say.

There are three saloons on Front Street at the navy end. I spend the next couple of hours drifting from one to the other and poking my head in now and then to check out the faces of the sailors and then hanging around where I can, outside in the shadows, and ducking the police when they come by, 'cause they'd take me as a boy-gone-bad and they'd nab me for loitering and street-roaming and for whatever they'd make of my weapon, though I'm ready to say my logger father needs it for work and I'm just trying to find him, the poor harmless drunk who's going off to the woods at dawn without his billhook. But I keep out of the way and nobody pays me any attention and though the sailor I'm looking for isn't around yet, I'm ready to wait till he appears and then till he's drunk and he can be taught a thing or two.

Finally, as I watch the sailors who got an early start at the saloon drifting out and back to their quarters, I realize they all have to go down Front and past the park. So I find a thicket of bushes at the street edge of the place and I kind of burrow in where I can't be easily seen but I can watch everyone going by. I wait and wait. And then I wake up with a start. I grab fast at my billhook and it's still there beside me. I look around. The street is quiet. It's very late. I come out of hiding and I go down Front and I look in at the three saloons and they're almost deserted. The guy I'm looking for isn't there, and I head on home. Ma and Pa are both still sleeping so deep that for a second I think maybe a crook snuck in while I was gone and killed them.

The next day I'm a perfect model of a schoolboy. I definitely don't want to be kept in, even for twenty minutes, 'cause when the final bell rings I go down the road and find the billhook all wrapped up by the tree where I left it and I slide around out of sight and wait for Miss Spencer to go by. When she does, I step out and follow her. Today I'm going to stick right behind her all the time. I'll take my beating for missing dinner and the damn beer pail and bedtime and breakfast, even. Not to mention I'll take my hanging, if it comes to that. If this bluejacket starts beating on Miss Spencer, even if he's cold sober, I'll go at him right then and maybe that'd be just as well, with the cause real clear to everybody.

She's moving kind of slow. She doesn't really want to go to him. I don't blame her. If only I was somebody, I'd just go on up to her right now and say, Come with me instead, and we could do that, we'd just walk off together. But she leads me down toward town and I can see the bay out in front of us looking real blue and peaceful, and then Miss Spencer does something I don't expect. She takes a path off the road and heads up into the hills, up toward the old growth on the edge of town that the loggers haven't got to. The bluejacket and her are meeting somewhere secret this time. He thinks he won't have to worry about people seeing him if he gets upset with her and he can do what he wants. It's good I'm along. We're on barely a walking path now, through a shaggy meadow coming up on a big wall of trees as tall as a Seattle skyscraper. I don't want her to know I'm around, so I hang back quite a ways and she never looks behind her.

We go on into the dark of the woods and I have to stay closer to Miss Spencer with all the turns in the path. But there's more places to duck behind, as well, and I tread real light, like a redskin, staying on the mossy parts when I can. We play up here sometimes in the summer. We sneak around with rifles carved out of wood and we hunt the Suquamish and the Chimakum and the Muckleshoot, some of us being the Indians, and when I'm Chief Seattle no one can ever find me till I plug them in the back and I never have to give away nothing to the white man. And there are real Indians out here, too, real off-the-reservation Indians, hop pickers mostly, farming and fishing between seasons. So we never know when we're going to run right into someone real, face-to-face.

I think about giving the bluejacket a few extra blows for making Miss Spencer come all this way alone. She's just turned out of sight ahead, beyond a tangle of dead trunks, and there's a strong smell of decaying wood in the air. I make the same turn she did around the dead trees and ahead of me the path falls down a little slope to a clearing where there's a couple of shacks close by each other made of waste slabs from the sawmill and Miss Spencer is heading straight for them. Then a couple of Indians step out to meet her and I jump off to the side so they can't see me. But I flatten out on the ground and crawl under a thicket at the edge of the clearing and I peek down on them.

The Indians are an old couple. The man, in raggedy overalls, is moving over to the second shack, which has cattails drying on the porch and woven hop baskets bunched up beside it. He goes in. The woman is wrapped in a blanket and her braids are hanging on her shoulders and she's real old. Miss Spencer has turned this way and the two women are talking. Miss Spencer lays her hand on that place below her stomach where he hits her with his fist. She's crying. I can see that from this far away. Then the Indian woman puts her arm around Miss Spencer and takes Miss Spencer's hand in hers and they move off to the other shack, the old woman talking low and gentle all the time.

It's now I realize he's not coming. This has to do with how he's hurt her. I don't like the doctor in town either. He comes with his black bag and never says a word and he looks over his glasses at me like it's my fault, even if I've got a broken rib. Maybe this Indian woman has some medicine that'll help Miss Spencer. And maybe her coming here alone means she's quits with him. I reach into the burlap and I squeeze the handle of the billhook and I think about catching this guy on Front Street tonight. And I wonder if maybe I'll find out what my pa is thinking when he does what he does to me. Of course, Pa's never actually gone and killed me. Or even hacked at me with a blade. But it's got to be pretty much the same. I'll lift my hand to the guy from behind and I'll strike at him over and over and he'll crouch down, bleeding heavy already from the first strikes and being too weak and drunk to put up a fight. He'll cry for mercy for a while and then he'll see it's no good and he'll just shut up and take it. That's him. But what about me?

I sit and wait, trying to imagine. What if I was Pa. And then it seems real simple. I hate your guts, is all it is. I just hate your guts. I'm starting to cry. And then there's crying from inside the shack. A sharp shout and then some crying like Miss Spencer knows I'm here and she can feel what a kid feels and she knows, and I'm ashamed of my own tears but they keep on coming. Say, don't I want to go help her, if she's hurting? But don't I realize that Indian woman is doing all she can and she knows things I haven't even dreamed of? And say, aren't I crying myself like the child that I am? So I get up and I drop that old billhook at my feet and I go on along the path through the trees, and to hell with my pa if he wants his old billhook ever again. To hell with him.

IN THE RUSH SHE WAS WED

Wife of Sixteen Asks for Divorce from Middle-Aged Hubby—Alleged Forced Nuptials

TACOMA (WASH.) AUG. 6—Ethel M. Custer, a 16-year-old bride, has brought suit for divorce against her husband, who is twice as old as she. Mrs. Custer tells how Custer literally forced her to a marriage by taking her to the Courthouse at Port Oxford, securing a license and marrying her despite her protestations before she had time to realize what she was doing.

She says she never wanted to marry Custer, and that his plan of courtship was irregular and extraordinary. Mrs. Custer was living with her parents in Vancouver, Wash., when she met Custer last September. Custer proposed that they go to Port Oxford to visit his relatives. When she arrived there, he asked her to go to the Courthouse to see those relatives.

All unsuspecting the young girl acquiesced, when to her surprise he secured a marriage license and coaxed her so persistently that she agreed to marry him.

from the front page of the *Los Angeles Times*
Sunday, August 7, 1910

A SUMMER GIRL

COPYRIGHT, 1909, MOFFAT, YARD & CO., N. Y.

THIS SPACE MAY BE USED FOR
CORRESPONDENCE

PORTLAND, ORE.
JUL 14
5 - PM
1909

Miss Pauline Muller
Baker City
Oregon

I GOT MARRIED TO MILK CAN

Portland, Ore.
Jul 14, 1909
5 – PM

Miss Pauline Muller
Baker City
Oregon

Dear Pauline, Arrived at Portland yesterday morning and it was such a relieve for we had an upper berth and I didn't sleep a wink. Well I got married to Milk Can and we are now on our honey moon. Mr. Watt is here and he looks stunning. Katie

It was getting close to sundown when I and the man I'd just married stepped onto the China & Japan Express in Baker City. We were right there in plain sight. If any of my friends had happened to be near the station, they'd have seen what I'd done. They'd have all come up and stood on the platform and I would have paused and turned to them and waved farewell with a gloved hand. Their little faces would have been like a row of sunflowers turned up to me, if sunflowers can have little eyes full of tears of happiness and amazement. Not too happy, for they'd have misgivings, my friends. And not too amazed, for Mr. Trimble had been publicly wooing me to beat the band.

But there I was, boarding the train that would carry me off—not quite so far as China, but to the great city of Portland for my honeymoon. I did happen to pause and turn, but simply to look past and above the station to the copper-clad spire of City Hall where the deed was quietly done, and then off to the roll of hills beyond my fair city, out to where Milk Can's dairy farm was.

I had never called my new husband by the name I'd always had for him in my head. Heavens no. Dear fussy sweetly preoccupied man that he was. He was "Mr. Trimble" even to the speaking of the vow just an hour ago. He gave me a little chicken peck on the cheek and my mama burst into tears and my papa folded his arms across his chest and beamed—I saw them out of the corner of my eye, since Mr. Trimble was kissing his bride on the justice-of-the-peace-side cheek. I said, softly, "Thank you, Mr. Trimble."

He said, just as low, "Thank *you*, Katherine. And please do call me Clarence now."

Not that he'd insisted on "Mr. Trimble" before, but he respected my formality till the last bow was tied.

It was I who wanted a small ceremony. Everyone was content with that, my papa especially. A penny saved is a penny earned. He came up and shook Milk Can's hand and said, "Now she's yours."

So we sat in the parlor car of the China & Japan Express, with velvet seats and incandescent lights and a cut-glass chandelier all aquiver from our rush down the tracks toward the Big City, and I was feeling I should feel grand. Milk Can was perched on the seat beside me as stiff as his collar and reading his evening newspaper—a comfortably settled married man already—and I turned my eyes to the Blue Mountains off to the west where the sun was setting. I cocked my head at the sun. There it went.

The last bit of its fire spilt on the mountains and then presto, it vanished. I sighed.

We'd met on a summer day one year ago, Milk Can and I, when he was still strictly Mr. Trimble. It was the afternoon of the July ice cream social at the Methodist church. They had a lovely big tent set up with tables everywhere and half the town was there and we girls were all so pretty in our white lingerie dresses, we half dozen or so girls with a little too much learning and a little case of the uppities who were getting on to be twenty-one or twenty-two years old and not yet married. I looked particularly nice, I think, with my hair in a Psyche knot and spinning a parasol on my shoulder.

How open I was to the future, standing there quite content with the image of myself, running my tongue through a cold groove of the ice cream in the pastry cone in my hand. And yet how oblivious I was to the import of that moment. I was about to encounter, nearly simultaneously, both my future husband and a man I'd not seen in several years, a man who nevertheless quite persistently kept popping up in my imagination, growing grubbier and more dangerous each time.

Just outside the tent, shuffling his feet awkwardly and standing all alone, a true outsider now, was Mr. Watt. He had grown a beard, it was true, and he had a funny little floppy Frenchy kind of hat on, but he had a collar and a properly tied four-in-hand and did not appear from this distance to be especially grubby. He raised his hand to his brow and shielded his eyes from the sun, looking into the tent as if trying to find someone without whose presence he would not dare to venture in. Odd, the little galloping that went on behind the lace insertions of my lingerie dress at that thought. I even fancied I could see the stains of oil paints on his hands.

And as I considered all this, a throat cleared beseechingly just over my shoulder and I turned to look into the eyes of a vaguely familiar man. I had to lift my gaze only a very little bit, for Milk Can is built low to the ground so he cannot readily tip over, and he closed his eyes at their first contact with mine and he dipped his face in a little bow, ripping off his derby to reveal a deep red crease around his sparsely furred head.

"Miss Hildebrand," he said, "I apologize for my forwardness, but your father encouraged me to approach you."

My reflected face appeared now in the train window, glowing a lovely shade of yellow. The Blue Mountains were sawtoothed against the darkening sky. Milk Can's newspaper rustled beside me. Of course my father had encouraged him.

"I'm Clarence Trimble," he'd said beneath the Methodists' tent. "I own the largest dairy farm in Baker County. I am not married."

I am my pecunious father's daughter. I cannot deny this was an interesting declaration, even as I thought of Mr. Watt peering in from the outside.

Ah, Mr. Watt. Pauline Muller and Mary Haight and I sat side-by-pigtailed-side in our school classroom, barely fourteen, and Mr. Watt—sans beard and Frenchy hat but occasionally with paint on his hands, I think—Mr. Watt was our teacher. Oh the giggly admiration that issued forth from the three of us. He had beautiful large cow eyes with long lashes and a chin that was as square and strong as a brick. He'd mumble his way through mathematics and then glow when we took out our drawing pencils. How sad it had been to move on from that year with Mr. Watt, and we kept track of him around town for a long while after that. Each time we encountered him on the street we'd furiously debate over which of us he'd smiled at most ardently, a gesture, of course, that revealed his secret desire. Then, with a big stir at the school, for he'd begun to profess quite liberal views, he went off to Portland to become a bohemian. Moreover, a bohemian *painter* with, almost certainly, unclothed models. Our giggling stopped, the three of us, and our thoughts grew quite serious about him, I'm sure. Mine did at least. Serious and just a touch resentful, I think. And then he was, in my mind, besmeared with paint and bearded down to his chest and his beard was full of crawling things and I shivered at the thought of his models.

I tried to focus on this man turning his derby round and round in his hand. "I'm happy to meet you, Mr. Dairy," I said, and the blush that came upon me was like to melt my ice cream.

He squinted at me closely, but before I could correct myself, his eyes widened in understanding and he started in to laughing. "Quite so," he cried. "Mr. Dairy, the trimble farmer."

I smiled wanly and he continued to be amused, his laugh rattling around inside him like a stone in a tin can. People were turning their faces to us. I glanced over my shoulder toward the place where Mr. Watt had been standing, and he was gone.

The newspaper suddenly smashed beside me now. I turned to Mr. Trimble. That is to say, Clarence, my husband. He was wagging his head fiercely.

"What is it?" I said. "What's wrong?"

"Mark my words," he said. "As of this moment, the world will begin its decline into oblivion."

I had no idea what he was talking about, precisely. But it seemed oh so true.

"Yesterday," he said. "It was proposed by the Congress to amend the Constitution so as to allow the federal taxing of income."

"Oh my," I said, and I could hear how concerned I sounded—the loyal wife affirming her husband's opinion—and he began to discourse at length on the dangers before us. My husband was no doubt correct. The decline had begun.

My married life began with an irony. In the last century, Baker City had been the belle of the Oregon Trail, the center of the gold mining region, and it had grown up fast, with dancing girls and saloons and houses of ill repute, and though most of that was gone from our town now, these things preserved me on my wedding night. They had helped make Baker City important enough to be an express stop for the Union Pacific, and since my husband—sweetly to his credit—wanted the luxury of a parlor car and a Pullman, he booked us on the China & Japan. But the only accommodation available was an upper berth to share. Not enough space, not enough privacy, and so we climbed our ladder together in our union suits and dressing gowns and squeezed in head to foot and merely slept.

Well, *he* slept. I lay awake, his stockinged and gartered feet beside my face. I folded my hands on my chest like the painting of the dead Juliet in the Opera House foyer and I closed my eyes and I waited out the night, the train engine chuffing distantly outside in time to the pulse I faintly heard in my ear. I tried to give Milk Can over to his own dreams and I just lay there *traveling*. I imagined our train as we crept through the mountains and then ran along the Columbia River and I could sense Portland lit up ahead like London or Paris or somewhere. He will take me traveling every year, my new husband, I resolved. There was a new world and a new century out there, and he was rich enough to have hired men who milked his cows. They did not need his touch.

The first time I stepped foot in the house that was destined to be mine, my mama and papa were at my side and Mr. Clarence Trimble, dairy baron, was bowing us into his parlor. I entered and took in the slightly tatty settee and the needleworked armchairs—things that eventually would have to go, being the taste, clearly, of his recently deceased mother. Her presence, too, was felt in the wide expanse of wall above the fireplace, as it was simply hung with a modest steel engraving of Moses descending with his tablets. Then my eyes fell to the hearth and fixed intently on an object just off to one side.

A five-gallon milk can. It was filled nearly to the brim with varied small objects. While the three elders spoke, I moved to the can, drawn there as if the thing were a powerful electromagnet. And then I saw the objects clearly. Quarters and dimes and silver dollars and Miss Liberty gold coins and a garnet ring and a necklace of pearls and on and on, finger-itchy stuff.

Suddenly Mr. Trimble's voice sounded just over my shoulder. "My future wife's little milk bank," he said. "I've been adding to it for a long while."

I cocked my head at the can. The jewels on top were no doubt once his mother's. It was a good sign, it seemed to me, that he had now simply thrown them in. I turned to face Mr. Trimble—this sturdy, capacious milk can of a man—and I found his unblinking gaze somehow comforting.

He was snoring now. I could no longer hear my own pulse, and even the train whistle receded behind the titanic honking of my husband.

Clarence Trimble is a gentleman. We arrived in Portland at dawn and I'm not a complainer. He had no reason to think that I hadn't slept as soundly as he, but he had booked our suite at the Nortonia Hotel so that we could go directly to our rooms, which we did, and there he discreetly kept his distance and allowed me to bathe and even to sleep a bit in maidenly privacy. I was grateful enough at this to slip my arm into his as we ascended by elevator to the roof of the Nortonia for a bit of light lunch. Though, to my shame, I slipped my arm instantly back out again when I was struck by a sight for which I was ill prepared.

We stepped into the open-air tearoom, which was sheltered from rain and sun by a blue-striped translucent tentlike cover strung with Chinese paper lanterns. Beyond was the roof garden, and sitting out there in the pale, cloud-veiled sunlight was Mr. Watt. I turned my face away at once, though an image of him lingered, as if I'd glanced into the sun itself. His beard was trimmed neatly around that wonderful jaw and his head was bare and his hair was tousled in the breeze and he sat hunched over a book on the table before him.

At the indifferent wave of my hand, my husband ordered lunch for the both of us and I tried to keep my eyes focused far off, away from this hotel top, out to, for instance, Mount Hood, which pushed up from the horizon, and when it seemed, in my overheated state of mind, to resemble a bosom, perhaps of an artist's model, I shifted to another object, nearer in, a man-made thing of great height and simple shape and earnest purpose and it too began to trouble me, and my husband said, "It can hold a million bushels of grain."

"Ah," I said.

"The Pacific Coast Elevator," he said.

I looked for something else to focus on, but suddenly he was there, standing above us and saying, "Forgive me for intruding."

I lifted my eyes to Mr. Watt and he was looking directly at me, though Clarence Trimble was addressing him. "Aren't you Matthew Watt?"

And Mr. Watt confirmed as much and explained how he once was my teacher and how bright and talented I was, how much the perfect model of a student, and I tore my eyes away from his, for they would not leave off looking at me. He said, "It's a pleasure to see how she has become a woman, bright and talented even still, I'm certain."

"To be sure," Clarence Trimble said, rather coolly. "Which is why I have only yesterday made her my wife."

I looked quickly back to Mr. Watt's face and there was a sudden hardening there, I swear.

"My best wishes to you both," he said.

"And you, Mr. Watt?" my husband said. "What business are you pursuing?"

"Not a business, actually," he said. "I am an artist." At this he waved his book—a sketchbook—before us. "You must stop round at my studio, if you have a chance," he said. "I am at the corner of Front and Everett, by the river." And then he bowed and he moved off, and I held very still, not watching him go.

"I despise a man like that," Clarence Trimble said. "You can't just run off from the world and be an artist. Not in this day and age."

The next afternoon I found myself alone in a cab, wondering what was getting into me. On the second night of our marriage—this one in a hotel room, in two beds, side by side—my husband had asked for nothing from his new wife. "You look weary," he'd said.

"Yes," I'd said, and I kissed him on the cheek in gratitude, and we had a long, deep sleep. If he snored, I was unaware of it.

The next morning we toured City Park in a hired motorcar, which put a stiff summer wind into my hair and made me feel quite wonderfully quick and free. And we went up to Portland Heights and looked out across the city to the distant Mount Hood and the Willamette River in between. I thought of Mr. Watt's studio out there next to the river, and in the afternoon Clarence wanted to take a nap at the hotel and he gave me a twenty-dollar bill and sent me off to the Olds, Wortman & King Department Store for whatever I wanted to buy.

I stared a long time at the greenback before I stepped into the cab. The horse nickered its disapproval at me. I ignored him and then we were off. Soon we wound our way through rutted streets full of Chinese people and laundry hanging from windows and vendors hawking their wares from carts. I shrunk back a little into the seat until at last the cab stopped on the corner of Everett and Front. I took a deep breath and stepped out.

I stood twirling my parasol before a tenement that was leaning so clearly to one side it was like to tip over and I breathed in such exotic smells of food and city filth that I might have indeed ridden the China & Japan Express clear across the ocean. But almost at once I heard his voice.

"Katie," he cried.

I looked up and Mr. Watt's upper body was thrust far out of a window, so far I was afraid he would fall on me.

He waved for me to come up and he disappeared. I summoned my courage and went up the stoop into this place and up the stairs. I climbed no more than a floor before I heard the clatter of his descent and he appeared before me on a landing. "Katie," he said again and offered his hand, which was stained with dark green and blue. I took it and, to be honest, I thrilled at that touch, even regretting I'd not removed my gloves before this. He escorted me up three more floors and I entered his studio.

There was sunlight slanting sharply through a wide wall of windows and there were two easels and canvases everywhere, though all stacked with their backs outward, and the place reeked of turpentine and paints, and I grew suddenly lightheaded, perhaps from the smells but more from the fact that I was alone in an artist's studio—in *Mr. Watt's* studio. I was taking none of this in clearly.

That phenomenon got worse. "Katie," he said. "When I saw you yesterday, I thought perhaps fate was intervening. Now that you're actually here, I have to speak my mind. I've been thinking about you ever since I left Baker City."

"Ah," I said.

"I came looking for you last summer, but I lost my nerve."

"Ahh," I said, drawing the syllable out a little farther, the best I could do to express myself at that moment.

He grabbed my hand, which I did not remove from his ardent grasp. "Katie, what have you done?"

"Done?"

"You've married an old man who milks cows."

"Not exactly that," I said, and it was unclear even to me in what way I was trying to mitigate his statement.

To Mr. Watt, however, it seemed quite clear, for he smiled and grew instantly calm. He kissed the gloved hand he still held, then whispered, "I will soon go east, Katie. To Philadelphia. There are artists there I've heard of who will understand me."

I knew what he was saying. An alternate future suddenly stretched out before me.

"Would you like to see my work?" he said.

I nodded, and he let go of my hand and loped across the room. He took up a canvas from an easel and stepped into the center of the floor, the canvas held with its face against his chest, like a sleepy child. It was a touching gesture. I was feeling as wobbly as a newborn calf.

And I must admit I had a waking dream as I stood there, the dream of a life in Philadelphia with Matthew Watt. It was a carefully managed dream, for the Portland tenement had become a swank Philadelphia town house in granite and marble and Matthew had cleaner hands. I even could see myself draped over a settee being painted by my famous husband.

Then Mr. Watt turned the canvas around.

I did not understand. I drew nearer.

He had painted a row of ash cans in a dirty narrow alley, perhaps behind this very building that was threatening to fall down around us.

"To hell with the French and their flower gardens," he said, bouncing up onto his toes.

I had no words. He propped the canvas against a chair and dashed back to the stack. Then, one after another, paintings appeared, and he chattered ceaselessly about people I'd never heard of and about trends of this and reactionaries of that. But it was all just fly buzz to me. What he was showing me were sweatshops and restaurant kitchens and alleyways and more ash cans and saloons and hanging laundry and still more ash cans, and there was not a pretty thing in sight, for all the canvas he'd covered with paint, not a single pretty thing.

Then I had still another vision of the future. I saw myself hanging over a fireplace, painted on a vast canvas full of light and beauty, me in a white dress with a parasol over my shoulder and all about me are flowers—it is a beautiful flower garden, perhaps in France. My husband would commission such a painting of me and he would take me to that garden and he would say to me, "Katie, I have big plans. This is the day and age of people like me and the things I can give to people like you."

And so I interrupted Mr. Watt. I thanked him for his time and trouble and I veritably flew down the stairs and into a cab, and I would stop at Olds, Wortman & King before returning to the hotel. I would buy a pretty new dress, which would please my husband very much.

WOMAN WHO DIED SUDDENLY MAY HAVE STARVED

A woman known only as Mrs. Brown died suddenly yesterday afternoon at 326 East 119th street, where she rented a furnished room. She came in at 1 o'clock and fell on the stairway. Mrs. Hattie Wuschofins and a neighbor ran to help her.

"Give me some bread—a bite of bread," she pleaded and fell over dead.

Dr. Richards came from the Harlem Hospital and said Mrs. Brown had been dead for twenty-four hours. Mrs. Wuschofins convinced the police, however, that Dr. Richards was in error.

from page 2 of *The Sun,* New York
Sunday, August 7, 1910

UNION POSTALE UNIVERSELLE
EGYPTE
CARTE POSTALE

I am awfully fond of this garden.
How pretty are those plants & flowers!
There is a grotto in this garden
I was afraid to enter as it is too dark
then, but at last decided. It is full of
passages the water runs over the walls
outside. With best wishes Yours sincerely
Clara

THE GROTTO

I am awfully fond of this garden. How pretty are those plants & flowers! There is a grotto in this garden I was afraid to enter as it is too dark there, but at last decided. It is full of passages, the water runs over the walls outside. With best wishes Yours sincerely Clara

I t was in the spring of 1914, while I still had salvias and hydrangeas and dahlias in bloom, that I went to Egypt. I had not left Mother's house for a long while. That is to say, not overnight. Her soul had passed into the bosom of God through her Savior Jesus in 1910. And yet, of course, much of her had remained with me. I decided to forgo seeing my plumbago and my oleander. I decided to whisper a good-bye to Mother for just a little while. There was a brief ceremony, I suppose you could call it. I stood before the window seat where mornings she would drink her tea and nurture a bit of breeze. The lace curtains would stir and she would draw one to the side and turn her face to the street. The Seth Thomas ticked heavily on the mantel. I said softly, "Surely it's of little matter to you now, dear. I will do this thing." She would not have understood. Though it is only a few dozen miles away, she considered even Mobile to be a foreign land.

I stood at the window of my room at the Savoy Palace Hotel on the Rue de la Porte de Rosette and I drew back the heavy linen curtain and there was no breeze but only a welter of voices from the street. My companions were laid low in other rooms about the hotel. I had not clearly understood how sturdy my constitution is until the other half dozen of us from the Ladies Literary Society and Garden Club of Bovary had wilted instantly at sea and by the time we arrived at Alexandria were still declaring, quite convincingly, that their deaths were imminent. The few married couples who completed our touring party fared little better, and all of them were on a regimen of bismuth cachets, and some were taking quinine as well. I myself had stood on the rolling deck of the *Laconia* and put my face into the sting of ocean spray and waited for the sickness to befall me, but it did not.

Not that I am without my frailties. The voices from the street below frightened me, terribly, as did the dark men in maroon fezzes and crimson sweaters that morning at the docks, all of them crying out at once, "Cook's tour man!" and "Cook's here!" and "Me Cook's!" As I understand it, few of them actually were from Thomas Cook and Son. They were full of pretense for the chance to carry your things away, perhaps never to be seen again. I was glad to have our own tour guide to shepherd us through this chaos, though he was a coarse man, provided by the agency in Mobile, who seemed simply to have memorized, imperfectly, snatches of the Baedeker we all had tucked into our bags. He needed to understand we were part of a literary society, many of us. We were capable of reading and had done so in our preparations.

I had some little difficulty in breathing as I stood at my window in Alexandria that first day. The air was fetid, the din unceasing. I let the curtain fall. I fended off the thought that Mother was right about the world. The noise would have been sufficient to make her nod with closed eyes, the gesture alone saying, There, Clara, see what I mean? What would soon transpire in this city far away would have truly alarmed her.

I was myself alarmed after Mother passed. Not long before, Halley's Comet had finally dimmed from view. It was a warm, early summer evening. The door was open to the yard, and the smell of the Confederate jasmine filled the kitchen where I sat alone at the table, her body laid to rest with our pastor's reassurances of the life to come, the last sympathetic visitor finally gone from our house, the countertops filled with brought food. I could hear the clock ticking in the parlor. A dog barked somewhere in the distance. The rooms above me were silent. I was forty-five years old. I never married. Father long ago left the two of us, Mother and me, well provided for. I had only to care for the woman who'd borne me and to tend the garden we both loved. Now there was only the garden. The ticking of the clock. To sit in the heavy fragrance of the jasmine and later the summer roses and later the smell of burning leaves and autumn coming on, and then, with winter, the tight smells of the house, the soap and the coal smoke and the starch. I could not imagine a winter of silence in this house. I began to weep, and I trembled inside much as later, in Alexandria, I trembled from a state of things quite the opposite of all that, with the cacophony of voices and the smell of wood fires and rotting food. I turned away from the hotel window. I had gently asserted the privilege my father had given me. I had arranged to occupy a room alone on my grand tour. The enforced physical company of other women in a similar state of life offered me no comfort, I'm sorry to say. They were clinging to each other even now. I did enjoy to read the same books as they. To speak together of flowers and fertilizers. I removed the white lawn waist and voile skirt that I had determined would be my traveling uniform, and I lay down on the bed in my chemise. An electrical fan hummed beside me on the nightstand. The air moved across my face and my neck. Be still, Mama. In spite of the warmth of Egypt in spring, I shivered.

My first night I woke in the dark and there was only silence in the room. I thought Mother had stopped breathing. I sat up and would have called for her, but then I knew where I was, in spite of the blessed, and so far uncharacteristic, silence. I went back to sleep. But I woke once more, to a lone voice crying out. A faint light was seeping into my room from the window. This time there was no confusion. Mother was long since dead. I was halfway round the world. The voice was a male voice but high-pitched, rising sharply and stretching out his words, long and ardent, and then falling to rise instantly again. It was, I knew from my preparation, a muezzin calling the Mohammedan faithful to prayer. I turned on my side away from the window, putting my face into the air from the electric fan, and I said the Lord's Prayer over and over until the voice outside ceased and I was asleep once more.

The next day one of the couples, from Mobile, whom I did not know, and one of my fellow literary ladies—Alice Fay Miller, a librarian at the Carnegie in our town—were ready to try their health in Alexandria. Given the smallness of today's party, our tour guide declined to hire a local dragoman but, rather, took us out himself. Consequently, I listened to nothing that was said. Whenever he would look my way as he muttered through his vague memories of Baedeker, I would lower my face slightly and he would vanish beyond the roll brim of my Panama hat. He was, however, efficient in securing the appropriate horse-drawn cabs for us. I credited him with that.

I spent the day trying to calm my unease at the boisterousness of the city. Wherever we passed, these people, dark of face and voluminously becloaked, were carrying on their lives in the streets, and there was much shouting and waving of arms and, as we passed, lifting and hawking of goods. Fezzes and postcards and shawls and embroidered cloths and woven baskets and pistachio nuts and dried fish and one man offered a parrot from his arm and another a monkey on a leash crying, "Buy monkey please, he is your Egyptian friend." And, of course, there were those who had no goods to sell, also beseeching us loudly for money, often, in appearance, no different whatsoever from those who at least offered something in return for what they asked. Those who clearly were much worse off, maimed or sick or truly destitute, quieter in their plea, made me uncomfortable in the show of our privilege, though we had been strictly instructed by the Egyptian hotel staff to resist giving money to any of these.

And there were others I could not block out, either, though they made no sound whatsoever. The women. We passed a donkey cart with a man leading, and inside were half a dozen Mohammedan women wrapped in their burkas so only their eyes could be seen, dark eyes turning to me and to Alice and the other woman in our cab, wondering, I daresay, at the nakedness of our faces. And thinking what of us? That we were brazen? A shame to God? Wicked and worldly? How little they could know of me. Or I of them, for that matter. The man who had just struck his donkey with a rod looked at us too, and I refused his appraisal, turning instantly away. These were the worst times for me during the day, of course, as I moved through the streets, the times when I felt most keenly the absence of that other rhythm of life I'd always known in our house on Wilkinson Avenue. How deeply those years had shaped me.

Not that I'd come to Egypt simply to find a quainter Alabama. But I was feeling keenly my own limitations. The limitations of an Old South spinster born the year that the war of secession ended, the Northern president was assassinated, and the Southern president was captured dressed as a woman. Two of these three events had always been forbidden as topics of conversation in my mother's home. As was, of course, the emancipation of a whole latent nation among us of people enslaved from this very continent, which also occurred in the year I was born. I never asked—perhaps I was afraid to—why this latter topic was also forbidden. From shame for that particular Southern institution, I hoped. But it is quite possible my father and my mother regretted its passing or, at best, regretted the relinquishing of the state-centered rights that helped perpetuate it.

Even away from the clamor of the streets, I was keenly conscious of who I'd always been. Before Pompey's Pillar, a red granite column seventeen hundred years old, as tall as the tallest building in Mobile, my eyes would not quit straying to the wide scattering of rubbish all around, some of it the broken fragments of other antiquities, some of it clearly the detritus of modern times, nameless things of stone and cement and rotted wood. This was as shameful to me as perhaps my naked face was to the Mohammedan women who passed in their cart. My lawn, my garden, my house were immaculately neat. At the Catacombs of Kôm esh-Shukâfa, down a winding wooden staircase in a circular light shaft, the chill of ancient death came upon us and I looked into the empty crypts shaped deep in the stone walls, heavily shadowed from the electric lights, and I thought only of Mother. Mother in the plain pine box she'd asked for. The lid closing to the ages. Was she presently shocked to find herself a fellow citizen somewhere with the Alexandrine soul whose remains once lay in this hollowed stone? This was not necessarily an ominous consideration. There were many early Christians in Alexandria. At the Museum of Greco-Roman Antiquities my guidebook translated the words on the Coptic tombstones as, *Be not sad; no one on the earth is immortal.* I wondered if, on the contrary, that wasn't the very reason to be sad. And in another room was the mummy of a Roman woman, her rather plain face painted on the head of the wrappings, her body deep within, but the cloth was torn away at the bottom where the bare toes of her left foot were visible, gray and wrinkled, and I was embarrassed for her. I was suddenly acutely conscious of my own body. I would be mortified to have my bare feet made visible to anyone. I despise the shape of my own toes. These were not the thoughts of one whose horizons have been broadened by travel.

Deep into the afternoon we were intending to return to the hotel, but our guide, to his credit, heeded the suggestion of our cabdriver and took us first to a vast public garden along the main canal leading from the west harbor. We stepped down at the stone-arbored entrance, and after the puffing of the horses subsided, I was struck by a clean, sudden silence, the silence of growing things. We drifted through the archway, and inside, we faced a wide, rolling, green expanse with quite a large pond and paths and splashings of floral color here and there and ringed about with higher ground and, far off among its trees, what seemed to be the fragment of an ancient wall. Nearby was an empty bandstand, and beside it, an active café. My companions, with no words spoken but being of one mind, moved off toward the café. The guide trailed along until he noticed I wasn't following. He stopped and took a step back in my direction. "Miss Summerfield?" he said.

"I'm going to explore a bit," I said.

"I should come along," he said.

"No." I'm afraid my reply carried my disregard for him in its firmness. "It's simply a garden, Mr. Fisk," I said, trying to soften my voice.

He looked at me dumbly.

"I insist," I said.

"Very well," he said, and he hurried along to the café, no doubt relieved to be acquitted of his responsibility.

I had not thought to feel uneasy walking in an Egyptian garden alone until this foolish man raised the issue. I recognized a faint fluttering in my chest now, but I considered the source and put it out of my mind. Besides, there were very few other people visible in the garden and I would simply avoid them. Things rooted in the ground had always been friendly with me.

I followed the main path along the irregular edge of the pond and wandered off, now and then, to stands of jacaranda and eucalyptus and sycamore and to a great gathering of oleanders, massive oleanders taller than a house, and to lovely runs of roses—musk roses and off-white roses I didn't recognize—and then, in a little dip of the green, around a curve of the path, I was astonished to find a profusion of Madame Pierre Oger, her pink cups nodding at me as if from my own backyard. I approached the nearest shrub and bent to her and I cradled one of her blooms in my hand. It was a dark pink, verging on red, darker than mine ever were. "What is it, dear lady?" I said to her, low. "This place has you wrought up, does it?" I lingered with her for a time. She was a sport, a rose that came into being accidentally, an abnormal impulse in a long-established other rose. Madame Oger's immaculate mother was La Reine Victoria. I was filled with a kind of tenderness about her that I often felt in my own garden. Her scent was heavy about me, like ripe pears.

I was reluctant to leave her, but I felt my qualms about Egypt were being pruned away in this place and I wanted more of that. I went on along the path, coming up to some poinsettia trees that were thick and dark. I wished I'd seen them in bloom, though if I had, my dear Madame Oger would have then been sleeping, and I was very happy for her reassurance. I moved through the poinsettias, Christmas in Alabama beginning to slip in at the edge of my thoughts. But the air now was still and warm. I put away Christmas. I was growing easy with the notion that I was in another country.

As I moved toward the far reaches of the garden, a sound was beginning to gather about me. It was the unbroken plash of falling water. I came round a bend by the lake, thick with boscage, and I found its source. Water poured over a stone wall that emerged from the trees at the side of the hill that rimmed the garden. And nearby was a portal, dark in shadow. It seemed at first glance to lead straight into the side of the hill. But among all the growth above and around and beyond the opening, I noticed hints of the asphalt paper that was laid over something, trellis work or cement or stone, that embowered quite a large space. It was a man-made grotto. How lovely, I told myself. How exotic. But I hesitated, surprised at an almost desperate clutching that had begun inside me. I was reminded, perhaps, of the dark openings of the crypts at the catacombs earlier in the day. I forced myself to take a step, and another. I tried to see this as an entryway into the very midst of all the verdancy around me. But I stopped again. It was a cave. An unnatural one, at that. Perhaps they had some dark-growing things within, but it would be mostly stone and hard surface. And the entrance was very dark. I turned to go.

What made me reconsider? I'm not entirely sure. I did hesitate once more. No doubt there was some undercurrent of the determined traveler in me. No one had forced me to leave Alabama, to pack a steamer trunk and board a ship and come to the African continent. I'd had enough of the silence of my house, enough of the momentum of my everyday life that rolled on as if Mother were still upstairs or as if she had never existed. Either condition would have left me doing the same spinstery things in an endless succession of mornings and afternoons and evenings. Standing now with the grotto entry behind me and the path back to the café and my fellow travelers ahead of me,

I must have yearned for some break with what had gone before. But it was a structured, managed break, free of actual risk, after all. A tourist's cave. I turned and squared myself up, pressed my Panama hat firmly to my head, drew my handbag to my chest, and I strode forward and into the dark gape of the grotto.

My first thought was that this is how it feels to die. A chill and a hush and a distant rush of water and dim striations all about of unfamiliar stone. I was not frightened. The thought was a calm one, a mundane one even, like turning over an unusual root in the garden, something growing unseen. And it soon faded. I had a choice of paths, one to the right and one straight ahead. I assumed, as I gathered my traveler's courage, that either direction would ultimately wind back to this spot, so I moved forward. Soon the path bent to the left and there was grainy tufa rock all around me and a pale electric-bulb light casting the tapered shadows of faux stalactites against the walls. Another turning and I felt the squeeze of anxiety tightening in my chest. I clutched harder there with my handbag, but I was keenly conscious of my withdrawal from the world. I knew the tufa rock, for I had used it some years ago in a corner of my own garden to create a small fountain, idle now, neatly kept though inoperative. So the rock seemed familiar and I focused on that. I walked faster, the rasp of my footsteps echoing thinly. And then I turned another corner into a chamber and a heavily cloaked figure was before me.

I gasped. A face turned to look over a shoulder. A dark face, an Egyptian man, tightly turbaned, with a dense black mustache and large dark eyes that considered me matter-of-factly. He was sitting on a stone bench before a wall with water sheeting down into a narrow pond. He seemed massive to me somehow. The typical layered cloaks he wore had seemed on other Egyptian men to encase a much smaller person. But this man was broad of shoulder and gave the impression of stretching heavily at his own wrappings. I retreated a step.

He leapt to his feet and turned to face me. I stumbled backward some more.

"Please," he said. "I am sorry. I mean not to frighten you, dear lady."

He spoke clear English, though bearing, oddly, both a latent rhythm of his native Arabic and, in pronunciation, a distinctly British accent. I was happy for his English but not at all comfortable hearing him call me a "dear lady." Still, he bowed his head at me, and my mind calmed even as my heart fluttered heavily on.

He came round the bench and made a grand, sweeping gesture at it. "Please. You arrive to a very charming place."

Once again I found myself suspended in the struggle between my fear of new things and my wish for them. "I was just passing through," I said.

"You may sit for a while," he said. "You may think peaceful thoughts."

Still I hesitated. I felt him trying to read me.

"I am going," he said. "You will stay alone."

It was a respectful offer. I credited him with that. And it prompted a similar feeling in me. Either way now, I would offend the man. If I were myself to go on or if I were to encourage him to go, he would surely think I was being critical of his presence. I knew from long practice how to correct the social awkwardness in a room. I straightened and came forward, making my steps firm, approaching him so that he could see nothing but confidence in me. "You must not go," I said. "I will sit on one end of the bench and be peaceful, and you will sit on the other and resume your own thoughts."

I went promptly to the far end and sat down. If he had not been here I would have done no such thing. I tried to calculate how long I needed to stay so as not to hurt his feelings. There was a rustle, and in the faint edge of my peripheral vision I watched him sit. I folded my hands over the bag in my lap and stared at the scattered points of reflected electric light in the flat tumble of water on the wall before me.

"Pumps," he said.

This made me turn my face to him, in spite of my resolve simply to sit and feign peaceful thoughts for a brief time as if he were not here. "I beg your pardon?"

"I am sorry," he said. "I have interrupted."

"It's all right," I said.

"Pumps," he said. "The water." He turned his face to the wall.

"They use pumps," I said.

"Yes," he said, looking back to me. "You understand."

"I do," I said.

"It is my official duty to explain," he said.

I was further relieved. I had not thought to suspect this man's motives for lingering here. But the formal sanction of his presence made it easier now to return my gaze to the cascade and begin to count in my head to a hundred, at which time I would depart.

"Is there some other question you have?" he said.

I looked at him. He had offered an opportunity to think peacefully. If I had, in fact, been so inclined, he was making that impossible. But I felt a hypocrite. I had been seeking no such thing. What *had* I been seeking? Here was a local inhabitant who spoke English and who was prepared to enlighten me in surely the very ways I had sought in coming abroad. But nothing came to mind. And I supposed he was merely soliciting questions about the grotto. After which, he would no doubt expect money for his information. He would turn into a hawker, lifting tourist-spot information in his hands at a passing cab. And he still frightened me, I realized, the massiveness of him, the foreignness. I was feeling foolish in my dumbness as this little string of contradictory thoughts gabbled its way through my head.

"It is all right, dear lady," he said, as if reading my thoughts. "I will not interrupt you again."

But of course he did not read my thoughts. He had a certain social perceptiveness, though he had himself created the awkwardness. "It's not an interruption," I said. "I couldn't think of anything to ask. It's a grotto."

"Yes," he said. "I know what you mean. I find it rather dull myself."

"I'm not being critical."

"You are very kind to say this, but it is Masud—this is me—that is being critical. It is not a natural place. It is for the tourist."

"*I* am a tourist," I said.

"I do not mean insult to the dear lady," he said with a rush.

"May I ask you where you learned to speak as you do?"

"I learn English from the English," he said, shrugging. "They conquered my country and they teach us what they wish us to know. They treat us like rather stupid children. But we learn these things because we must survive. I work for some years in an English bank."

He looked at me, pausing, I think, to assess what he had just said. He had not dealt with the essence of my question.

He shrugged again. "You see now the reason I no longer work in an English bank. I speak what is in my heart."

"Do you value this quality?" I asked. "To speak what is in your heart?"

"It is how Allah made me," he said.

"Then may I say that it causes discomfort to a woman to be addressed as 'dear lady' by a stranger?"

He furrowed his brow to take this in. "I believe for a long time this is a friendly way to speak," he said. "I heard these words said by the English."

I realized at once the problem. I was sorry to have broached the subject. If this had been an English banker in collar and three-piece suit, I could instantly have been a "dear lady" and thought nothing about it. "Of course," I said. "I understand."

He rose abruptly. I must have flinched, for he grew solicitous. "I am sorry. Yes," he said. "I will leave you. . . ." He hesitated very briefly, suppressing another *dear lady* I'm sure. "You can have now your peaceful thoughts."

I should have let him go. But once again I felt I was causing offense. "No. Please," I said. "I did not mean to complain. It was a small semantic point. I was prompted by your courage to speak one's heart."

I could see him react to my assertion of his courage. He smiled and sat down again. As soon as he did, however, I thought of how he must see me. In my preparations I had read what these people believe. He could call a woman from the infidel culture *dear lady* because she was already, automatically, so far outside the boundaries of moral behavior that it did not matter. My face should be hidden. I had no place in public alone.

I looked at the thin veil of water before me. I determined to wait a few moments only and then leave. I did not belong here. And with this, Mother whispered in my head. *You see, dear. My dear Clara. My dear daughter. There is no place in the wider world for you, not for either of us.* Then I could see her. Her face was turned to the thin sheeting of water down the window. The wider world had long since ceased to be an issue. It was raining heavily but quietly. There had been some thunder at first, in the distance. But now it was just the flow of water down the windowpane. She watched from her pillow. I sat beside the bed, the soup bowl still full in my hands, burning faintly at my palms. She'd taken only a few spoonfuls. I knew she would die soon. She watched the rain and I watched her watching the rain, her eyes sunken now, her face gaunt, a woman I had to struggle to recognize. Finally I turned to see what she was seeing. The lace curtains. The blur of water. Nothing visible beyond. I began to tremble now, in the grotto. As I had the day she would not eat her soup and she would not acknowledge me with her eyes. "Mother," I said, looking back to this face, though I had nothing to say to her. I just wanted her to see me instead of the water on the window. "Mother," I said. "Yes, dear?" she said very softly, but she would not look at me. I waited. There was only the sound of rushing water.

And I began to weep. I bowed my head in the grotto in Alexandria and I wept. I quickly pulled a handkerchief from my handbag and covered my face. It smelled of Yardley's lavender, my mother's smell. It was my smell too. I knew I should rise up now and rush down the corridor and out of this place. But I did not have the strength. I was weeping and trying not to make a sound. It wasn't easy. The image of Mother had vanished from my head and my most conscious part focused on not sobbing. A stranger—this Egyptian man—was nearby and I tried to summon my strength to leave, but it was all I could do to moderate the spectacle.

"Have I somehow caused this?" he said.

"No," I said, shifting my handkerchief only enough to see him. "No. . . . I should leave."

"Can I do something?" he said.

"Nothing. Perhaps . . . since I can't seem to go . . . for some reason. . . . " I was short of breath and my voice would not hold steady to speak.

"Yes," he said, rising once again. "I understand. I, Masud, will go."

Twice before he had offered this, sincerely and appropriately, and both times the offer had led me to encourage him to stay. This time I did not stop him, but neither did he go. And then, unexpectedly, I said, "I haven't done this for her. Not properly."

I covered up again and wept on for a time, not thinking of Mother, really, not thinking at all. At some point I sensed his return to the bench. And then, finally, the tears began to slow and I lowered my hands from my face. I knew he was closer to me now. I glanced. He was being very discreet. Not looking in my direction. Still an arm's length away. He seemed a nice enough man.

"My mother," I said. "She died."

He spoke something quickly, almost to himself, in Arabic. Then he turned to me and said, "Allah called my mother one year ago. *Allāhu akbar.*"

"I'm sorry," I said. And I was. For both of us. I pressed at my eyes with my handkerchief, trying to dry them. The very clothes Mother wore into the grave smelled of lavender. This man's mother would be sharply critical of that, no doubt. She dared not go off to her god scented in this worldly way.

I looked at the man next to me. His eyes were glistening in the electric light with his own tears. He loved his mother. She loved him. I wanted to say now that she was all right. She was in heaven. He too seemed to be struggling to find words. "Allah . . ." he began, and stopped. I thought of the woman who never knew Jesus. He looked into my naked face. We both of us remained silent. Finally he said, "I am sorry also."

Our eyes held for only a moment more, as if we were passing in the street, thinking briefly that we recognized something familiar. But no. I was a tourist here. And he was from another world. Then I rose and said, "Good-bye."

"Good-bye," he said.

I followed the path back the way I'd come, rushing, the air dank, difficult to breathe. What did I know of eternity? Mother was on her own now. Masud's mother as well. He would soon prostrate himself at the cry of the muezzin. I would kneel this evening beside my bed in the hotel and pray the Lord's Prayer. It was not up to me to sort this out. One more turn in the path and then light was ahead. I pressed forward quickly, a few steps more, and I nearly leapt from the place at last. Outside, among the sycamores, with a faint scent of roses in the air, I stopped. I lifted my face to the light, desperately grateful for the sun, which I knew was even now rising over my garden in Alabama.

MAKES FACES IN CHURCH

Deacons Want Court Injunction Against Expelled Member Say He's Revengeful

KANSAS CITY (MO.) AUG. 6—On petition of Lewis B. Major, and other deacons, a temporary restraining order was issued today by the Wyandotte District Court, prohibiting William V. Jones from attending the Armourdale Baptist Church. The deacons, in their petition, alleged that since his expulsion from the church in September, 1909, Jones has persisted in attending services and by "facial grimaces and noses," aroused the congregation.

from page 2 of the *Los Angeles Times*
Sunday, August 7, 1910

and soon. from
Beulah Hurshel

Feb. 14, 1909. Hello Miss Maude
how are you standing
the time all O.K. I guess
please excuse me
for not ans. sooner
wish I could see you we
are all well except bad colds
Hurshel had
the bull up by mountain
was it ringff or to preaching
and is now learning to make
his a.b.c. I said when he
got through preaching he would
Mr. J.R. Jeburn. he was going
to start up a thought he said
ask you if you if it would suit
bring Charlett down some thing
I was coming

POST CARD

THIS SPACE MAY BE USED FOR
CORRESPONDENCE

FOR ADDRESS ONLY

FOREIGN

SPARTA
FEB
15
6 PM
1909
TENN

Miss Maude Knuble
Walling
Tenn
Route #1.

UP BY HEART

Sparta, Tenn.
Feb. 15, 1909

Miss Maude Knowles
Route #1
Walling, Tenn.

Feb. 14, 1909. Hello Miss Maude how are you standing the times all o.k. I guess please excuse me for not ans sooner. Wish I could see you we are all well except bad colds Hurshel said he had the bible up by heart and was fixing to go to preaching and is now learning to make his a.b.c. said when he got through preaching he wanted Mr. P. for a clown. he was going to start up a show. he said to ask you how it would suit to bring Charlie H. down some Sun. he was coming any how and would bring C.H. with him will close ans soon Beulah & Hurshel

S o he's coming again tonight, the stranger in the white linen suit and with the razor burn on his cheeks, like he prefers keeping a big beard and he's not used to shaving, and he's pretty much said who he is, though I knew right enough 'cause I've got the Bible up by heart and I've done my preaching and spoke the word as it's writ and not just the words you pick out to suit you, and he's done this before, now and then, he come to Moses plenty and he even rassled Jacob in the dirt, which is told in the book of Genesis, chapter 32, and Jacob rassled him to a draw and some folks who won't hear the real word think it was only an angel rassled Jacob but when Jacob asks his name, he says, "Wherefore is it that thou dost ask after my name?" and instead of saying, he gives Jacob a big blessing, and then Jacob declares, clear as can be, "I have seen God face to face." Jacob also gets himself a shrunk sinew in the hollow of his thigh from one of the old man's holds, which is dirty fighting down in our part of Tennessee, like biting a nose or gouging an eye. But that's one of the things I know about God, from hearing all the words. And from looking around me. This is a fierce neck of the woods, the planet Earth. And God's a roughhouser, all right. I ain't afraid to say it. We got to live in the world he's made for us. Every living thing is eating some other living thing every second of the day. It's just how it goes. I myself ate old Jeb just last week, who was as personable a rooster as you could find and who'd walk right up to me to say howdy whenever I come near. But times is lean and we had to eat him. Though often I had to hold it against Jeb, for in Proverbs, chapter 27, it says, "He that blesseth his friend with a loud voice, rising early in the morning, it shall be counted a curse to him." In the midst of all the carnage you need to keep your voice down in the morning. That's the word of God.

Beulah helped me. She is my helpmeet. When I hadn't got my abc's, she read the Bible to me over and over, and the words of God were like sticky burrs on the pant leg of my mind. I have walked through his field, and though I stumble on the rocks in his high grass, I am covered with his burrs. Beulah my sweet wife. Who is sleeping now in our bed and my sweet boy Charlie sleeping beside her, for the bad dreams he's been having. I think about the bad dreams of a boy and I think of my visitor coming tonight and of my pa. I had bad dreams for a long while as a boy from a riddle my pa told me and he wouldn't tell me the answer of it. "Old Pap coming down the side of the hill. He has my gait, he has my face, the trees fall before him and there's no place to hide." What's that riddle mean? I'd ask my pa, and he'd just laugh low and shake his head, and over the years I been thinking the answer to the riddle is my pa himself coming to whup me, 'cause we looked alike, him and me, everybody said so. Charlie looks like his ma, which I count as a blessing to me and to him.

I don't know what God is wanting with me next. He ain't said real clear yet and I suppose I'll find that out tonight. I finished putting up the Bible in my head this past winter and then I decided to spread his word like I understood it from the spirit. It moved me one night in February to say to Beulah, "I've got it all up now, hon," and I tap the side of my head with my forefinger.

"Hurshel Hudgens, you're a right wonder," she says in reply, closing the Bible and reaching across the table and placing the palm of her hand on my cheek.

"You're the wonder," I say, "for putting up with me."

She just pats me with that hand laying there against my face.

"You know what I got to do now with all these words," I say.

"You're going to go out and do like Billy Sunday," she says.

We had went to see him in a tent in Chattanooga. But I knew there was words Beulah read me from the true and holy scripture of God that even Preacher Billy Sunday wouldn't want to talk about. For example, Billy hated drink. But Paul said in his letter to Timothy, "Drink no longer water, but use a little wine for thy stomach's sake and thine often infirmities." I stand ready to drink wine every time I am tempted to take water, but Billy wouldn't, I'd wager. And he slipped on around the word of God in Proverbs where it says real clear that kings and princes shouldn't drink, but for all the regular folk, you should "Give strong drink unto him that is ready to perish, and wine unto those that be of heavy hearts. Let him drink, and forget his poverty, and remember his misery no more." That's right there in chapter 31 and I know a bunch of boys in these hills who, in their misery, are more godly by the word of scripture—which you aren't supposed to subtract even one syllable of—than Billy Sunday is ready to allow for.

"Maybe not like Billy exactly," I say to Beulah.

"You need to quit at the mine?" she asks, very quiet and helpful, like she wishes to put no stumbling block in my way if God's word is calling on me. At the time and for a few years before, I was working at the sandstone caves mining saltpeter.

"Work's irregular now anyway," I say, and so it was.

"Things happen for a reason like that," she says.

I put my hand on top of hers, which had recently gone back down to the tabletop.

"What kind of preacher are you fixing to be?" she says.

That was a good question.

I went on to spend a while studying that. You can't go putting your light under a bushel. God always made a good show of it, with the pillars of fire and the floods. And hanging his own flesh-and-blood son up on a cross was quite an attention-getter,

I don't need to say. Billy Sunday played baseball for a living when he was young and when he'd get to preaching real fierce he'd wind up and pitch his words right at us from the stage, going through the motions of his work. I thought for a time about that, but sweating out sandstone cobbles from the wall of a cave don't look all that interesting in mime. Though I come to realize the prophecy in my work, saltpeter being a pretty holy thing, having within it both the Old Testament and the New, as it makes both gunpowder and a potion to keep your pecker from rising. It tokens both the God of Moses, Joshua, and David, who between them wiped out more nations from the earth—man, woman, and child—than pretty near anyone, and the God of Paul, who would, if he had his druthers, stop all the peckers of a holy world from rising. Both of which, of course, is one God. Like saltpeter.

Well, I tried out a few things for a preacher show.

I went into town and down to the general store where the boys hang around of an afternoon if the mines don't have any work, and I go in and some are playing checkers and some are sitting and whittling things that might be graven images if you'd ever figure what they're meant to be, the boys of our town saved from perdition by their poor knife skills. My friend Ernest Porter was hanging around the pickle barrel sampling a gherkin on account and I go over to him and I say, "Ernest I'm fixing to be a preacher now that I've got the Bible up by heart and I'm trying to work out the show of it. I'm thinking a Church of Humility is a good way to go, since we're facing some tough lessons and there's no use trying to stand up proud to them. So let me try washing your feet."

Ernest stops right in the middle of a bite into his pickle and he sort of holds it there thinking about what I've asked. The checker game has also come to a stop. "You boys too," I say to the players. "Elmer. George. Come on over and let me wash your feet. This is like Jesus done." I look at the whittlers, but they're keeping their eyes hard on the sticks in their hands.

"Listen here, Hurshel," Ernest says. "I appreciate your wanting to be humble and all if you're fixing to preach, but my feet are shy boys. They're not much for other fellas working at them."

"That's just why you're the right man for the job," I say. "Ain't we done foolish things together plenty of times?"

This was true. For example, we made up like clowns in a show for the orphan home they started in Sparta. These very feet Ernest was being shy about did a hopping-mad dance in the show and then he went to winding up to hit me, his right arm going like a windmill faster and faster and me standing there, my own fists up like to block his blow, and then all the sudden he kicks me in the shin and the little orphan kids laugh like they're going to shake off all their buttons. If I could find some words about clowns in the holy scripture, I'd do him and me up both for my preaching. But for now I just say, "Ernest, have another gherkin and sit on down there on that barrel and let me do this."

Ernest was just finishing off that pickle he'd already started and he sighed and took another and sat down. "Roy," I say to the groceryman. "I need a bucket of water and a bar of that pumice soap."

"Wait now," Ernest says. "Don't you go rubbing the skin off."

I say, "This ain't no job for pretty perfume soap, do you think?"

"You're going a shade more than humble, ain't you? No need to go a-scourging."

"Just leave it all to me," I say. "I'm trying to work this out."

So I get down and unlace Ernest's shoes and take them off and his socks too, which are in bad need of mending. As are poor Ernest's feet, which are twisted and gnarly like a lost soul and in plenty need of washing. So I grab up the soap and I dip it in the water and I take to rubbing pretty vigorous, 'cause I'm always one to do a thing right and thorough, and I'm trying to think of a passage from scripture on that virtue and I'm hoping to find something along the lines of "Blessed are they that do a thing right and thorough." I'm feeling sure there is one. But instead, all I can think of is Moses in the book of Numbers, chapter 31. He was full of wrath at his captains come from the battle where they'd killed every male among the Midianites, who happened also to be descended from Abraham, and who happened to take Moses in and protect him when he was running away from Egypt after killing a man for smiting a Hebrew, and whose priest gave Moses his daughter to be his one and only wife. But Moses was in a serious lather 'cause his captains had killed all the men in Midian but they kept the women and children alive. They hadn't done their job right and thorough. So he went ahead and had them kill all the boy children and all the women who weren't virgins and then he gave all the virgins to the captains and his men. Which wasn't as thorough as he done with most other of the tribes in his way, but what's a fella to do when the help don't get it right the first time? He treated those captains right kindly. Ernest is starting to make an awful racket. Not in words exactly. To his credit, once in for this job, he isn't trying to back out. He's just wailing a little in pain. But like Moses with his captains and the virgins of Midian, I figure I can go a little easy on his feet. Besides, I'm getting kind of shaky, thinking, as I have been, about one of the tougher lessons of the holy word.

"Why don't you leave him some skin left," says Roy who's standing watching all this.

I look up at him. Now, Roy has a bald head, not a hair on it. I'm a little touchy about my calling from the Lord and consequently not ready to take casual criticism, so I'm about to make a comment on the scant leavings at the top of his skull. But scripture come to me once again. I think of God's beloved prophet Elisha who's walking along the road right after healing Jericho's water supply and, as it says in Second Kings, chapter two, "there came forth little children out of the city and mocked him and said unto him, 'Go up, thou bald head. Go up, thou bald head.' And he turned back and looked on them and cursed them in the name of the Lord. And there came forth two she bears out of the wood and tare forty and two children of them."

And the mood I was looking for with this here foot washing has sort of disappeared. Ernest is still whimpering. Old Baldy—I keep that nickname to myself—is watching with a critical eye. I'm not even going to consult the checker players and the whittlers. I just put down the pumice soap and look Ernest in his watery eyes. "You're a good and true friend," I say to him.

"That I am," he says.

So I give Ernest's feet back over to him and I go on out of the general store and head back to home, and I'm still working on what sort of preacher to be as I come down a little gully on the dirt track to our place, and up ahead a bad-boy rattler is crossing from one side to the other, not in any real hurry but slithering along kind of meditating about snake things, maybe. Now, by rights, though it's one of those mild days that can come once and again to Tennessee of a February, he should be in a cave somewhere waiting out the winter. I take it the Lord has sent him forth just for me, 'cause I'm put in mind of another kind of show. Jesus himself says of his preachers in the book of Mark, "They shall speak with new tongues. They shall take up serpents, and if they drink any deadly thing, it shall not hurt them." The rattler has already heard me coming—maybe he's even heard me thinking—and he's stopped in the middle of the path and has curled up to consider the notion with me.

So I come near and he lifts his head and sticks out his tongue and takes to shaking his tail something fierce. But I don't back off. I come up even closer, till I'm right inside his striking range, and he's rearing back in amazement like he can't believe I'm doing this, and then I crouch down to his level and look the serpent straight into his beady little eyes. He's making so much noise I expect his rattles are fixing to fall right off.

"What's it to be?" I say to him.

He flicks his tongue and sways his head back and forth.

"You gonna let me take you up?" I say.

He's not acting like it. But I think maybe that's how it's supposed to be. If the serpents you take up just roll over like pups, it don't make a show of any kind. The folks might not think it's the Lord's doing but that you found you a sick snake. I'm fixing to put my hand out to grab this here rattler by the throat, to the glory of God.

And then I think what kind of world it is that's been created all around us. Roy the groceryman lost his only grandson to a rattler bite just last fall. When he's not killing children, the snake's eating lizards what's eating bugs what's eating other bugs and them snakes will get eat up by a weasel and that weasel will get tore up by a coyote who's going to end up a wolf's meal who's a good dinner for a bear and everybody's young ones are apt to die by somebody else's tooth or claw, the wolf taking the baby bears in return, and that snake is also going to end up a pair of good boots for some old boy. Not to mention the stars exploding out there in space, which Beulah has read to me from a newspaper, and it don't surprise me one bit. So I think of the gospel of Matthew in the fourth chapter when Jesus says, "Thou shalt not tempt the Lord thy God," and it seems to me that's just what I'm fixing to do, finding a test for him which is about this here rattlesnake not biting me. All the sudden I don't see me being a preacher of that sort and I say, "Okay, old boy, you just go about your business," and I back away real slow, still in a squat, and the serpent lets me. Praise the Lord for that.

"You're welcome," a voice says from behind me.

I jump up quick and turn around and he's standing there fresh-shaved in his white linen suit without a spot and he's an old boy with a weathered-up face you'd expect to find behind a mule or, cleaned up like this, behind the bench in his robes at the county courthouse in town. A razor nick on his chin is starting to scab up and there's a strong smell of bay rum about him, like he's only recently splashed it on. I bet it burned that nick. All of which doesn't even near explain how there's a powerful something about him. His face is in the shade of a white, flat-brimmed Stetson but I can see his eyes burning dark under there and it sinks in that he read my mind about being thankful the rattler didn't strike.

"You have something to do with that?" I say.

He chuckles at this like I should know the answer.

My heart is about to pound its way out of my chest by now and there seems to be one of two possibilities for who this old boy might be and one of those is a good sight more well known for making an appearance.

"You from these parts?" I say, which ain't half the question I'm really trying to ask.

"I'm from all parts, as I think you know," he says and he pulls out a cheroot from an inside pocket and lights it up and blows the smoke through his nose.

"Now see, that tells me something, what you just done," I say.

"No it don't," he says. "You'd expect the Lord your God to have a good set of lungs, wouldn't you? And a taste for tobacco? I made the stuff, didn't I? Praise me for a good smoke, if you're of a mind to do some praising."

"So you're saying you're the old man himself?"

"Yes I am. That fella you're rightly concerned about don't go around claiming to be me, does he?"

"Ain't heard of that."

"Goldurn betcha, you haven't."

I feel my face puckering up to consider this and I know he's reading my mind again.

"Hurshel," he says, "Jesus died for your sins."

He pauses a moment to let that sink in. Then he says, "The other boy would never say such a thing, would he?"

"No he wouldn't," I say. I'm looking in my head for the verse about that, but this is common knowledge, no doubt about it. Old Scratch can't even say that name without gagging.

"And I'm here to encourage you to go a-preaching," he says.

"You are?"

"Yep," he says, blowing a tight little ball of smoke that I expect is going to open into a ring but instead stretches up and down and out to the side to make the cross of Calvary. "Take this as your calling."

"I been called?"

"By the Lord your God personal. You done heard me in my holy word better than most. So I'm telling you to stop trying to turn my church into the Hippodrome and preach the words. In the beginning was the word. I've always been a talker."

As all this is sinking in and I'm believing who it is that's standing there conversing with me, I'm suddenly having trouble catching a breath and I'm feeling my knees going all wobbly. Of course, he knows all about it.

"Hold on there, Hudgens," he says. "Don't go falling down."

And my knees stiffen up instantly and I'm breathing normal again. I say, "Should I get down on my knees like in respect?"

"We're not standing on ceremony here," he says. "Just shake the Lord your God's hand, boy." And he sticks the cigar in his mouth and thrusts out his hand. "Put her there."

I grab his hand in mine and he's got a firm grip, but not too firm, just right, and we have a good shake, with him saying, "Go on now and preach that word."

"Yes sir, I will," and we're still shaking.

"And when you done your first big meeting, the night after, I'll come pay you another visit and we can see what's next." He gives my hand one last big pump and he lets go.

We look each other in the eyes for a moment and then he sort of shifts his gaze over my shoulder. "Say," he says, "what's that over there?"

I turn around and all that I can see is the path home. I look back to the Lord my God and he is gone.

So I go on home and find my boy Charlie playing in the front of the house without even a coat on and he comes running, which is his way whenever he sees me. I take my son up in my arms, him running full out and fixing to be seven and not too small a boy for his age. But I can take up my big boy and stay on my feet and we pretty much start speaking in tongues, him and me, "Oooh li'l spookum flibberty," I say and he says, "You big ole barrwangle gibbet." And then I go ahead normal and say, "How you doing?" and he says, "Ma made me drink the Castoria," and I say, "It shall not hurt you."

I put Charlie down on the ground. "You should have a coat on outside."

"It's warm today," he says.

I say, "Neglect not thy cloak in winter."

"Is that in the Bible, Pa?"

"Lest a wind come suddenly up and freeze thy butt," I say.

Charlie laughs. "There's nobody's butt in the Bible," he says.

"You'd be surprised what is," I tell him, but I clear up one thing. "Still and all, that was a 'Sayeth your pa' you just got."

"And your ma," says Beulah who's standing on the porch and I'm feeling real tender about her.

"Beulah," I say, "thy nose is as the tower of Lebanon which looketh toward Damascus."

She makes a sorrowful face.

"It's Solomon talking to one of his wives," I say. "It's real good."

"Thank you for the interpretation, Pastor Hurshel," she says. "You know I'm touchy about the size of my nose."

"The tower of Lebanon was a beautiful thing to King Solomon," I say, "like as your nose is to me, Beulah Hudgens."

She shrugs her shoulders and we go in and I'm all in a bother through suppertime, not knowing what to say about meeting the Lord our God in a white linen suit. Then finally Charlie is sleeping and he's doing okay, sleeping real quiet without the bad dreams, and Beulah and me sit down together at the kitchen table with some coffee and the Bible out between us.

Beulah sighs and sips at her coffee. "He just won't take his Castoria, even if his tummy is acting up. He says it'd be better for him to be cured by faith."

So I say, "You remind him that when Jesus cured the blind man outside the temple in Jerusalem, he had to spit on the ground and make some clay and put it on the man's eyes and then the man had to go and wash off the clay for the miracle to work. So you might could use some Castoria and it still be the hand of God."

Beulah touches the Bible and cocks her head a little.

"Gospel of John, chapter nine," I say.

Beulah smiles. "You're ready to go do that preaching, I'd offer."

It's come time to tell her or not. And I have heard the words of God as written in scripture, every one of them true and holy, and in Deuteronomy, chapter four, God's beloved Moses says, "Ye shall not add unto the word which I command you, neither shall ye diminish aught from it," this right after he's destroyed every man, woman, and child of Bashan, which was about threescore cities' worth, after doing likewise to all the folks of Heshbon, and so you got to think God's pretty serious about that point, and since he is, you have to consider how Paul says to "suffer not a woman to teach, nor to usurp authority over the man, but to be in silence." So if I was to ask Beulah to tell me what to think and what to do about this visitation, I'd be putting her in a position that's against the word of God. If enough of these things add up, who knows what might befall Sparta, Tennessee, and thereabouts. Besides, if I told her about God talking to me and smoking a cigar, she'd think her Hurshel done gone crazy. I would hate that.

"I do believe it's God's will," I say.

"Praise the Lord," Beulah says.

I'm feeling bad. This is my beloved Beulah. I'm feeling special, too, like God and me have a secret, but I'm feeling bad holding back from this woman that read me every word of the Bible over and over so that I could get it up by heart. And now

I'm feeling like it's all going to disappear anyway, the words I've heard and remembered and the calling to preach, it'll just up and vanish like the way the Lord my God did on the path.

"Well," I say to Beulah, "if it don't work out I'll just get Ernest Porter, and him and me can go back to being clowns."

And Beulah says, "You're good at anything you put your hand to."

Beulah always was one to encourage me.

"If there's things I need to do on my own . . ." I say and sort of hesitate.

"You do those things," Beulah says to me right quick.

"Or keep to myself . . ." I say.

"This all is between you and the Lord," she says, and I like to jump up and kiss her right then. But we just hold hands across the table.

Then over the weeks that follow I go to finding myself a place to put up a big tent for my preaching, and I have to choose between the valley all along through Sparta, or off a few miles in the Cumberlands, up the mountains among the shortleaf pine and the white oak and the chestnut oak and the sourwood, which I love to be among. But I choose the valley after all, not wanting to make an expedition out of it for folks. So I put my eye on the picnic meadow on the bank of the Calf Killer River just south of town, mindful that "no prophet is accepted in his own country," as Jesus himself said in the gospel of Luke, but these here are the souls I care most to save from the wrath of God by them hearing and heeding his true and holy word unvarnished.

So I get Beulah to do up some posters and I go all around White County, even unto Walling and Bon Air and Doyle Station and Yankeetown and Onward and Peeled Chestnut, and I tell all the folks around these parts that the word of God will be preached without leaving out the tough things and that's the way God wants it and they should all come to listen.

And a good many of them do.

Yesterday night I finally do my preaching. The only little bit of show I set up isn't really show at all, it's just like having a singing leader or something. Ernest and Roy agree to sit on opposite sides of the congregation and start off the Amens whenever I say something that a right-attentive group of revival-goers should offer up a spiritual you-betcha for. And there's pretty near a couple hundred come to the tent, and I know the old man in the white suit has a hand in the turnout. He has put it on quite a few hearts to come. Beulah is in the front row and Charlie's beside her 'cause if you shouldn't spare the rod on a child then you shouldn't spare the word either, no matter where it leads.

It's sundown and we light candles on stands for when the dark comes along, and I have got up a big old wooden cross at the preaching end of the tent, and after a time, everybody comes in. I suppose I should do a few hymns just to make people feel sort of comfortable, but most all the hymns are the words of men and this is the church of the word of God, and so when they settle down and are quiet, I start to preaching. And I follow the advice of Jesus himself when he sent his disciples out to preach: "Take no thought beforehand what ye shall speak, neither do ye premeditate, but whatsoever shall be given you in that hour, that speak ye."

So I just clear my throat and look out at these folks from my county and I say, "It says in the Bible more times than I can count, 'Thou shalt fear the Lord thy God.' And I do, brothers and sisters."

And I start to tell them all the holy words that have been running around in me for weeks, about the people of Midian and of Bashan and Heshbon but also Makkedah and Libnah and Lachish and Gezer and about all the other cities and nations that were destroyed down to every last woman and child by the chosen tribes, and these destroyed folks had the wrong ideas about who God was and all, but they didn't have any chance to think otherwise, and even when God sent Moses to Egypt to perform miracles so they'd know the tribes of Israel was in touch with the one true Creator, God said he'd make a point to harden the Pharaoh's heart—he didn't soften his heart or even leave it up to the Pharaoh himself—God personally hardened his heart—and all those other nations, God didn't even give them a chance to see a sign or wonder or hear his own true words, if you was in the way of the chosen ones and you been left to figure out the world for yourself 'cause nobody ever come to you with the truth, then you're doomed to be slaughtered, in this life and the next. And I'm careful as I preach all this to quote the words in the books and the chapters and the verses that's in the holy scripture, and the first few times that I say something like "we took all his cities at that time and utterly destroyed the men and the women and the little ones" Ernest or Roy would give me up an Amen, but that soon stops and a terrible silence comes over the folks out there before me. But these are the words you can't add or subtract from, and I go on to tell about how even if you're worshiping the one true God, you got to watch yourself. 'Cause God said if a guy gathers some sticks on the Sabbath, kill him. If a guy curses, kill him. If a child is stubborn, kill him. There are no Amens about this. There's even some stirring in the congregation, and a few are starting to slip along the rows, kind of ducking a little, and heading for the exit. I'm looking out at the people and I say, "These are the words of God, what you're supposed to do. There's nothing in the Bible to take them back. Jesus himself said, 'Think not that I am come to destroy the law or the prophets.' The Bible don't tell you to do some of this all the time and do some of it when you're of a mind to. Here's two things the Bible says, one right after the other, Leviticus, chapter nineteen, verse eighteen says, 'Thou shalt love they neighbor as thyself,' and verse nineteen says, 'Thou shalt not sow thy field with mingled seed, neither shall a garment mingled of linen and woolen come upon thee.' And then just a few verses later— all of this is put out equal and forever and holy—'Ye shall not round the corners of your heads, neither shalt thou mar the corners of thy beard,' and then two verses later, 'Do not prostitute thy daughter.' You've loved your neighbor, but have you minded the mixed cloth in your clothes? You looked after your daughter, but what about your beards? And me standing here bare-faced, I know. I'm afraid for all of us. And some of you shouldn't even be in a church, by God's commandment. If you're wounded in the stones—men, you know what I mean—then you got to get on out of God's house. If you was born out of wedlock or your daddy was or your granddaddy, all the way back ten generations. You got to get on out."

By now they're running from the tent.

"Which is probably me too," I cry. "My own granddaddy was none too reliable in that way."

Beulah is beside me now, taking me by the hand.

"Maybe we should give an offering," I say.

"It's okay, Hurshel," Beulah says real soft.

"God asked for five golden hemorrhoids once as an offering," I say. "It's there in First Samuel, chapter six."

"Let's get on home," Beulah says. "We're fresh out of golden hemorrhoids."

It's not the way I expected things to go. So here I sit and night has fallen and my family is asleep and I'm waiting for God to knock on my door in a white linen suit. Am I crazy? I think I even ask this out loud, here in the kitchen, sitting alone at the table with the holy word of God lying there before me and whispering away in my head even still. "The blueness of a wound cleanseth away evil," I say, which is right there in Proverbs. I'm bruised all over, is what I'm thinking.

Then there's a knock at the door.

It's low, just for me to hear. He knew to come round to the back. I fear the Lord my God. But I rise and cross the room and I open the door and there's God in his linen suit with no wool mixed in, for sure. "Evening, Hurshel," he says.

"Evening," I say.

We look at each other for a moment through the screen and he says, "Ain't you going to invite me in?"

My legs are fixing to crumple up underneath me again.

"You didn't disappoint me," he says, which was exactly the fear I was having, that I did.

I try to speak, but no words come out. And still I'm just standing there with the screen door between us. I smell his cigar smoke, though he doesn't seem to have one lit.

Then he says, "Behold, I stand at the door and knock. If any man hear my voice and open the door, I will come in to him and will sup with him and he with me."

Which is Jesus' words that John heard in his own head when he had a vision of his Lord in the book of Revelation, which means I'm still dealing with God here, no doubt about it, to be quoting Jesus like that, and he's maybe telling me I'm not crazy, 'cause John wasn't crazy, was he? In spite of his going on to see a beast with seven heads and ten horns and one with two horns like a lamb and speaking as a dragon, whatever that's like? Let him who has ears hear, I guess.

"Buck up, boy," God says and my legs suddenly straighten, and I push the screen door open and God steps into my kitchen.

He looks around and sort of sniffs at the air. "Pot roast," he says.

"Yesterday," I say.

He nods like he knew that.

"You like to sit?" I say.

"Sure." And he does, taking off his Stetson to show a full head of thick white hair with a tight rolling wave in it like he'd gone to town and had it marcelled.

"Coffee or something?" I ask.

"Nope. Sit down, Hurshel, and let's talk about how much you love me."

I sit. "You are the Lord my God," I say.

"That's right. But do you love me?"

And I'm put in mind of the time when the children of Israel were tired of running around the desert and wanted to go back to Egypt and God was ready just to wipe out the whole bunch of them—this was in the book of Numbers—and Moses more or less said to God, Oh no don't do that, you'll look bad to the Egyptians if you wipe out the people you've just delivered. Everybody'll talk and they won't know what a compassionate and swell God you are. And God changed his mind. You have to curry the old man up a little sometimes.

And even as all this is going through my head, he's watching me close. "So?" he says.

"You bet I love you," I say.

"So you'll keep all my commandments," he says.

"I'm real sorry about the beard," I say. "It didn't come to mind till last night. Beulah has always liked to touch me on my cheek."

He waves his hand. "Later," he says. "I've got one for you right now."

"Okay."

"You did what you could last night. I hardened their hearts."

"You did? I thought it was me."

"Of course it was. But they weren't supposed to hear, and you were supposed to make a fool of yourself for me. That's love."

I nod and try to sort this out.

He goes on right away. "Here's what you need to do. Tell me about the twenty-second chapter of Genesis."

And all the sudden the blood feels like it's drained right out of me and into the floor and I try to think this isn't really God sitting in front me but just a few moments ago he even quoted Jesus and I have the knowledge of who he is sitting in my heart and I know just how he's acted all along, pretty much from the beginning of the world and down to the bugs in the field, so what he's saying is next shouldn't surprise me.

"Speak up," he says.

"That's when you asked Abraham to offer up his son's life on the altar."

"You bet," he says.

"But then you stopped him," I say.

"Don't go assuming anything about that," he says. "I had real plans for Isaac. And if Abraham knew what you know—if there was a previous time when I'd let the father off—then Isaac would've had to die. Otherwise it's not for real, his being willing to make this sacrifice God's asking him for. You see my point there, Hurshel?"

I'm afraid I do, but I keep my mouth shut. My hands have taken to trembling 'cause I know what's coming next.

"Okay," God says. "You shall love the Lord your God more than anything. So take now that there butcher knife on the counter and go up to thine only son Charlie, whom thou lovest, and cut his throat in his sleep."

I feel like Lot's wife must have felt turning around and peeking at Sodom. It's like I've turned into a pile of salt. I'm heavy and hard inside, a stack of something you could just shake out onto the ground and the wind would blow away. I'm looking God in the eye and he's come to me personal, which don't happen all that much. Even Peter and Paul never spoke about seeing God face-to-face.

"You been chosen is why," God says. "I pick the humble to love me the most. You know that."

Then all the sudden I get my strength back. I'm full of a jerky jump-up kind of energy and I push back from the table and I step over to the counter and pick up the butcher knife and I turn back to God and hesitate for a moment, and once more he's right there in my head dealing with my hesitations.

"Cut her throat too," he says.

I feel my head nod yes.

"I'll wait for you out in the yard," God says.

Then my legs move me around the table and across the floor and through into the hallway and down along to our bedroom, and it's dark but I know the way and I don't even have to look to step over a tin truck of Charlie's, I just know it's there, and I would've had to fuss at him in the morning for leaving it where his pa could trip on it coming in to bed but there's no need for that now 'cause he ain't going to have another morning, and I'm quaking inside something fierce now and tears are streaming down my cheeks, I realize, 'cause the Lord my God is a savage God and he is a needy God, and I'm in the bedroom and crossing the floor and the bed is before me and Beulah is curled up on her side facing this way with the sheet hooked over her shoulder, and there, on his side, his little face floating-like in front of Beulah's bosom, is Charlie, and I am before them and my heart is pounding like an automobile engine in my ears and backfiring loud bang bang my eyes are blurred so I can hardly see and I lift the knife in my hand for love of the Lord my God who's sitting off somewhere waiting for me to do this terrible thing that fits right in with the world he's fixed up for us to begin with, and Charlie makes a sigh in his sleep and stretches his neck a little and mutters a thing from his dreams that I can't make out, my little boy sleeping, my beloved son, and he's a sweet little boy who might leave a tin truck in his daddy's way without thinking but who cups his hands around a lizard on the kitchen wall and carries the critter outside to set him free, and who loves his father, and I struggle with my hand that has risen up and that wants real bad to go forward now and do the will of God, but I am a weak man, and maybe I don't love God enough but I struggle hard now with my own right hand, and I have the use of my left hand and I grab the wrist above the knife and my right hand wants something powerful to obey its creator and it has plenty of proof that's the way it should go, 'cause there's countless people who went under the knife for somebody else's righteous love of God, and all my left hand can come up with is that "God is love," which comes into scripture pretty late, and elsewhere in the holy word the love of God has a bad outcome for a whole lot of folks, but I stand above the bed where my wife and my son are sleeping and I struggle on in the dark and my boy murmurs again in his sleep, and it's Pa he's saying *that there's my pa,* and I pull hard at the knife hand trying to get it away from my son and then all the sudden my right hand just lets up and falls.

I stand huffing like a dray horse for a moment, and then I turn to the door and I cross the bedroom and go out in the hall, and a sharp pain jumps into my right big toe and I think it's

God starting to pay me back. But it's Charlie's tin truck. I grab my foot, being careful with this here butcher knife, and I hop on down the hallway some more till I can walk again. Then I'm in the kitchen, and I put the knife on the table, and I go out the screen door. He's standing in the yard in the full moonlight smoking a cigar, the smoke hanging all around his head like a cloud.

"You disappoint me, Hurshel," he says.

I'm stripping off my shirt. "Come on," I say. "Too damn bad, old man. I'll rassle you right now."

He goes "Ha!" and his coat and shirt is off in nothing flat and I rush at him and plow my head into his chest and it's like hitting an oak tree, I just bounce off, my head crowned in pain, and he grabs me round the waist and lifts me up and the moon is dancing in my eyes up above, and the stars, and he's got me round the waist tight and I start pounding on his head with my fists, denting his Stetson but just hitting the cushion of his fancy-man's hair underneath, and he throws me down bang on my tailbone and my head bounces and he leaps at me but I roll away and he thumps down in a cloud of dust and his arms come on out and grab at me, and I look him in the face, which is clear before me for one moment, and I lift my hands and thumb him hard right in the eyes and this time I feel something to the touch at least and he kind of grunts and lets go, and I jump up and there he is already in front of me and he grabs my throat in his hands choking hard but my own hands are free and something comes to me to do and I start winding up my right arm, going round and round like a windmill faster and faster, like I'm fixing to give him a big blow. This amuses him. He lets go my throat and stands there before me, staying in striking range, smiling and chuckling, And my arm is going faster and faster spinning around. He casually puts up his dukes, his two fists hanging big as melons in front of him. I know what to do next, of course. But there's very little about shins in the holy word. A man's stones is another thing. So while my arm is still spinning around, I work up all the strength I got and I aim right between the old man's legs and then I kick as hard as I can. And he vanishes. Just like that. Only the smell of a cigar remains, and a wisp of smoke.

So that was the end of my preaching days. I may be nothing more than a clown. I may not love God enough and I may burn in hell for my shortcomings. But I do love my son. And my sweet Beulah. She's taken to reading me a book called *Great Expectations* of a night, and I nearly got it up by heart.

TAR AND FEATHER ACTORS

Farmers Thus Protest Against the Jokes of a Barnstorming Company

WASHINGTON, PA., AUG. 6— Angry because itinerant vaudeville actors used questionable language at a show given in the Brownlee schoolhouse at Wylandville last night, a band of young farmers tarred and feathered six of the actors, ducked them in a creek and later drove them from the village.

The vaudeville troupe was billed for two nights, the affair being advertised as a "clean performance with four big acts." The schoolhouse was jammed. An attempt by one of the actors to produce a laugh by an obscene joke drew a protest from one of the young farmers. The protest went unheeded.

A majority of the farmers led their sweethearts from the building. Later, every young man in the neighborhood reappeared with buckets of tar and some feathers. They coated the six offending actors, not sparing the two women of the troupe. Following the tarring all six were dumped into a creek and then told to hasten out of the village. They walked eight miles to Washington after midnight, but were told there to keep moving.

from page 2 of *The Sun,* New York
Sunday, August 7, 1910

Bryan, Texas, Dec. 27- 1907

My dear Carmelita —
Today I sent you
a little package
by mail, I have
pictured the contents
— hope you will like
them. I think I shall
have to call my
candy shop "The
Sign of the Sugar
Pecan," don't you?
Did you have a good
time Christmas &
was Santa Claus
good to you? You
must write to me
soon & tell me all
about your holiday.
Did you get my letter?
Love to all from
Elelele

Good
"la Needa"
Andrew!
100 yards to
I reckon"

POST CARD

THIS SIDE FOR THE ADDRESS

BRYAN
DEC 29
9 PM
TEX.

Miss Carmelita Drexel

2898 Vallejo St

San Francisco

Calif —

UNCLE ANDREW

Bryan, Tex.
Dec. 28

Miss Carmelita Dresel
2898 Vallejo St.
San Francisco, Calif.

Bryan, Texas, Dec. 27, 1907
My Dear Carmelita,
Today I sent you a little package by mail. I manufactured the contents. I hope you will like them. I think I shall have to call my candy shop "The Sign of the Sugar Pecan," don't you? Did you have a good time Christmas & was Santa Claus good to you? You must write to me soon & tell me all about your holiday. Did you get my letter? Love to all from Elsbeth.

Good old "Uncle Andrew" 100 years old I reckon.

Missus ask me to look there and I don't even know she is around, so I turn, and my hands is trained real good, trained from long ago, and one of them take off my hat to Missus. That morning she done give me some candy. And I been having some deviling thoughts ever since. Though maybe them thoughts got nothing to do with the devil. I ain't even certain I think there is a devil like we all been taught to believe, 'cause you surely have trouble picking him out of a crowd.

And if this was Old Master's daughter, if Old Master was involved, I'd not be thinking nothing about it. My hands and my feet and my whole body just do what they suppose to do and never mind anything else. I know that is true, and knowing it make me squirm around inside myself pretty bad right now, which is what all this recent thinking is coming to. I am too old. I got too much cluttering up my head.

She take my photograph with her camera and she say, "I'm going to put you on a postcard and send you around. Old Uncle Andrew. Still going strong."

"Yes'm," I say. And even with all my thinking of that day, my mouth and my tongue don't judge me proper enough, and they go and add, "Yes, Missus."

Then she is gone on down the path and I am standing there holding my hat. And feeling a kind of tremble and shiver start in me, like it's long ago, like I'm fixing to be beat all afternoon long, on my back and my legs and the soles of my feet. Not like that happen to me personal so many times. Only about three or four. And Old Master weren't happy to do it to me. He say so right out. There was many others take the whip on the plantation and they live with it regular, the field slaves that was, they get beat by the driver, who was just another slave all in all, and Old Master, he never let the driver have at me. Thinking kindly of Old Master should calm me down, like it can do. But I'm shivering on.

I put my hat on my head.

Old Master taught me to read and write, which was some special gift to a slave I don't have to say. I was only a few years old, just a child, when Old Master take me into the big house 'cause he say he like my eye, how I watch things close, from how he ask me what I see one day and I say how that bird kind of crouch himself a little before he lift up to fly. Old Master laugh and he take me off of Mammy Sukey, who watch all of us children through the day. Mammy Sukey was not my real mammy. I don't know my real mammy, though I believe I suck at her breast all right for a few years. I don't remember none of that. She and my pappy was sold off separate when things got a little bad with the plantation. Sukey told me these things some time later when I was a young man and Old Master's body slave, and Sukey was fixing to die. I don't think to ask these questions before that. There was no one to ask them to.

He even tell me the year I was born. Like it mean something. 1820. Old Master say to me, "Andrew, I will tell you a thing. Not for you to get uppity about it, but I have made you special, and most of your kind will never have this knowledge. I remember when you was born because I had a run of good calving that same year." And he tell me. Then he laugh and say, "So I should've expected more like you."

But there weren't. There were only one of me that year.

This all was in Louisiana.

I put my hat on and I watch Missus go on down the road and I try to stay put in my head, try to crouch down and stay put. I go on along to the little cabin I live in. Missus, I know her from when she was born, which was after the war, after I become a hired servant making my own money. Her daddy own me for some few years, once Old Master pass on, and her daddy hire me too, for a servant, after there was no slaves, till I had got just enough of my own money to leave his house and go up to Marshall and become a barber for the Negroes in that town, some of them going to Wiley College for Negroes that start up there and where I find some books to read. When I first come to this Texas farm, this little cabin was just rough logs daubed up with mud and nothing in it but the fireplace and howsomever many beds there was slaves in here, the beds just wood planks put up and rough pillows full of horse combings. I don't live in here when I was a slave. I was bought for two thousand dollars for a house slave what can read and write, and so I live in the big house where Missus live now. When I was a slave I live in a beautiful house and now I live in a slave house though I am a free man. Still enough, I made this a place for me. I have a table and a chair and a kerosene lamp and I have my books, which I can read. I read Mr. Frederick Douglass, who know what I know. I read Mr. W. E. B. DuBois, who never been a slave but who also know what I know.

Old Master died. He died in 1856 and I was thirty-six years old and I had a wife—even though we was not allowed a law-ful ceremony for that, we know in our hearts what we was to each other, and Old Master know it too—and I had a small child, and I daren't not let myself even think one thing more of them for fear I will die from the thinking of it, to think even what they look like or what their voices sound like talking to me, for when Old Master died he say very clear in his last will and testament that my slave Andrew and Andrew's wife and Andrew's child are to be sold together as a family, but Old Master's wife, the Missus, she has nothing of that, she and her own children want to sell the plantation and its chattel to the highest bidders, and I am brought into a showroom in New

Orleans with my wife and my child and fifty other slaves and they look at our teeth and they make us take down our shirts, my wife too, all the women too, and they look at our backs for scars to see if we be unruly and then they sell my wife to one man and my child to another and they sell me to Missus's daddy who live in Texas. And I never to this day see my wife or my child again.

Old Master's wife, the first Missus, I sleep for some years under her bed in a trundle. From the start I do that, in the big house in Louisiana. Old Missus keep me under her bed to fetch her bedpan and to massage her feet and to dance to her music box. Jump up, Andrew, she say. Jump up when you dance. And then she take off her stockings and put me down there to rub at her bare feet.

I am trembling again. I am sitting on my chair in the little cabin I rent now from my own labor and it is all these many years later and I am remembering about massaging Old Missus's feet, and my hat is in my hand, this memory coming on me of a sudden before I can even put my hat on the table, and the hat is trembling something fierce and I start in to grinding my teeth and pounding a fist onto my leg, which is something I don't feel like doing for a long while already, for a very long while.

The present Missus, she never own me and never whip me and never has a cross word for me and she come and give me some candy, and I am losing what little I have done cobbled together over the years as a mind. 'Cause she put on her gloves. Which made me start to look at how I got by all my life. Some very small thing like that. The morning when she took my photograph, she come earlier to give me some sugar pecan candy that she made with her own hands in her own kitchen. I look out of my window and see her lift her hand to touch my gate, but before she do, she stop herself. Her face go all sour. In her other hand is the paper bag with the candy in it, though I don't know what it is at that moment. She step away from my gate and she is still looking sour and her hand with the bag is waving a little back and forth like it don't know what to do. So she look around and she don't see nobody and she don't see me watching 'cause I'm in the shadow, and then she tuck the bag up under her arm. Both hands free now, she dip into her dress pocket and pull out some gloves and she put those gloves on her hands. Then her face smooth out, and she take the bag from under her arm and she touch my gate and open it up.

I am eighty-seven years old. I was born a slave and spent pretty near half my life in slavery and I have done suffered more indignities than any man can count. But maybe being that old make a man weak. 'Cause while Missus is walking up my yard to my door I am thinking all the sudden about how she never, in all the years, touch me with her hand. I do odd jobs for her around the big house so that I can live in a place till I die and have a little food and she done took me back in here some few years ago when I can't cut hair in Marshall no more and she never say a cross thing to me, but she is coming up to my door and I see her putting on a sugar-pecan face, sweetening up enough to make your teeth ache, and I find myself riling up 'cause she will not even touch Uncle Andrew's gate or hand him a bag of candy with her bare hand, and this is how it has always been.

She knocks on my door. I move to it and I am taking in to quaking like a newborn calf. I open the door. She has done backed off beyond arm's length. She do this always when she come to my door and never do I give it a second thought. I see it now. I am grinding rough inside. But I hear myself speaking like the man I always been. "Missus," I say. "Lordy, you shouldn't be troubling yourself come all the way here. I can come to the house to do for you." I am bowed forward now, keeping my eyes cast down.

"No, Uncle Andrew," she say. "It's nearly Christmas. I want you to have some of my special sugar pecan candy I have made myself."

And the bag is hanging there in front of me to take. Which I do. Which make me shuffle my feet like in pleasure. Jump up when you dance for me, boy. I shuffle and I say, "Thank you, Missus. You is the kindest Missus. Old Uncle Andrew is mighty happy for the candy you make."

"Merry Christmas," she say.

"Merry Christmas to you and all your family," I say.

Then her face get fixed to do something necessary and she step a little forward and give out that gloved hand for a handshake. I give out my hand and shake hers and then she is turned around and going up to my gate, her hands held away from her 'cause her gloves is soiled.

I close my door and I am worrying about myself. I can't bear to live like this. They is too many things been done for me to start seeing them now.

And Christmas is coming on. I keep that paper bag of candy on the center of my table, not even looking inside. It come to Christmas Eve and the bag sit there. And I light my kerosene lamp and I read a little about how Mr. W. E. B. DuBois ask himself, "Why did God make me an outcast and a stranger in mine own house?" I put my book down. I do not know all that much about God. Christmas ain't no special time for me, not in my heart. I come to religion later in my life. My wife believe, and she teach me about how things are in heaven. Before that, from a little child to a young man, I have Old Master teaching me everything. And he is giving me everything I got. And he is taking away anything he sees fit to take away. And he feed me, and he beat me. And sitting in my cabin on Christmas Eve I want to think kindly on Old Master, who owned me body and soul. Anytime I think on heaven, I see Old Master there, waiting for me in the parlor, waiting for me to come in bringing him his whiskey and water and his box of cheroots. He done rung his bell for me to come in. There ain't nobody at all in heaven when I picture it but Old Master in a white robe waiting for me in his parlor.

I look at the candy sitting on my table. I am partial to sweets. But I do not open that bag up. I got no hunger for candy done up by Missus's hand. Don't be uppity, boy, Old Master whisper in my head, and he looking shocked, he looking like he don't even know me. Him and Old Missus are off in another part of the house yelling at each other something fierce. Then he come in to me and ask if I stop off rubbing Old Missus's feet when she specifically ask me to keep on. And I say, Only for a moment, Massah, I done took up rubbing again when she told me. A second time she told you, he say, don't be uppity, boy. I am going on fifteen at that time. I always know my age. Old Master give me that. He say, Don't be uppity, and then he take me to the place where they beat the field slaves and he have me strip off my clothes and he tie me down. And he beat me. This was one of those few times.

And I look at the bag of candy. And he say in my head, maybe from heaven, Don't be uppity, boy. And I take that bag. It is Christmas Eve and so I take that bag and open it up and I take a piece of that candy and I put it in my mouth and I search out my good teeth and I let it sit there and it is sweet as can be. I'm partial to a sweet thing. I let it sit there and I don't chew it, but the voice stop in my head.

And now it coming up to be New Year's Day. It is December 31, fixing to be 1908. The seven years I been back to this place where I was sold to when Old Master died, each day before a new year, Missus come out to see me. She bring me some tin of ham to eat. I am sitting in my cabin and she will come to that door anytime now and she will have her gloves on, I know. I am thinking about those gloves like a crazy man. I am going over all the times she shy off from me and I am going over all the times she put those gloves on, right in front of me, and I don't even see it happening at the time, and I am talking to those gloves now and saying, You are a whip to me, and I am looking around my house and I am a stranger here.

And a knock come. A soft, muffled knock of her gloved hand. I don't stop to consider what to do. My body just stand up now and I cross the room. My body know so many things to do that it learn from this life I done led. I feel my body moving like it always do and my voice fixing to say what it always say. I cross to the door and I open it and she is standing there back a ways with her face all sweet smiles and she is holding the tin of ham with gloves buttoned all the way up to her elbows.

These are her good gloves and I will get no handshake this time, I know.

"Uncle Andrew . . ." she begin to say.

And I shut the door in her face.

I stand trembling inside the cabin, like I suppose she is doing outside. But she say nothing more. I think she is moving away pretty fast. I can barely stand up from my body not knowing what to do next, now that it has done a new thing. But I gather up and I put one foot in front of the other like a little child walking, and I sit down at my table and I lay one hand upon it. And into my head come a vision of heaven. The bell ring and I rise up in the kitchen and I look at the tray with the whiskey and the water and the cigars. I am dressed like a gentleman. I am dressed in evening clothes and collar and tie, and I have on a pair of white kid gloves. And I leave the tray where it is and I go into the parlor and Old Master see me and he rise up from his chair. I go to him and stand before him and his eyes narrow at me. But before he can speak, I take off my gloves, first one and then the other, and I lay them together, and then I lift those gloves and I strike him across the face.

BROTHER NAILED HIM IN ATTIC

Boy Hungry Four Days— Story of a Princely Ancestor

MILWAUKEE, AUG. 6—Huddled on a heap of rags in the attic of a cottage, where he had been nailed in by his brother and forced to remain four days and nights without a morsel of food, George Glaser, nineteen years old, was found yesterday by patrolmen who had been sent to serve a vagrancy warrant on him and his brother Henry, sixteen years old. The boys will not work, it is said, because they say they are descendants of a German prince.

from page 3 of the *New-York Tribune*
Sunday, August 7, 1910

Ellis Island, New York

1917

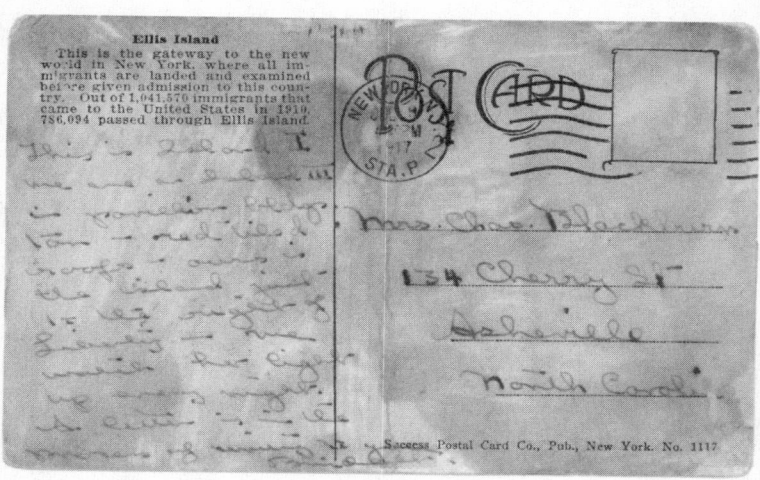

Ellis Island

This is the gateway to the new
world in New York, where all immigrants are landed and examined
before given admission to this country. Out of 1,041,570 immigrants that
came to the United States in 1910,
786,094 passed through Ellis Island.

Mrs. Chas. Blackburn

134 Cherry St

Asheville

North Caroli

Success Postal Card Co., Pub., New York. No. 1117

TWINS

New York, NY
July 8, 1917

Mrs. Chas. Blackburn
134 Cherry St.
Asheville, North Carolina

*This is Island I. We are on Island III in pavillion bldgs
tan—red tiled roofs—ours is the island just to the right
of Liberty—we watch her light up every night. A letter is
in the process of writing to you*
Bridget

There is another of me. I always assumed she and I would live and die together, side by side. How could I think otherwise, even as late as last night as the sun went away and the electrical lights of New York City flared up and we waited for the rest of our life to begin. Identical we are. Twins that surprised nearly to death our mother and our father, as they tell it. And so it is always Bridget and Caitlin then. I look into my own face every day. And sometimes—as she sleeps and I am awake—I feel I am a ghost, I feel there was ever only one of me and now I am after dying and stepping out of my body and I am looking back to see what it is I am leaving.

I love her. But she is like myself and so I love her not, as well, for I know my own shortcomings, which I long to make right. Sufficiently for a good Catholic girl I do not honor my mother and my father. I despise my place of birth and all it would make of me. I despise it though I cannot but be its daughter, and I despise that as well. I despise its cringing submissiveness to the English, and what good is its resistance? Parnell torpedoing his country by sleeping with another man's wife. Those fools going to war without even possessing their guns on Easter last year. Not that there won't be more bloodshed. After the Germans are done with and Home Rule starts up again, there'll be plenty, and make no mistake. But even beyond the violence there's merely and only a life of potatoes and turnips and turf fires. And the baking of soda bread, which is all I ever seem to be doing. And a life surrounded by Irish boys with brains of sod who won't even marry when they at least still have their good looks for fear of another famine, this many decades later. Sure and it's the life of an Irish farmer and his family, after all, but for Bridget and Caitlin there's not even the coal mines to get away to, like our oldest brother did. So I persuaded Caitlin first and then our father and our mother to let us go away to America. Our aunt in Asheville in the county of North Carolina was only too happy to rescue us as she was after rescuing herself. To my father's credit he let us go. With ten American dollars in each of the shoes on our feet and with our clothes in wicker cases we boarded the *Celtic* and made off for New York.

Caitlin took some persuading. A myth it is that identical twins have always the same thought. In some ways Caitlin is more the girl I am supposed to be. Closer, sure, to my mother. And more accepting of the farm and of Ireland itself. But she is also my twin, and so she came to see how we should start anew. She even left a sod-brain behind, which her own fine brain knew was the right thing to be doing, but her heart was soft and she cried for a long while. I can see now how this fool of a boy brought about all our present trouble.

Steerage on the *Celtic* was crowded, and though what I heard of the Atlantic passage before the war was far worse, things were bad enough for us. When we boarded in Queenstown there were already hundreds crowded belowdecks, and they weren't even English, many of them, but were people from all over the continent fleeing the war, and they were after passing through a thing or two. We slept on bunks with straw mattresses among foreign tongues and ragged children, and also among much wailing and vomiting once we started rolling in the waves of the North Atlantic.

Caitlin and I suffered only a brief day of queasiness, and after that we stayed on deck as much as possible, for most of the others remained sick and in hiding and we could find a place on the rail a bit away from the others and surrounded by the sea. We would talk.

"It's afraid I am," Caitlin said on our third day out.

"Only from the strangeness of it," I said.

"You feel it too," she said, which was no bit of a question at all. She knew well enough I did.

"It's finished I am with the familiar," I said.

She looked away from the sea and straight into my eyes. "*Familiar* is too pale a thing to call it."

"True enough."

"Our family, our land."

"Your lad," I said.

She did not begin to cry until I mentioned him, which is why it's him I blame. We cried together over family and country

at Queenstown, before we were thrown so intimately together
with all these others, and I didn't even mention him in all that.
If I could but go back to the deck of that ship and stay her hands.
She began to cry and she turned her face to the sea and then
she was rubbing at her eyes.

"He isn't worth it," I said.

"And don't I understand that?" she said and she wiped first
one eye and then the other with her fingertips. I feel sure and
certain this was the moment.

Which brought us to last night and beyond. How long was
it already our custom—our fate?—Caitlin and I, to fall asleep
at the same moment. Last night she left me to go in and I lingered for time. She feared there was nothing for her across the
harbor. Those great and mightily bestarred buildings. Liberty
herself, nearer at hand. She was lighting up, too. Her torch was
aflame. Though 'tis true she had her back to us now. We knew
we must find our way to one more boat and across this last bit
of water to see her face again, as we did so full of hope on the
morning of July the Fourth. All of us from steerage crowded up
onto the deck and we all cheered together at the sight of her.
Catholics necklaced in rosaries and Jews draped in prayer shawls
and even a few Mohammedans nearby doffing their fezzes. That
very first night, anchored in the harbor and awaiting the ferries
to Ellis Island, we watched the sky over New York fill with exploding stars and pinwheels, and at the tip of the island was a
vast blinking sign urging us to drink Lipton Tea. America calling out to us in a very loud voice.

Last night, looking across the harbor, she took up my hand
and she whispered to me, "I'm sorry."

This is not something we are accustomed to say to each other. When it is called for, we know it already.

Sitting wrapped in blankets at the fumigation center in Queenstown, for an example. Wet and shivering we were, from the cold showers, from standing naked together among dozens of other naked women in the rush of icy water from pipes in the wall. Who could imagine ever being in such a situation? Well then, Caitlin and I were sitting there, each inside her own tightly held blanket—clinging to our separate bodies but reading each other's minds—and she said, "All of this torture so that we might drown."

"The end of June it is," I said.

"He told father there was more to it," she said.

"Whiskey and more whiskey," I said.

"You would have us die," she said, leaning close and hissing at me like the thin spikes of cold water that came from the walls.

Then she blinked at me and pulled back. She did not have to say aloud that she was sorry, for we always knew so much more than anyone could hear. In this instance she was speaking of the *Titanic* and I of the vanished icebergs and she of our father's uncle who worked upon the ship in Glasgow and who felt this ship never was unsinkable and I of the everyday foolish drunkenness of this uncle and she of the wrenching fear she had from the thought that *any* ship might be holding rivets fastened by a drunken fool, a fear such that Caitlin blamed me in advance for anything terrible that might happen out at sea when in fact she was just miserably cold and wet inside her blanket and oddly unsettled—as I was—at having been naked with all these strange women.

Last night she said she was sorry. She began to pull away to lead us inside. I touched her arm and I said to her, "Sure and we'll be fine. Caitlin and Bridget in this new land."

But she made no reply and went on. I did not. I stood for a time alone on the edge of America. If he was to blame in the usual manner, if he put a swimmer in her belly, that would be one thing. We could have the wee one over here and go on. But it was her eyes. The fear was her eyes. We arrived at Ellis Island and they drove us down the gangplank from the ferry and into the Frenchy palace on Island One and they took away our possessions and stripped us and showered us and dressed us again, having wadded our clothes into wrinkles, and we were after passing under the gaze of many an official, blue-clad in round hats or done up in white to give them leave with our bodies. One of these latter it was who used a buttonhook to flip our eyelids. And they drew Caitlin aside and were going to send me on in another direction, but they took a second look at me and at her and I said, "I must be with her," and the man in white nodded, a man with a flushed round face who himself once fled our green isle, I suspected, and sure he had a familiar lilt in his voice when he said to me, low, "Not to worry then. It might be nothing," and he nodded me along after Caitlin.

Trachoma was what we feared. Trachoma that you can get from somebody else. Picking up something from somebody else and not knowing it's upon you and then touching your eyes to wipe away the useless tears shed for a useless fool of a boy. Trachoma, for the contagion of which they will send you away from America and make no mistake. Send you back home to rooting up potatoes and cutting up peat and waiting for the bombs and gunfire and the stupid aging bachelors finally to get up the nerve to have a life. Because your eyes were violated by strangers from other lands carrying this curse along with them. They say there's no cure and you can someday lose your sight. They put us both on Island Three, the Isle of Contagion, with the tuberculosis and the scarlet fever and the other suspect eyes. When they knew for certain, they sent you away. The very uncertainty about Caitlin told me it was that moment on deck with the tears when it happened.

There's hardly a blade of grass on this island. This struck me shortly after she pulled away and vanished inside. I was growing critical of America, I suppose. For the present, though, it didn't matter about the grass, as the night was coming on. The water went dark and electrical light was all there was in the world. You can look up at the stars in the sky, but pale and pathetic they are, compared with the things Americans make with their own hands, what they raise up and light up for themselves. But still and all, the first look of a morning, there was not a bit of green anywhere to be seen. And 'tis true Ireland is drunken lush with green, and twice now I was stripped naked in a room of stone and drenched with water and it made me to think what I missed, how the part of me that drove me out to sea and toward a new land, how good and sweet it would be if, before I left, that very same part of me was after driving me alone in high summer to the far rolling field in a fine mist of a rain and I strip me naked for my own self and lie down in the thick grass. Would Caitlin do such a thing as that along with me? How could she not? How could I see myself naked in the grass alone?

I looked to the near end of this other island now, the one we were waiting to reach. The sky was dark behind it, blocked by all the light. I'll hold you, nothing is green over there either, I thought. Lipton cried out to be brewed and drunk down, cup after tasty cup. I strained to hear the city, but only the faint murmurings of the sick people about me were filling my head. It would be different in North Carolina, of course, which was alleged to be as green as mother Ireland. On board we went up on the steerage deck at the rear of the ship at night and you could hear the orchestra from first class, faint over the sound of our wake, faint from the privileged sanctums of our ship where those who already were after getting ahead danced to music of the salon. Breathless is what I became. The music took away my breath and I turned to my other self, my twin, and distracted she was in her own way, looking out into the dark. I did not know what it was she was thinking, which frightened me a little. But I did not ask.

I drew away last night from New York. Turned from the light and faced the sleeping pavilion of our Island Three. A few years ago there was gunfire down the road. We could hear it from our kitchen. Some of our boys had it out with a squad of English soldiers, and lads we knew died and were hauled off in a donkey cart, though we realized none of this at the time. We fell asleep that night, my sister and I, telling each other how it was hunters, how the rumors of something else was all fairy sneezes. And so it was that I went in last night with a final thought that my sister's eyes were simply tired, that they were irritated from saltwater baths on the ship, that some lesser thing was happening to her, which is why we were here now and not on a ship home already.

With this final puff of fairy breath, I went in. I lay down sweating in the hot July night with Caitlin on her side in the next bunk. Her back was turned to me, like Miss Liberty outside. We had nothing to do but to sleep and to wait.

And with the morning came the news. Caitlin has trachoma. The nurses cried. We liked the nurses and they liked us. They made over us being the wonder I suppose side-by-side we are. They regretted their country's decision to deport us. Though strictly speaking, it was only Caitlin the country was intending to deport. The doctor sat us at his desk and finally he made that point clear. Caitlin was infectious and had to return to Ireland. Bridget was checked carefully and was free to enter America if she wished. He glanced from her to me and back again and shrugged his shoulders. Then he said to Caitlin, "The White Star Line is responsible for returning you at no charge to yourself." He looked at me. "Under the circumstances," he said, "I'm certain passage can be arranged for you as well."

"Can she be cured?" I asked.

"No," he said.

Caitlin was beginning to cry. Her face was bowed. And my only thought was that it was upon me now to take my own hands and touch the contagion in my sister and bring it into myself, for as we sat there on Ellis Island, her eyes and mine were suddenly different.

The doctor said, "You'll need to decide in a few hours. The *Britannic* has space for you departing this afternoon."

Well then, we stood beside each other, Caitlin and I, out on the veranda among the deck chairs where the tuberculosis patients lounged like first-class passengers crossing the sea. We put our backs to Ellis Island and looked across the harbor. My twin sister surprised me. She knew the names of all the big buildings we were seeing. The Whitehall and the Washington. The Bowling Green and the Manhattan Life and the World. The Singer, which was particularly beautiful, even from this distance, with red stripes running up each corner to a dome and spire. The Woolworth, a little further north, the tallest building in the world. Her doctor taught her all these. When she was off being looked at, she was flirting with her doctor, my twin sister. And she spoke these names to me as the names of objects of wonder.

I said, "I began to think somewhere along the way that I wanted this more than you."

"No," she said. "How could we not be the same?"

She knew I clenched up tight inside at this. It surprised the both of us. I began to weep, though I took no notice of it, letting the tears fall without wiping at them, without letting them summon forth a single sound from me, without acknowledging them whatsoever. I never did this before and I never saw Caitlin do this before. She was crying too, now, noisily. I looked at her and she did the usual thing. She lowered her face and covered her eyes, her afflicted eyes.

"You should go ahead," she said.

"I can't," I said, very low, trying out this obvious notion.

She nodded once at this, accepting it without a fuss. I seized up again, with a little bit of anger this time. The matter was done. So it seemed. I turned away from my sister and toward the island of Manhattan. Scarcely could I see the big buildings now for my tears. I felt compelled to wipe the tears away.

I did not know what was on my hands. It was only a short time ago I was ready to take on this affliction with my sister. My hand began to rise. But I stopped it. I held it back. And then I began to tremble terribly.

Caitlin put her hand on my shoulder.

And I had but a single thought: I can be one of a kind at last.

God forgive me.

And Caitlin knew. She slipped her arm around my waist.

"I'm sorry," I said.

"It's America," she said.

IN BATHING GARB ON CARS

Stormbound Women Cause a Stir at Stamford, Conn.

STAMFORD, CONN., AUG. 6—Professor C. B. Davenport, in charge of the biological laboratory at Cold Spring Harbor, took a party of friends, most of whom were women, out in a motor boat yesterday to study nature on the Sound. All wore bathing suits.

The wind blew hard and the waves dashed high and seasickness came. The occupants were glad to make a landing here at Shippan Point. The lack of street attire became particularly embarrassing when it was found that return to Cold Spring on the boat was out of the question, and further that there were no accommodations for all of the party at Shippan Point. Nine or ten had to board a streetcar and ride into the centre of Stamford, where they finally succeeded in obtaining quarters at the Stamford House.

The natives exhibited a lively interest in the pretty women who trouped through the streets, their bathing costumes showing beneath the cloaks they had borrowed. The party returned this morning to Cold Spring. In it were Professor Davenport, Mr. and Mrs. Walter, Miss Hartman, Miss Mellet, Miss O'Sullivan, Miss Naughton, Miss Blossom and Miss Squier.

from the front page of the *New-York Tribune*
Sunday, August 7, 1910

POST CARD

PLACE
STAMP
HERE

CORRESPONDENCE HERE   NAME AND ADDRESS HERE

1919

SUNDAY

Sunday Aug 7th 1910

I love *The New York Times* here on my lap, I love this canvas chair I'm sitting on and I love this beach and I love all of Coney Island—the press of this multitude of bodies about me, each set free in bathing flannels, not to mention Coney's temples and pagodas and fountains strung with a million and a half electric lights—I love the nickel red hots in buns with mustard, especially the several I've recently consumed—though they are not loving me in return, they are clogging the center of my chest and whispering slithery hot little sausagey secrets—I love the Fourth of July, the rockets' red glare, which now will mark forever, year after year, not only the birth of our country, which I also love, but also my wedding day, which I had long since given up hope ever to have, and of course I love my sweet young wife—I especially love her—my Lillian, my Lily. I don't love the thought that she will one day be a widow before being an old woman—I am forty-eight years old and she is twenty-three—but she loves me and says this is all right, and I wonder at how I came to find the nerve to ask her if this might be so. Presently she is out somewhere laughing and splashing amidst the throng, amidst ten thousand temporary exiles from the city, out in the

Atlantic Ocean with her friends and former fellow type-writers, most of whom still work under my direction.

A short time ago, we all stood together in the ocean, up to our waists, all of us from the Manhattan Life Insurance Company, along with dozens of strangers, and a young man, one of the strangers, took our photo from the lifeguard's perch and we cried together, "Hurrah!" as if it were the Fourth of July. We were countrymen, all of us. How I love my United States of America. I began with so very little. I passed through Castle Garden, long before Ellis Island opened—though I barely remember it, which is all right with me because in fact my life began that day—an official who could not write our family name even gave us a new one, which we gladly took on—and my parents and I were soon stuffed with two hundred others and a dozen languages and a thousand rats into the tiny spaces of a tenement on the Lower East Side and there was no light and there was no air and there was only the stink of the water closet down the hall and the garbage down the air shaft and cholera took my mother soon after, though I clearly remember my mother, the vast sheltering bosom of her, her unblinking eyes fixed admiringly on me with the flicker of candlelight there, her long hair always gathered up in a knot—I don't remember ever seeing her hair unloosed, which I regret—and then there was another mother, who was a good woman, and there were years of striving, and I love my country because now I am an office manager at the Manhattan Life Insurance Company and I have an apartment uptown nearly to Houston Street and it's on the first floor and it has windows and I have at last married a woman and she loves me.

An eddy of people swirls by me now, a party bearing wicker baskets and blankets and already-squalling children. I will welcome such a squall one day. These are my country-men too, and I smile at them as they pass, though they are unaware of it, for they do not give me a glance. I lift my smile to the sunny sky above me. And the red hots shift in my chest. I resolve to revisit the red-hot stand later, to push these along with more of their kind. It is Sunday. I am at leisure. My wife is somewhere nearby. I lift my paper. *The New York Times. New York, Sunday, August 7, 1910. 64 pages.*

Why do I love so much to read the newspapers? They are always full of clouds. At the top of the page to the right, how-ever, Sunday has no clouds: *The Weather. Fair Sunday.* But of course there's always tomorrow. *Unsettled Monday.* I'm happy there are sixty-four pages. Tomorrow is unsettled. Yesterday was full of well-chronicled strife. But I can sit safely here in the middle and read my newspaper in the bright sunlight and let all these lives full of striving flow around me. Tomorrow I will have been married for five weeks. On Independence Day we held hands, Lily and I, and I placed a ring on her finger and we kissed and that night we sat in the Battery and watched the sky light up for us. Later, in the light from the gas-mantle lamp of my apartment, my wife unfastened her hair, slowly pulling out the pins and placing each one between her lips and I could hardly breathe, but I asked if she would turn her back to me so I could see her hair, and she did, and the last pin was gone and her hair rushed free and fell, breaking for a moment on her shoulders and then cascading far down her back. Thinking now of her hair, I once again am struggling to draw a breath.

I close my eyes and I wait. The joy in me finally settles down and I open my eyes. I lift my *Times* and begin to read. The lead story headline first, directly beneath the unsettled Monday: *SOLDIERS DISPERSE PRIEST-LED RUSTICS*. The dateline is San Sebastian, in Spain. I've been following this. The government of Spain and the Vatican are struggling for power. Under their present Church-State agreement, public expressions of any faith besides Catholicism are illegal. And there is a heavy national tax for the Church. The new premier José Canalejas and the young King Alfonso are trying to disengage the State from the Church and ease the tax and allow other religions to express themselves, and as a result there are great political struggles and even cleric-inspired public uprisings. It seems so much of my life that I remember is by artificial light in a small room. My father with the kerosene lamp trimmed low on the table between us. "More people have murdered each other in the name of God than anything else," he said to me. "Harold," he said, "give me your hand." And he laid his own hand, palm up, in the center of the table, next to the lamp. I put mine on his and he closed his hand, holding me tight. "You must think clearly," he said. "Always. If God exists, he is either too savage for our respect or no one in this world knows the first thing about him."

Lily and I go to a church on Avenue C most Sundays. But we married at City Hall. We pray, each of us, at times, but I'm not sure who it is I'm speaking to and he does not fill me with as much joy as holding Lily or bathing in the Atlantic Ocean or watching the Stars and Stripes flying up over the grandstand at the Polo Grounds. Or seeing the Giants win, for that matter. I can wait no longer. I thumb back to Section C of the *Times* and my heart is fluttering as I head for yesterday's game. I pass by a full-page announcement of Macy's Furniture Sale where *The Prices Do the Talking* and by news of the *New Ruler of Morocco, Who Is Torturing and Killing His Subjects* and an *Opera War in London* and tourists turning away from Paris in favor of Berlin and stories on Mahler's new symphony and dwarfs in New Guinea and the divorce rate in France, and at last I arrive at the sports page to find that my Giants, who I love, have won, beating the St. Louis Cardinals 5 to 4 in eleven innings with Fred Snodgrass slashing the winning single to right field.

I am about to return to the front page—my habits are fixed with my daily newspaper, to skim all the news stories commencing with page one and then return later to read them in full until I take in every word—but first I seek out a story a few pages back from the sports in Section C. The Giants have won. I have that to support me as I face the trials of life recorded elsewhere in *The Times.* The Moroccan king. I read the lead paragraph: *The question is being asked in Europe, and asked with more and more insistence, How long is the brute who is now the ruler of Morocco to be allowed to torture and kill his subjects?* I glance farther along. It's about politics, not religion. A struggle for power. A rival thrown to lions. The man's wife shackled and hung by her wrists for weeks. When will Europe intervene?

I close Section C. I am touchy about a wife in peril. The pressure in my chest resumes. Marriage is making me prone to strong feelings, it seems. I move back to the first section, glancing inside briefly. I'm heartened by *An Immense Purchase of Muslin Underwear* at Greenhut & Co. with the resultant savings passed on to an eager public, of course. And for those who are victims of the bad news today, the Stern Brothers have big savings on *Imported Mourning Millinery*. And I am at the front page again.

A great shout goes up and I lower the paper. On the edge of the shore three young men hold two other young men on their shoulders while another young man climbs up their backs to the peak. But half a dozen young women who stand before the construction project all turn in a perfect line and face the same way and they bend forward at the waist and lift the hems of their bathing dresses. They wag their bottoms like music hall girls and the quite considerable crowd of onlookers raises a loud, delighted cry. The pyramid strives for a better view and crumbles. I lift the veil of my front page and turn my eyes to the left-hand lead story. A tale of political corruption: *HUGE BRIBE OFFERS TOLD OF BY INDIANS*. A Choctaw chief and his son have testified to a Congressional investigative committee about bribes offered by lawyers holding government contracts seeking to buy 450,000 acres of Indian land rich in coal. I drop the veil to see a mound of bodies, limbs waving, the onlookers storming in. Even the vice president has been mentioned as having personal interests in the contracts. This, too, is my country.

I raise my paper. The news once again replaces the crowd, the beach, the sea, the far horizon. *The Times* is merely crowned with the blue sky above. I'm growing unusually agitated by the wider world today. I like the heat, the sun, even the crowds of

August at Coney. But I'm sweating unusually and there's a restlessness in me, in my limbs, in my throat. I move my eyes across the top of the front page to the third column, and crime is flourishing in this very place where I've brought my wife. *MAYOR HEARS CRIME THRIVES IN CONEY.* This story I read word for word at once, continuing on even after my fears abate somewhat. It's simply a matter of pickpockets—which I know already to beware of—and short-change artists working as waiters in the less reputable eating joints at the far west end. These aren't places where we'd go anyway. But there's more corruption, as well. I follow the story to its continuation on page two. The mayor and the police commissioner are struggling. The mayor has ordered the police on duty to wear uniforms at all times, the plainclothes operations having facilitated the collection of bribes and extortion money by bad cops, he says. The commissioner says he needs the plainclothesmen to catch the short-changers.

My father whispers to me. In my right ear. Among the laughter and the calling out and the women's voices babbling behind me and an accordion playing in the distance and a dog barking, I hear his voice clearly. "Harold," he says. I turn in that direction. The door of the apartment opens wide and he stands there with blood on his left temple and a bright red abrasion on his cheek. My second mother screams. He is sitting at the table now and I am standing near. His forearms are resting heavily before him. Then a policeman in a dark blue uniform, his buttons flashing gold in the lamplight, is standing in the doorway. My father drags himself up and crosses to the policeman and lifts his right arm and the policeman does too, and they grasp hands and they shake. "Thank you," my father says, and the policeman says, "We caught him over on Orchard. He took a beating from resisting. A severe beating." "Thank you," my father says again, lower this time, emphatic, and he shakes the policeman's hand once more. Then they both look in my direction.

I flinch. I am on the beach at Coney Island. I am surrounded by strangers. I am holding my *New York Times*. It is still lifted, wide open to pages two and three. I heard my father's voice with perfect clarity, right here beside me. I listen, but he does not speak again. I look back to the newspaper, returning to the last sentence I read at the foot of page two, a numbering of the police force. I lift my eyes to the top of the page. *DENTIST SHOT DOWN TALKING IN STREET*. But he seemed to know his assailant. *No Attempt to Rob Murdered Man—Police Believe the Motive Was Jealousy*. Dr. W. F. Michaelis of Chicago, what could have possessed you to do what you seem to have done? *Miss Inez Wilcox, a young stenographer employed in a downtown office, was at the office of Dr. Michaelis until within half an hour of the time of the murder. She had been employed in clerical work by the dentist, she explained, and was so occupied until 10 o'clock last night. She left the office at the same time as Dr. Michaelis, and parted from him in the street. Half an hour later he was shot to death.*

I'm starting to grind inside again, rather like I did thinking of the Moroccan wife hanging by her wrists. But I skim on. The dentist's wife was away in Indiana with their three daughters, and love letters were discovered in a mailbox at Dr. Michaelis's office. *He was dapper in his dress, always wearing gloves, both Summer and Winter.*

I put the paper down. I lean forward and peer through the passing bodies and the posing young men on the water's edge. I look out into the breakers, searching for my wife. I don't see her or her three girlfriends from Manhattan Life who took her off to splash and gossip.

My indigestion's getting worse, clutching its way up into my throat, and further, making even my jaw ache. I sit back. Lily worked for me. Typing on her Remington brilliantly, her back straight, her fingers flashing like a great pianist's. It took me a year to struggle with the impropriety of speaking to her in the way I finally did. A warm day this past May, the tenth. The windows of our office were flung open. I was a lowly clerk in this very office when our building was the tallest in the world, sixteen years ago. It still gives me great pleasure to stand beneath it. It towers up in granite and terra-cotta and brick to twin domes and then farther up still, 348 feet to its lantern top and the American flag flying above, and I am a lucky man to work high up within this wonder, on the twelfth floor.

It was during our lunch break on May the tenth and Lily was standing before the window, looking out to the west, toward the docks and the Hudson River, and then her face turned to the south. I knew what she was seeing. I had hesitated so many times before, but this time I stepped up beside her and shared her gaze: Miss Liberty in the harbor, lifting her torch. "She's beautiful," I said.

"Yes," she said.

"Did she welcome you?"

"I'm native-born," she said quickly, firmly.

I held on fast to the windowsill. I'd finally spoken and I'd instantly made a terrible mistake.

But Lily read my face. "I'm not saying that's better."

"Some do," I said.

"I don't," she said. Her hand fluttered out toward me but found nothing exactly to do to express the reassurance it intended. I'd made another mistake, pressing this issue. I wanted very badly to take her hand, but I couldn't. She withdrew it and looked at me closely. "And you?" she asked. "Was she there to welcome you?"

"No. But only because I came long ago, as a child."

She smiled. "So you've been an American longer than she has."

I laughed. Softly, and I knew how much I loved her.

"Harold," she whispers. Here beside me on the beach. She's come back from the ocean and her friends, and I turn to her, but she's not here. Passing bodies. A blur of bare arms and bathing costumes. And a white-knuckled fist is clenching in my chest. Let go, I say inside my head. Please let go.

I need simply to return to what I was doing. Harold, she says. I want to marry you, I say. Yes, she says and we are lit by moonlight on a bench in Tompkins Square and I have forgotten to go down on a knee, which I scramble to do, and she puts her hand on my shoulder. No, she says. Just sit beside me.

At the top of the page of my *Times*. My arm is hurting. A sharp pain is running down my left arm. At the top of the page: *AVIATION MEET AT ASBURY PARK*. World-famous aeronauts. Including five professionals flying for the Wright Brothers. Brookins and Coffin and La Chapple and Johnstone and Hoxsey.

I am panting with the pain inside me. I will take Lily to Asbury Park. We stood high in the air when I first knew I loved her. I will take her flying someday. The paper is quaking. The pain will pass. Please let it pass. I realize I am praying. Beside this story is another on aeroplanes. *MIMIC WARFARE IN AIR. The bombardment of a warship and two submarines before a grandstand filled with people and a long line of parked motors.*

Please let go. My newspaper falls. I try to rise up to find Lily. But my arms are very heavy and someone is squeezing the center of me *my father's arms are around me his rough cheek against mine Daddy please he hugs me too hard and now his face is very still in the flicker of a candle he is lying on the bed and I bend near to him and call for him, Papa, and he is silent and there is weeping beside me, Mama, my real mama, is here in the room and her hair is pinned up tight and I think to ask how she is still alive, where have you been, but before I do she looks at me and puts her finger to her lips and I am holding Papa's hand and leaning into the rough cloth of his coat and Mama is on my other side and the street is full of passing bodies, dark clothes, flowing skirts, the smell of coal fire and horses and rotting fruit and Lily's cheek touches mine I cannot breathe from the happiness of her cheek against mine and I look, and the room is dark, this place where I live, the room is very dark and it is large and at the far end is a sudden tiny flare of light Mama lighting a candle and she straightens and her hands rise to the back of her head, the gathering there, and then her hair falls and beyond her the night sky blooms into great flashing white spirals of light, bombs bursting in air.*

DEATH AT CONEY

Amidst the revelry yesterday at Coney Island, a man quietly died on the beach. Harold Smith, 48 years old, an office manager, of 173 Ludlow Street, Manhattan, was found dead in a canvas chair of apparent natural causes. His demise went unnoticed for some time, in spite of being surrounded by Coney's largest crowd of the season. Smith worked for the Manhattan Life Insurance Company. He is survived by his wife, Lillian.

from page 3 of *The Sun,* New York
Monday, August 8, 1910

WITHDRAWN